To Jerry & Dianne,

I am always happy
when someone reads this
who knows the experience.

Hope you enjoy it.

Joe

Galhattan Press
270 East 10th Street, NY, NY 10009

ISBN #0-9640300-1-2

First printing

This book is dedicated to Julia King and Katy King,
slavedrivers both,
and
to the girls with whom I attended Santa Catalina and remember
with great love and respect.

NOT QUITE PERFECT

With great thanks to Todd Mueller, Aline Ozkan, Fred Wistow, Suzanne McElfresh, Cordelia MacIntyre, Andrew Elliot, Julia Perkins King, Julia Darst King, Andrew Nahem, Jordan Nogee and Katy King.

FRESHMAN YEAR

"Up up, up up." The nun's voice insisted firmly.

I sat hunched-up, staring at my knees, and started to absent-mindedly consider where I might have put my jeans. Then I remembered. No jeans. No pants. The new rules. At all times, we were to dress in a "ladylike fashion." As I put on my pink and green cotton bodysuit with matching wraparound skirt and green sandals, the information passed down the hall, by osmosis, that we were to go to Study Hall and get our class schedules.

The pale, slender nun came down the hallway again.

"Meeting in the Study Hall in twenty minutes for all freshmen."

Surrounded by girls similarly dressed in light summery flowered dresses, I timorously walked across the main parking lot, up the stairs and past the long, low, Spanish hacienda buildings. Blood-red bougainvillea wound around the white-washed brick buildings and overflowed the walkways.

"Right this way girls." Sister Aaron nodded her small pale-freckled head.

Jennifer, whose straight dark hair fell to her waist, was sticking close to me. The sun glinted off her gold barrettes. Maybe this was an unsettling experience for someone else besides me.

"Girls, girls," the slim nun steered us, her arms spread, through an open-air walkway and toward a set of glass doors leading into a modern, concrete cathedral-like hall. The room was filled with row upon row upon row of precisely lined-up desks. The front wall was all glass, looking out on the carefully tended grounds, green grass with perfectly spaced thick-trunked live oaks.

My hands were folded on my desk, and I looked straight ahead as the nun, birdlike, glanced at the pristine sheets then quickly walked down the rows to hand one to each freshman girl. I glanced curiously down at my new schedule. The classes were the same as grammar school: English, Math, History. I can handle that, I thought. Spanish. My stomach gave a lurch. I was totally positive the much more advanced girls in this school had had language classes since first grade in their very elite and ultrasophisticated grammar schools. Then I noticed a small H by each class. I wondered what that meant.

"Those of you with H's are in honors classes," the nun said. "If you think you should be in honors classes and are not, you can speak to me after this meeting or anytime today."

Think we should be in honors classes and are not! What if we are absolutely positively sure we *shouldn't* be in honors classes? Already, I felt terrified and panicked again.

"You may go."

We all pushed for the door, to get back out in the sunshine. I was frantic. My head was spinning with the horrifying information that I would be competing with the smartest students, girls (I knew! My mother had told me!) who were from the wealthiest families, girls who were well-educated world travelers, taught in the best schools and sometimes even by tutors! What was I going to do! I felt a small slip, the ground slid from under me, I tried to regain my footing but *woosh*! Bang, slam, I was lying on the ground on my back. My classmates' smooth, lovely faces arrayed themselves in a circle above me, looking down with totally humiliating concern. How was I ever going to be in the "in crowd" if I acted like this?

Many hours later, I mustered the courage to approach Sister Aaron (someone had reminded me of her name once again) although I was still not fully recovered from my physical mishap. I was deathly afraid that I had already established my character, the personality that I would unwittingly be saddled with during high school: a klutz, a clown, a laughing stock. As if I weren't already handicapped by being not so smart, not so rich and not so pretty.

"Sister Aaron . . . ." I ran down the hall to catch up with her.

"Yes, June?"

"Uh, Sister Aaron. I believe a terrible mistake has been made. I have all honors classes, and I am positive I'm unqualified."

"Let me see." She took the schedule I had been frantically clutching and studied it, then looked back up at me, obviously concerned. "What grades did you get in English, History and Math last year?"

"All A's, Sister Aaron, but that doesn't mean . . . ."

She smiled slightly and handed the schedule back to me. "Try this, and if it's too much for you after a few months, we'll do something." She clicked off down the hall in her square, black nun shoes.

I stared slump-shouldered after her.

A few months? By then I would be totally flunking all my classes. I was never going to be able to keep up here.

I saw Jennifer coming down the hall.

I don't deserve to be here, I thought. I will have to work very diligently to make them let me stay and not embarrass my mother and father. I'd heard my parents talking about how expensive the school was. I knew they could barely afford to keep our house. My mom always said heating twenty-five rooms was impossible, and on top of that they had the back-breaking expense of the gardener and maid. Aloud I said, "After I get settled, I will go to the surrounding households and take in their laundry to help out financially."

Jennifer just looked at me. Luckily the statement was so far-fetched, I think she decided immediately that she must have misheard.

2

Sister Aaron tiptoed down the row of rooms, pulling aside the canvas curtains. "Time to get up," she firmly whispered. "June, June. Time to get up." I didn't like early morning rising, but after not quite a week I'd gotten quite used to it. Not to say that I bounded vigorously up each day, but I did usually awaken a few minutes before Sister Aaron's morning foray and lie motionless listening to the other girls sleeping.

Eating was also a completely new experience. We were assigned to a table with ten girls. The meal was wheeled out on trays by white-jacketed server boys, who must have been about our age, but looked somehow different than, for example, my brothers. They looked unappealing, rougher. They quietly placed heavy white serving plates of eggs, bacon and coffee cake on the table. The coffee cake had crumbles of cinnamon streusel on top and a delicious bit of chocolate swirl.

By the end of the first week, I was still a little foggy on who the other students were besides my roommates, and so it startled me when another girl at my table exclaimed, with surprising venom, "Can you believe it? Joan Frawley is going on a diet." I didn't understand how going on a diet could be so newsworthy. From my discussions during the summer with my cousin Brooke, I had gathered that all women dieted, and if you didn't, you would never be able to wear a bathing suit again. In fact when she'd first explained it to me, I was nervous that perhaps I had been starting a bit late.

A couple days later, I heard a girl in my honors English class with long curly black hair and green eyes address another girl as "Joan." I looked over, instantly on the alert. Maybe that was her. The diet girl. I noticed that the girl addressed as Joan had long straight hair, glasses, a funny nose and bad skin. Still, somehow she was quite pretty. Her face was thin and she had thick dark eyelashes framing sensuously shaped, half-closed eyes. She slowly turned her head and looked straight at me. Well—I *had* been staring. I blushed and looked down.

It didn't take much longer for me to figure out that, in fact, this was Joan Frawley. She was in many of my classes—not just English, but Honors Spanish, History, Algebra and Speech. After you had a certain amount of classes in common, the rest just fell into place. The problem, I discovered, the maddening element of Joan dieting, was that she was *already* super-skinny. She was 5' 6" and weighed eighty-five pounds.

Some of the girls talked of getting a group together to bring the matter up before the nuns. Perhaps Sister Aaron would *forbid* Joan to go on a diet. This was a major topic of conversation for about a week, but then it solved itself—Joan's diet resulted in a weight gain of fifteen pounds.

3

One Saturday morning I woke up at 7:30 like just about everyone else. I stretched and yawned. I could see my roommate, Diane
Hull, was already dressed and standing by her mirror putting gold
hoops in her pierced ears. Diane was pretty in an angelic way, with a
high forehead and light brown hair. She looked serene, and in fact,
so far, I'd have said she pretty much *was* a serene sort of girl.

I got dressed in my navy-blue and red diamond dress, black
stockings and blue flat heels. I knew the color blue of the shoes was
not exactly the same as the blue of the dress, but when I scrutinized
myself from several angles in the full-length mirror hung inside the
closet door, I decided I liked the contrast.

"Diane?" I asked.

"Yes?" she gently answered.

"You sure are a quiet roommate." I was immediately frightened
that maybe she'd be insulted, although I certainly didn't mean it that
way.

She laughed. "Well, don't get used to it. We won't be roommates long."

"What d'you mean?"

"We switch five times a year. Each time, you fill out a form with
a list of whom you do and don't want. I hear you are far more likely
to receive someone from the latter list."

"Oh. Hmmm." I tried to digest this new information. What did I
know? Changing roommates must be the thing. De rigeur, au
courant. "Are you ready to go to breakfast?"

"Not quite, why don't you go on ahead?"

"Okay."

As I emerged into the sunlight, I spotted Joan and Ann Drendel just ahead of me, wearing flowered dresses and nude nylons, heading to breakfast.

Joan looked back. "Not you again," she said in mock disgust.

Joan and I had the same English class and I could tell she'd approved of me ever since I answered "Hera the Horrible" in a rare fit of derring-do to a mythology question. I smiled. Now I knew for sure she liked me.

"Do you think they'll have donuts again for breakfast?"

"We'll have donuts for breakfast every Saturday from here until the end of the year at least," Ann firmly declared. "One of the Beardsleys is a sophomore day student and a couple more are in lower school."

The Beardsleys were famous in California for having twenty-one kids. They owned a bakery and evidently, at least this was what I thought Ann was implying, the Beardsley childrens' tuition was partially paid in donuts.

"Great." I was *totally* obsessed with donuts. In my family, we had very strict donut rules: only on holidays, and my dad only bought two for each person. By the time I groggily arrived in the kitchen midmorning, one of mine would have mysteriously disappeared.

Even more fabulously, breakfast on Saturday and Sunday at our school was cafeteria style, all the food laid out on stainless steel and glass shelves for our supreme viewing pleasure. I'd only eaten cafeteria style once before in my life, when the Blackwells took me to Perry Boys Smorgasbord. I'd liked it that time too.

Following Joan and Ann, I took a tray and considered all the foods available: fried chicken, mashed potatoes, peas swimming in brown gravy in their stainless-steel bin, pepperoni pizza, melon, cottage cheese, chocolate cake, lime jello, orange juice, coffee or tea. I sauntered down the row of glistening donuts, carefully choosing three glazed, thrilled with the knowledge that I could return as many times as I liked.

Breakfast lasted until lunch for Ann, Joan and me. The donuts stayed out the whole time, all kinds, Boston creme with vanilla middles, cinnamon, chocolate-covered (my favorite), plain, pastel-sprinkled and glazed (tops shining under the fluorescent lights). By two in the afternoon, when the cafeteria workers were tiredly pulling the food back into the kitchen, I'd eaten thirteen donuts, three pieces of pizza and a small bowl of cottage cheese. Joan had had two helpings of lasagna and two pieces of blueberry pie. Ann had eaten four pieces of pizza, a chocolate chip cookie and four cups of coffee.

"I feel sick," I said. Indeed, my blue and red dress, made of stretchable jersey, was having a hard time straining across the bloat of my stomach.

"Do you?" Ann Drendel perked right up, her dark eyes shining. "I can help you. Let's go back to the dorm."

"I'll catch you later," Joan said. "I'm going to shuffle off to the library."

I rushed to keep up with Ann's pace as she enthusiastically led the way in the back door of Long Dorm and to the bathroom. She stuck her head surreptitiously around the door.

"Good. It's empty." Ann was a big friendly girl with a square, open face. She had the big shoulders and strong torso of a swimmer because she'd been on the pre-Olympic team, trained by a coach in Reno.

"Okay, look," she demonstrated in the open area. She leaned slightly forward as if bending over a toilet bowl. "Just stick your fingers down your throat and it will make you throw up."

What a great idea! Why hadn't I thought of that? So simple, and yet so effective. How totally great. Everyone should know about this really great thing. It was like spending all your money and then finding out your bank account was still full. Afterward, I felt a hundred times better, and I also felt strong affection for Ann.

"Everyone does it," she assured me.

4

"Ahem." Sister Carlotta called the student body to attention with an imperious throat clear. The remote green through the glassed wall of the Study Hall framed her. A fake smile pushed her puffed-out face even tighter, and her intense, small blue eyes peered out from the shiny flesh. We all stopped talking immediately. Inside the black and white nun's uniform her body seemed not exactly a woman's body but more the shape of a woman, like a dressmaker's dummy. It was impossible to believe, and I didn't, that if she took her clothes off, she'd have two breasts or nipples or a belly button. Instead, it would all be smooth and beige-colored. Not surprisingly, I was frightened of her.

"As you all know, today is the first deportment meeting of the year. The freshmen should be made aware that four times a year you will be given a card, and on the card will be your marks of deportment indicating behavior results in four separate areas. Each girl will come up individually and receive her deportment card from me."

She smiled again without warmth or humor, without any emotion, just the painful pulling back of her lips toward the sides of her face, exposing small dingy teeth.

I groaned inwardly. Each individual girl going up? This was going to take the rest of our lives. If I'd known, I would have snuck some licorice into my assigned desk.

Arrayed behind her were the other nuns: Sister Humpbert in the middle, Sister Jane Fox, Sister Clare, tiny-freckled, light-eyelashed Sister Aaron, Sister Malcolm, Sister Jane Ferdinand and Sister Jean. They were all thick with too much smooth flesh except Sister Jane Ferdinand, with her gaunt medieval face, and Sister Aaron.

"Jessica Andrus."

Jessica stood up and walked to the podium until she and Sister Carlotta were standing side by side, with Sister Carlotta situated just a bit closer to the microphone. They turned to face each other.

"Very good work, Jessica. Your mother must be proud."

Jessica smiled. She had a pixie haircut, long face and oval wire-rimmed glasses. Her mother was the head librarian and looked a lot like Jessica but sterner. "Thank you, Sister Carlotta," her voice mousier because she was farther from the microphone.

"Teresa Barger."

"An outstanding record, Teresa. Keep it up."

Teresa politely kept her head down on the way back to her desk.

"Karen Biehls."

Sister Carlotta was already wearing a little frown even as Karen walked up grinning.

I couldn't understand why Karen would grin at a time like this, except she was pretty much always in a good mood. She stood next to Sister Carlotta, still smiling her head off. Sister Carlotta did not smile—she looked like a viper ready to strike.

"Karen?"

"Yes?"

"Is it possible that you're in the wrong school?"

Karen looked confused. "Wrong school?" We could barely hear her, "No, my sister came here and . . . ."

She trailed off.

"Your sister had some idea of what a Catalina girl is." Now the sarcasm was unmistakable. Sister Carlotta thrust the behavior report at Karen as if she were repulsed to even have touched it.

"It would be nice if you would at least try to measure up."

All of us were holding our breath. Karen walked back to her desk, no longer smiling. Her face looked unfamiliar; I'd never seen her not smile.

"Basia Belza."

Then some more blameless people. Actually the freshmen had pretty good records, most of us hadn't settled in enough yet to cause any trouble.

"Lisa Ehrlich."

Well, there were exceptions, I thought. I'd even heard a rumor that Lisa was sometimes meeting one of the server boys under the dining room terrace and making out. What an idea.

"What? A server boy?" I asked the person who told me. "Wow, I never would have thought of that." Making out with a server boy would no more have crossed my mind than having an affair with a bedside table or a sofa. I had to admire her.

We all watched as Lisa walked up to the front of Study Hall, it seemed in slow motion. Each time her foot hit the floor it echoed against the glass and the ceiling. Surely the nuns couldn't have found out about the server boys yet, I thought desperately. How badly could she be punished?

"Lisa?"

Lisa looked sullen. She may have been through this trouble thing before.

"Answer me." The command was short and flat.

"Yes."

"Maybe you could explain to me how this is even possible."

"I don't know, Sister."

"Sister Carlotta." Sister Carlotta corrected her.

"I don't know, Sister Carlotta, sir."

We couldn't help ourselves, some giggles slipped out. Sister Carlotta's gaze shifted and her ire became general. Then her attention shifted back to Lisa, even more dangerous, even more intensely poisonous. Seconds ticked by in dead silence.

"Next time you'll do better." Each word was in its own box, wrapped in matte black and ominous, like a scorpion loaded with deadly venom, poised to strike. Lisa got the point, took her card and sat back down, her face dead-white.

5

It was about that time when, much to my delight, I detected who the in crowd were. Actually it was easy to tell—they were the most sullen and had the coolest clothes: Laura Fee, Lisa Ehrlich and Deedee Rosencrantz. Lisa Hale too, but before I had a chance to make an amiable approach, she got kicked out of school for shoplifting.

I waited for an opportunity to befriend them. One thing I'd learned from weaseling my way into what passed for the hip crowd in grammar school (which had been far less of a challenge since there were only thirteen girls total in the class) was not to rush things. Hang around on the edges and slowly but surely insinuate yourself, make small amusing jokes.

Sure enough, they let me hang with them, and then Laura Fee, the head of the in crowd, asked me to her house in San Francisco for October break. I was ecstatic. My mother and I had driven up each year to San Francisco to go to *The Nutcracker Suite* and see the Christmas tree at the Emporium, but I'd never been in anyone's house there.

Laura's family had the penthouse apartment of a building on Nob Hill. When we pulled up in a taxi, a man in a blue and gold uniform silently appeared, glided out of the building and smoothly held open the door.

"Evening, Miss Laura," he said.

I wondered who he was but didn't ask. We paraded past him into the lobby. Bone white marble with gilt trim.

"If my mother's not here, Emma will make grilled-cheese sandwiches for us." Laura casually informed me as we rode silently up in the matching gold and white upholstered elevator.

"Okay." I said.

What would happen if her mother *was* there?

Her mother was there. She was tall and had the same dark hair as Laura, but her eyes were more like a cat's. She wore a green suede coat and black suede boots.

"Laura," she exclaimed, smothering her daughter in hugs. As she turned and hung up her coat, the tiniest scent of expensive leather wafted over to me. Turning back around, she looked at me. "This must be your friend June."

She held out a long elegant hand with nails perfectly done in light peach. I was wearing a canary yellow skirt, yellow and orange vertically striped shirt, yellow stockings and orange shoes. I'd thought the outfit the height of chic when I'd bought it at the Dandelion boutique in Santa Cruz the year before. Laura's mother coolly shook my outstretched hand and smiled in a haute couture way.

"Welcome to our home."

Laura grimaced and jerked her head to the left like, "Let's go," so I obediently followed her to her room. I was shocked to see blue- and yellow-flowered wallpaper and a four-poster bed draped in matching material. In fact, all the furniture was royal blue. It was quite surprising, considering the tough, dark, cynical personality Laura displayed at school. I had thought her bedroom would be more Gothic.

"We'll both sleep in here, so put your stuff down, umm . . . let me see . . . ."

I waited patiently for her to make some deprecating remark about the decor, but she seemed oblivious to its incongruity.

Laura had opened the door of a closet stuffed with about a million dresses, peered seriously inside, then indicated that I should stash my suitcase.

"Are you hungry?" she asked as we went back out toward the front hall.

Laura's mother was coming down another hall toward us.

"Emma is heating up the salmon and string beans we had for supper. I'll sit with you while you eat in the kitchen."

We went down a long narrow hallway with wallpaper of cream silk shantung; then we crossed through one kitchen, sparkling clean and a bit oversized, with a big sink and a gleaming white Formica island in the middle; through another kitchenlike area with glass cabinets filled with different kinds of china and glassware; through a white swinging door into a room with a big white table and white wooden chairs with very high backs; and on the far wall an almost vertigo-inducing floor-to-ceiling window with a view of all of San Francisco. It seemed their house was pretty big. You could see the Golden Gate Bridge way in the far, far background.

Laura and I sat down. There were two places set with white linen napkins and very ornate, heavy silver forks and knives. Emma brought in two plates with salmon, very small green beans and potatoes russe.

Laura's mother seated herself across from me in a place with no silverware.

"Tell me darling," she looked at Laura. "How is school?"

"I hate it," Laura unequivocally proclaimed.

Her mother recoiled a little. "Oh, but dear, it's the best."

6

The next morning, we didn't get up until ten. When I opened my eyes, Laura was looking at me, smiling. I felt surprised, not used to seeing her happy.

"What'd you think of our apartment?"

"Apartment." I thought in my mind. Yeah, that was the word for what this kind of house was. "Far out," I said.

"Today we'll go to the park," she announced.

I felt a small jump in my stomach. She'd told me stories about the hippies who hung out in the park near her house doing drugs. Was that the park she meant?

We had waffles for breakfast, served by Emma in the kitchen again, and read the *San Francisco Chronicle* her mother had left there on the white table, along with *Vogue*, *Bazaar* and *Life*. We went back to Laura's room and lay on her bed for about a half an hour.

"D'you think your mom is going to let you change schools?"

Laura scowled in the way I was more used to from Catalina. "She better. Otherwise I'll starve myself to death."

We both silently contemplated that possibility. It might take a little longer than it would have if she'd started right away when she got to school: Catalina girls had a tendency to put on a little extra weight, and neither of us was an exception.

"I think a lot of our class won't come back next year," I said.

"What about you?" Laura asked.

"I guess I have to. The schools in Santa Cruz are too bad academically for me to go to them." I hated to sound uncourageous, but my parents had started talking to me about going to Santa Catalina when I was 7 years old, and it was difficult for me to imagine doing anything else.

We got up and dressed in our much-missed blue jeans. Mine were a pair I'd gotten last summer and had just adorned with my first patch, a piece of red-, green- and orange-striped material sewn in yellow thread over a small rip in the knee.

We were silent as we walked the few blocks to the park. It wasn't far, just up Nob Hill a bit.

Although on top of a hill, the park still managed to have peaks and valleys, all covered in lush green grass. Laura quickly walked up a small rise and sat on a stone bench.

"Sometimes if I sit here long enough, someone comes and offers to sell me some grass," she whispered without looking at me. I knew not to reply. We both gazed steadfastly straight ahead, our hands resting formally by our sides, trying to gape inconspicuously (at least I was gaping, for Laura I imagined the scene was old hat) at the rolling hills of San Francisco covered with elongated gingerbread houses edged with candy-colored trim, each smack dab up against the next, all tilted at impossible angles as your gaze went down a hill, then up again, then down some more until finally the view emptied into the jewel-like blue of the San Francisco Bay. Everything was brightly colored, everything was clean.

I slid my eyes a bit to the side, returning to my more immediate view of the park. There were some hippies dancing in a dale. I contemplated nudging Laura, but in the nick of time I noticed that a guy had materialized on the other side of her and was talking to her earnestly.

He had long, dark wavy hair, almost to his waist (not too many split ends I noticed) and a beard and mustache. Definitely he was good-looking and had a good body in blue jeans torn slightly at the knee and a flannel shirt.

"Hey. I bet you girls like to smoke," he was saying to Laura, as he looked me over with one eye.

"Yes, maybe," Laura coolly replied.

"I got some righteous herb back at my pad."

A thin shiver of fear and excitement ran through me.

Laura didn't answer him.

He moved his hand a little closer to where her thigh was pressed against the stone bench.

"C'mon. It'll be groovy. We can get high and talk, the three of us."

Again his glance flickered over to me.

"Where do you live?" she asked coldly.

"Down on Haight," he answered. "It's straight downhill."

"No, we can't." She'd decided and I could tell by her tone that the decision was final.

He looked at her for a minute hesitantly, then shrugged. "Hey man, that's cool." He got up and walked away.

The hippies, a guy with long gray hair, a beard and no shoes, and two blond girls, one wearing a tie-dye T-shirt and the other a fringed leather halter top and many Indian bead necklaces, were now about twenty feet away. They were rolling gently in the grass and laughing for no reason. Every time one stopped, they would look at the other two and begin giggling again. We watched them while we waited for another handsome young hippie man to come along and ask us to smoke some pot. Nothing happened.

"Want to go home for lunch?" Laura finally asked.

"Sure," I said, partly saddened that something *really* exciting hadn't happened, but mostly satisfied with the feeling that we'd been very, very close.

7

On Sunday night when we got back to school, it was time to change to our winter uniforms. The summer before I began high school, my mother and I had gone to Mrs. McElroy's shop in Carmel, a tiny boutique that had been ordering the kilts from Scotland for Santa Catalina girls since the school opened in 1955. Sandwiched between a riding shop and the famous French restaurant L'Escargot, Mrs. McElroy's had light pink and white walls and thousands of girly things—cashmere cardigans and ruffled white silk blouses. Although my mother yearned to dress me in such frippery, I had long since determined to sneer at all that smacked of "girly," no matter how well it might suit my round Victorian face and curly hair.

Buying the uniforms had been a bit painful for both of us, me because I was already just a tiny bit too hour-glassy to have an easy time shopping for clothes, my mother because the price, once we had assembled the many pieces listed as "Bare Minimum," was quite high.

The most expensive single piece of the four-outfit, multipiece uniform set was the green and red kilt imported directly for each girl from Scotland. Not that this was what my parents would have bought instead, but it was the price of a color tv. Then there was the green blazer (only slightly lower in price), the red cardigan sweater, green and red kneesocks, dark oxfords, the two summer uniforms— one blue and white, one pink and white, the white knee socks, the light oxfords, the white pique Sunday uniform (nude stockings and white shoes could be purchased elsewhere, Mrs. McElroy disapprovingly informed us)—and the gym uniform, which was a bargain at the price of a high-end turntable.

I was accustomed to wearing a uniform from my Catholic grammar school, and the only one that disturbed me was the two-piece white Sunday uniform with its round-edged collar, white pearl-shaped buttons that fastened down the back and rather conspicuous front bosom darts. The two bows over the cut-out V's on the bottom sides of the top were a bit too much decoration and the straight skirt down to past my knees made me look frumpy and about 50 years old. I was not mollified when I donned it for my first Sunday mass at school and saw that all the other girls looked just as much like over-stuffed sheep.

It was a few Sundays before I said anything about it. I looked over at Diane and considered. She looked perhaps more angelic, but not more attractive—a serene but lumpy, awkwardly shaped angel.

I pulled at the shirt. "These are kind of weird," I said, not wanting to say "ugly" or "bad" straight out.

She laughed. "Yeah they are, aren't they? I suppose we'll get used to them."

8

After I'd been at school for a couple of months, the class as a whole started to take some form for me. I noticed that Teresa was a natural leader and everyone looked up to her. Usually there would be at least two leaders in every class, but so far another one hadn't shown up in our class. Every girl was very different from each other and we seemed a strange mix.

As I was walking from Study Hall back to the dorm thinking about this, I noticed Teresa coming over and looking frighteningly like she was going to talk *directly* to me.

"Hey, June, wanna help me?"

"Sure," I eagerly replied. She'd pushed the right button.

"Okay. I have to write an article for the newspaper about the Senior/Lay Teacher basketball game this afternoon."

"Well, uh . . . ," I began, frantically trying to figure out how to renege.

"No, c'mon. You can do it easily. Just come to the game with me, then we'll go to my room and do it together."

"Alright." I figured she would do all the work and I'd just agree with whatever she suggested.

After the game, we settled ourselves on her bed. Her bedspread was a faded purple and white cotton Indian print, the second most favorite style among the freshmen (I had the first most favorite—corduroy in bright primary colors, red, blue or yellow).

"Okay." She had a yellow legal pad between her crossed legs and a pen loosely held in her fingers. She tapped her knee and I noticed that she didn't have fat bulging on the inside edges there like I did. "We need some kind of angle to make it interesting."

"Interesting?" I replied robotlike, then I was hit with a wave of silliness. "Interesting is as interesting does."

She stared at me. "That's it! That's it!"

I had no idea what she meant of course.

"We'll use cliches. We'll use as many cliches as we can."

The sun was shining pretty as a picture on the day the fiercely determined Senior Navajos and their equally ferocious opponents, the lay teachers, gathered for the basketball game—a basketball game that would go down in history.

Leslie Redlich started out quick as a wink with a brilliantly Machiavellian pass to Ann Powers. Ann dribbled with great panache down the

length of the court and passed the ball, smooth
as a baby's behind, faster than you could say
Jiminy Cricket, to her teammate Nancy Crooner.

The lay teacher team, not to be outdone, were
on top of the situation and soon gained the
upper hand.

Mrs. Grisham parlayed the ball across the
court in a path that was crookeder than a
horse's hind leg and then reluctantly relin-
quished the ball to her illustrious compatriot,
Mrs. Bartlett. Obviously rarin' to go, Mrs.
Bartlett, a shining star on the court, proceeded
to strut her stuff. Inning to inning the game
got increasingly more devil-may-care, and the
audience was on the edge of their seats.

"This is more fun than a barrel of monkeys,"
these intrepid reporters exclaimed as we watched
the seniors score one last breathtaking point to
pull out all the stops in a dramatic photo-fin-
ish. What a game. Hats off to the senior
Navajos and the Lay Teachers for this rousing
premiere performance. All members of Santa
Catalina, students and teachers alike, should be
proud as peacocks. All we can say is Viva la
Savoir Faire!

When we turned the article into Sister Humpbert she didn't
smile once, but I was proud (as a peacock) reading it printed in the
school newspaper.

9

"Psst. Pssssst."

I heard a whisper cut through the quiet of Study Hall. Somehow I knew it was for me:

"Hey, hey. Are you going to the dance?" Pam Phillips asked.

I looked up from my Spanish book. "No." I hoped that'd be the end of it.

Half an hour later when I was walking back to the dorms, Pam came running up.

"Why?!!" she asked me. "Why aren't you going?"

"I don't want to."

"C'mon June, it'll be fun. We're all going. Look, look at this list." Pam waved a sheet of loose-leaf notebook paper with various girls names scrawled on it in all different handwriting styles and colors of ink.

Somehow she'd appropriated the sign-up sheet.

"You better put that back, you could get in trouble," I admonished. "You could lose it, and then no one could go to the dance."

"I just wanted to show you one thing. Look—you can ask for whatever height boy you want." She pointed to the sheet, showing me the column where the girls had entered their height preferences. After the name "Cleo" was 5' 8" or taller. That was generous of her, I thought, Cleo was at least 5' 10."

"I don't want to go. I'm very busy," I said.

10

Less than a week later, the nuns put up the sheet of dates for the dance. The first I heard of it was Saturday morning as I tanned myself down at the pool with my ultracool friends, Laura Fee and Deedee Rosencrantz.

"June, June," I heard a little voice calling.

Oh God, I hoped it wasn't going to be a nerdy person trying to be friends with me.

"Ju-une."

It was Pam.

"Yes. " I smiled to see her. Pam *was* lovely, a bit like a young Natalie Wood everyone said. I guessed Natalie Wood had huge dark eyes and straight, short, lustrous black hair with bangs, because that was what Pam looked like.

"What is it?"

"You're on the list for the dance."

I was shocked. "How can that be? I never signed up for it."

"It's worse than that. The guy you got, everyone knows about him, his name is Horace Herbert. Laura Knoop got him last year and she called him Mr. Onionhead."

"Oh, no." I got up and pulled on my royal blue culottes over my bathing suit and hurriedly buttoned my matching blouse. "I'm going to ask Sister Humpbert about this, there must be some mistake."

Pam ran beside me as I rushed up the hill. "And you know what June? Cleo is not on the list even though she *did* sign up."

"It's simple then, she'll go instead of me."

It wasn't that simple. Sister Humpbert smilingly said, "It will be beneficial for you to go," but I suspected there was a hint of malevolence in her smile. There was no recourse. I got dressed as nicely as I could in my orange and red, scoop-neck, paisley A-line dress, all the while furiously swearing to myself that I would ignore my date as much as was politely possible.

It was with a dour face that I waited to board the rickety bus that was going to cart us to Robert Louis Stevenson.

"I will have fun. I will have fun," I started chanting to myself, but then I forgot what I was doing and a few minutes later, as we pulled into Pebble Beach, I found myself accidentally chanting "I will be run. I will be run." Oh, God, I thought. What was I going to do? Time was already dragging more slowly than a bad math class.

I was still trepidacious when I stepped down off the bus. A pride of newly shaven, freshly combed boys stood awaiting us, practically pawing the ground, excited to see which little morsel was theirs. I saw us as pigs, pink and squealing, milling together as a prehistoric sense warned us that we were being led to slaughter.

"Bella Zimmerman. Scott McPherson." Sister Humpbert called and the two paired up and were shoo-ed down a concrete path by a man proctor (or whatever they called their nun-equivalents).

"Megan McDonnell. Trig Duryea."

Hey, they were kind of a handsome, normal-looking couple I thought. They were the only ones.

Finally she called me. "June Smith. Horace Onionhead." Of course his last name wasn't really Onionhead, but it might well have been. He was a thousand feet tall and weighed about three pounds. He was wearing a bright green plaid wool suit and brown shoes, and his hair on his round head was so thin and blond as to be practically invisible. He bounded zealously toward me. I cringed.

We walked down a concrete path toward the dance, which was being held, I presumed, in what was normally the dining hall. Horace was clutching my hand in his sweaty palm. As we entered the hall, I noticed there were large translucent balls being bounced from one RLS student to another. I wondered what they were.

"Don't worry. I'll get them!" Horace yelled, waving his impossibly long cartoon-like arms about.

I didn't have the foggiest what he was talking about.

"Hold my coat," he said, turning toward me.

A second later I regretted my instantaneously polite response of accepting the coat, as I gingerly held the green plaid monstrosity—reeking of aftershave—over my arm. I saw Horace climb onto the shoulders of a rather beefy fellow and the two of them attempt to walk, Horace swaying precariously, his onionhead now about thirteen feet in the air as they went toward the side of the gym or dining hall or whatever this room usually was, and tried to rescue some of the large flesh-colored balloons that had gotten stuck in oversize bronze sconces.

I felt sick with embarrassment.

When he finally got down, after attracting the attention of everyone within a five-mile radius, I made a brave attempt to converse.

"So, uh, how did you come to be at Robert Louis Stevenson?"

"Oh, gosh, just lucky, I guess. My dad was a stonemason here at the school, he was old when he had me and he's retired down in Fresno now, but they said they'd give me a scholarship anyway." And then he threw his head back and brayed. At first I thought he was in pain, and I stared in horror at the tendons vibrating thickly in his neck, but then it dawned on me that it was a *laugh*. My dismay increased.

We stood along the side of the room and watched as two or three courageous couples danced.

"Would you like to dance?" he asked me.

Thinking that anything would be better than further conversation, I agreed. He took my hand, his giant teeth grinning in his onionhead and led me out into the middle of the dance floor. He held my hand out, his arm straight, and with a flourish began. At first I tried to dance in my normal way as the band played a not-that-great rendition of the Association's "Windy," but after a few minutes I felt that my contribution as a dancing partner was super-fluous. Horace was whirling, his long arms flung out, twisting and diving in an athletic but quite emotive imitation of a dying eagle. To top it off, his dance had absolutely no relation to the beat of the music. I edged myself over to the side of the hall and tried to look unperturbed, as if there were no connection between us. Fat chance of that here. At the end of the song he made a beeline for me and stood, his cheap white button-down shirt plastered with sweat to his bony, heaving chest, at my side.

"What happened, June? That was a great dance, but you seemed to tucker out halfway through." He moved his few tendrils of hair farther back on his head, bobbed his head three times, then continued. "Maybe you'd like to come back to see my room."

OH MY GOD! I couldn't believe it. I mean, not only would I possibly get kicked out for doing the very thing we'd been told specifically we were *absolutely* not allowed to do, but on top of it, Horace was possibly the least physically attractive boy I'd ever met. The mere suggestion of any type of physical intimacy made me faint with dread.

"Oh no, thank you," I sweetly said. "We're not allowed to leave the dance area."

We stood beside each other in silence, watching the other dancers a few minutes more, then he turned to me again with his eager grin, his head swaying precariously at the end of its long skinny neck.

"June, I beg you, please will you do me one favor?"

Although it was not like me, I was cautious. "What is it?"

"I have some friends, and they don't have dates."

I swear at this point he practically sobbed and brushed a small tear away.

"Yea-us?"

"And I wish you would do me the favor, the very small favor of agreeing to dance just once with them." He pointed to a group of boys standing by the edge of the floor.

I peered over. As near as I could tell without my glasses those boys were kind of cute. Still they were Horace's friends. I softened anyway. "Alright."

We walked over, Horace with a big happy broad smile on his face. He stopped on a dime, militaristically. In fact, his friends were much cuter close up, particularly the one right in front of us.

"This is my date, June," he said. "She'd like to dance with you."

I watched the expression on the cute boy's face change from idle curiosity to pure panic, much like the emotion I was feeling toward Horace. If only I could turn and run. But where? Out onto the Pebble Beach golf course? That would really help matters—then I'd be stranded for days. They'd probably send a search party of dozens of Horaci out to hunt for me. I stayed there, my smile frozen on my face. The cute boy and I danced. Rather stiffly.

11

A bag of nice crisp potato chips sure would taste good, I thought. No, I admonished myself. You can't have them. I stared at the blackboard and wondered how much coffee cake was left over from breakfast. I felt regret that I hadn't had any when it had been so temptingly there in front of me. Now it was too late. I could almost taste the soft streusel coffee cake and sweet crunchy nuggets in my mouth. The first lunch period was during English, maybe Sister Aaron would let us out early, she would just give us an assignment and I could go right over to the dining hall. That probably wouldn't happen. Maybe I could cut English since we weren't having a test. Maybe there would be pizza for lunch today. Definitely there would be blueberry yogurt on the salad bar. That was a delicious food. I could almost smell the milky aroma and feel the cool smoothness sliding down my throat.

Sister Aaron was writing on the blackboard, "Two Old Ladies." She turned around and addressed us.

"Now, when did the two old ladies dressed all in black first appear in <u>Heart of Darkness</u>?" She surveyed our faces. "Cleo?"

"In the waiting room when Kurtz went to get his appointment."

"That's right. And what do you think those two old ladies symbolized?"

Well, I thought, they were wearing black, a dead give-away that something was not all happiness and light. This discussion bored me. I knew Sister Aaron was going to assign another paper today and I would have to worry about writing it. The best thing to do was to stick to my diet and then I wouldn't have to study because I would be beautiful. When I got out of school, I could go to some second-rate college where only a few months into my freshman year a special scout looking for models who were not that tall would discover me and whisk me off to a life of beautiful clothes, fast planes and exotic locales.

12

By the beginning of November, Lisa Ehrlich had gotten thrown out, Deedee Rosenkrantz had unfortunately turned out to be not much of a conversationalist—in fact everything I said seemed to surprise her greatly—and Laura Fee had become completely obsessed with her lack of bowel movement, and my upbringing was such that constant talk of bodily functions was frightening. I could stretch myself to a mention once or twice, but for a friendship with excretion as the *constant* and *only* topic, I was not equipped.

One day I came home from class to find my top drawer out just a bit more than it had been when I left it in the morning. This was not suspicious. We had to leave our drawers open for inspection purposes and often the nuns opened them further to look at the contents and see if they were neat enough. I curiously pulled that drawer open to see how it looked: Would Sister Aaron have given me a "minus" for neatness? Something looked immediately funny.

I went and got Laura.

"Hey, look in here. Does anything look strange to you?"

"No," she said sharply. "How would I know anyway?"

"Well, look at this." I pulled out a bottle of vitamins. "This vitamin bottle was full this morning and now it's empty."

"Maybe the nuns took them to test for drugs."

"Ha, ha," I said, not quite sure of what attitude would display the proper level of cool. Maybe the nuns had gotten the wrong idea about me. Still, I didn't want Laura to know that not only had I never done drugs, but at the shamefully advanced age of 14, I hadn't even been kissed. What made me even more uncomfortable was that truthfully I did not want to get in trouble with the nuns, though it appeared I might be getting tarred by association.

Quite coincidentally, I decided right about this same time that maybe I'd have more fun if I got some cheerful friends.

13

Sitting in the Study Hall, longing to be back in my clean white room at home in Santa Cruz with my big, blue goose-down comforter reading an Oz book, I partially listened to the announcements.

Janet Miller was the big-boned, authoritative sister of Marian Miller, who was in my class. The upper-class girls who had sisters in our class stood out more to us. "And during Father/Daughter weekend, we have Saturday sports. So remember, it is very important that you go see your class president at her desk and sign up for the sport you want," she was saying.

Engaging in organized sports with my dad was not a happy thought. I was pretty sure it would horrify him too. My father thought that football and cheerleading were two of the more repellent aspects of American culture. In fact, my father was not that big on backslapping, rough-and-tumble camaraderie in any form. What kind of sport choices were they going to have? Baseball, soccer? Golf? In my family to even ask the question "Does he play golf?" conveyed extreme disdain. Sure enough, when I moseyed over to Teresa's desk, there it was, basketball, baseball and golf.

"I'll sign up for 'other'," I joked.

"Okay," Teresa quite seriously replied and marked me down in the box quite amazingly actually labeled "other."

Walking back from the Study Hall, I realized I now had a new problem. What "other" would we do? I knew! I had it! My father would love this—we'd go shopping!

14

By the time Father/Daughter weekend occurred, I'd made friends with Teresa and Joan.

Teresa was taller than me, about 5'7", with curly black hair, the kind that went wave, waved to the end, then curled, a pointy chin and a pointy nose. She looked like a movie star from the silent films, Theda Bara maybe, white skin, black hair and hazel eyes. Black Irish. She was the youngest of six kids.

Her father was a geologist from North Dakota who met her mother at a 4-H dance when they were both teenagers. I imagined her father as a hardy sort, traveling in the desolate plains of the Northwest by primitive transportation—old, barely working trucks or sturdy, faithful horses. Soon after they married, he left his young bride in North Dakota to go to Saudi Arabia and travel there in the desolate Sahara by camel, where his persistence led to the discovery of oil. For the first two years of their marriage, Teresa's mother and father communicated only by mail.

By the time Teresa was born, they were well established in Saudi Arabia, her father the president and founder of Aramco. At night, after Study Hall, Teresa told me exotic tales of their life in Dhahran, the sand, the compound, the huge company store that carried everything: blue jeans, rice, mulchers, cosmetics, cigarettes and hammers.

I wanted to have also been there and felt the dry, spare heat and seen the uncounted millions of grains of sand—golden, extending unblemished as far as the eye could see. I wanted to slide down the dunes in back of the house, sneak under the chicken-wire compound fence, the sand beneath quickly eroded by storms that so easily slid the sand away. I wanted to be lost in an endless planet of sameness. I wanted to grab the thick, knotty fur of camels, resting for a minute from their lope-y gate, smell their fetid smell. I wanted Teresa's memories to be implanted directly into my brain; I was so hungry for travel, not just more stories.

Joan had grown up in Beverly Hills, or more precisely, Holmby Hills, the good part of Beverly Hills. Joan's dad was the head of some megalith with a million companies under it, including Schick Electric. Evidently, or this is the story Joan told me late one night, he'd owned all of Shick but the campaign contribution he gave to Richard Nixon was outmatched by a rival. Some very dirty deal went down wherein Mr. Frawley was on vacation in Ireland and suddenly an antitrust suit was rushed into court and he had to sell half the company in a period of time so short only one person—the dastardly rival—came forward with an offer.

Mr. Frawley also owned Hanna Barbara and Classic Comics, which I found far more impressive because I had been personally interested in the products before I met Joan.

"My father used to be an alcoholic," Joan said in a serious tone, but really you could never tell with her.

"Really?" This was a new one on me. As far as I knew, I'd never met an alcoholic before.

"Yes, he was the type of alcoholic who would have trucks pull up to the house with cases of Dewar's and cigarettes, which were unloaded and stored in the basement."

This was also difficult for me to imagine for more than one reason. Cases? Really? I imagined men in blue uniforms, made tiny in comparison with the truck, seriously unloading case after case of liquor. And a case of cigarettes, not just a carton, which my mother occasionally purchased, but many cartons together in a cardboard box. Crazy. But the most interesting part of the story for me, the most difficult to imagine, was Joan having a basement—because although I'd read about them, I'd never actually seen a basement.

15

Friday night of Father/Daughter weekend, we went to

L'Escargot with Teresa, Joan, Mr. Barger and Mr. Frawley. It seemed as though my father liked them very much, except the part where Mr. Frawley cornered my father after dinner and insisted on demonstrating the effect alcohol has on Arctic foxes by squeezing my dad's wrist very hard. Mr. Frawley had strong beliefs, and my father is a bit (like his organized sports thing) against that. Luckily, it didn't go on long because we girls had a curfew.

The next morning, bright and early, as the other girls put on white sports costumes, I donned my smocked red-and-blue-diamond-print dress and went to wait for my father in the parking lot. He wasn't even that late.

We drove straight to Macy's at the Del Monte Shopping Center. As we pulled into the parking lot, surrounded by Monterey pines, I was bouncing in my seat with excitement. This was going to be really fun.

I pushed open the glass door of Macy's department store and streaked down the wide linoleum aisle toward "Young Juniors." Light glinted off glass cases containing gloves, hats and jewelry. The smell of new clothes filled the air. I quickly gathered a bunch of dresses, the vibrant colors piled high on my arm.

"What do you think of this one, Dad?" I asked, holding up a pink and orange horizontal-striped shift.

"It's quite nice," he replied, but not as enthusiastically as my mom would have. Maybe he didn't understand the fashion statement of red and orange.

It took me a long time to get in and out of the dresses. For some reason, they all seemed quite tight. I had to squeeze them over my shoulders and smash my breasts, straining the fabric, then there was another struggle at the hip zone, but I dutifully went out and showed my dad every dress. He'd found a green plastic armchair to sit in.

After several hours, we hadn't found anything I liked. Finally, when I spotted a clock on the other side of the store over the shoe section and realized it was almost time for Father/Daughter cocktails and further mingling with the other fathers, I was relieved. I tried on one more dress—a midi-length blue jersey that was no sooner over my shoulders when it ceased to fall in a smooth straight line like it had on the hanger and instead bulged and ballooned out in the most unseemly places. It was starting to occur to me that not many clothes looked good on me. I felt wilted, and my hair and face had gotten greasy even though I'd taken a shower that morning.

I trudged out and showed my dad the last dress, standing in front of a mirror while my dad stood off to the side.

"What'd you think?" I asked, hoping he could give me some refreshing perspective. The thin material of the dress bunched hideously at my bosom, the three cute buttons strained at their buttonholes, and at my hips and upper thighs the slightly ribbed texture of the dress actually pulled out so the stripes looked wider.

My dad looked very seriously at me in the large department store mirror. He seemed tired too.

"You have very beautiful ankles," he said.

*   *   *   *   *

That night at the Father/Daughter dinner they served us white California wine. After eating, there was a brief award ceremony and then the tables were moved out of the dining room and we danced.

"Your father is a beautiful dancer," said Dominique, a girl from New York, more times than was really necessary. I think she liked him because they both had red hair.

16

"Have you noticed how great Irene de Forge looks?" Michelle Farrar asked me. Michelle was part of the beautiful rich girls group in the class above me. She, with her honey-colored skin and dark eyelashes, had grown up and hung out with Patty Hearst and Trish Tobin practically since they were born.

"No, uhn uh," I replied.

"Check her out. She looks beautiful."

Later that day I did see Irene, a delicate girl with white blond hair and dark eyelashes and eyebrows. She'd never been fat, but most of us ate more sweets than were good for us. Now she was wondrously svelte and the delicacies of her features stood out. Her skin was nearly translucent and she had a beatific look on her face as she floated toward Study Hall.

Polly O'Melveny and Dana Hees were walking close to her. "You look great Irene," I heard them say.

A week later, Dominique and I were on our way to classroom 6B for a freshman meeting after dinner.

"Did you hear what happened to Irene?" she asked.

"No, what?"

"They took her to the hospital this afternoon. She weighed seventy-eight pounds and she couldn't eat anything. They're feeding her intravenously."

"Can you gain weight by being fed intravenously?" I asked.

17

Christmas vacation had come and gone. It had been strange to be back with my family, who had Christmas just the same as always.

I hadn't been all that sorry when the Sunday after New Year's my parents dropped me back off at school.

          *   *   *

A couple weeks later, in the middle of January when the weather in Monterey is in the 50s, chillier than usual, Teresa and I were sitting on the stairs. I had my plaid skirt pulled down over my knees. We heard a clatter behind us. We both looked up and I moved aside. Standing above us was Susie Tucker; she of the fabulously developed yet athletic body; she of the kinky, long, honey-blond hair, hypothalamic gaze and the biggest, most sensual lips I'd ever seen on a white person, particularly a Catholic. Teresa and I both stared after her as she trounced off. She appeared to be wearing a chocolate-brown velvet slip with a golden brown chiffon overdress and brown clogs. I desperately wanted to comment on her great beauty, but I didn't know if that was allowed, one girl about another, so I stayed silent.

I had seen Susie Tucker's mother at the Fall Fashion Show. My job had been to open the glass French door to the dining room (which had been supposedly transformed into a couture salon) for the mothers as they entered. And enter they did, the sophisticated mothers in their Chanel suits and huge diamonds, often more lovely and certainly more put together than their fresh-faced teenage daughters, who were awkwardly playing hostess.

Mrs. Tucker was a perfect case in point, just as beautiful and a thousand times more elegant than Susie: an ocelot coat and dull gray suede gloves, just-stiletto-enough gray suede pumps in the same shade, a hat like that from a forties film noir, with a feather. She swooped in and stopped at the first table, close to where I was standing. Her honey-gold curls were piled atop her head. She opened a clutch in matching dull gray suede, and I could see her checkbook, also open, inside it. In her gloved hand was a slim Waterman pen, and as she wrote a check I saw the name on her checkbook. "Mrs. Forrest Tucker."

"To whom do I write the check?"

About a month later I watched a Western with Forrest Tucker listed on the credits. He had been one of the main cowboys, I wasn't sure which.

I asked Susie Tucker, "Is your father a movie star?"

"No," she fiercely answered.

It was only a couple of weeks after that, right before midterms, that insidious rumors began to be whispered up and down the halls of the dorms after lights out. Susie Tucker was in trouble and so were some of the seniors.

"Seniors?!" I hissed, disbelieving, to Katie Budge. "Are you sure?"

The senior class was so far above us, so perfect, it was only by a great stretch of the imagination, no it was not possible, for me to conceive of them doing something wrong. Something so wrong as to account for the 2 a.m. lights and mysterious cloaked figures that crisscrossed the campus. Katie Budge and I timorously held the curtain aside and peered out my chicken-wire-reinforced window in Long Dorm, ignoring the chill of our bare feet on the cold floor. There were men in jeeps driving back and forth across the campus.

"Susie Tucker was pulled out of bed by Sister Humpbert a few minutes ago because . . ."

"But, what . . ."

"Shhh." Katie Budge crouched down on the cool linoleum floor beside the end of my single bed. We heard the whisk, whisk, whisk of Sister Aaron's feet. The rings on the canvas clattered as she pushed aside the curtain near the head of the bed.

"June?" Sister Aaron softly but firmly asked.

I kept my eyes closed in what I fervently hoped looked like sleep. She must know I always woke up when she called my name this way in the morning. The curtain rings clacked softly again as she let the canvas fall, but I didn't dare breathe a sigh of relief. Katie and I remained motionless for another half hour before Katie finally worked up the courage to slowly unbend herself and tiptoe back to her room.

"Hey, Katie," I whispered very, very quietly. "Who were those men in jeeps?"

She moved over close to me and said softly right into my ear, "That's the Houston Patrol. They're always there at night driving around. To protect us." She waved ruefully, slipped silently through the door and was gone.

The next morning it seemed like everyone knew before I even woke up. Five seniors, Susie Tucker and another sophomore—a day student I'd hardly noticed—were in big trouble.

I walked past Susie's room. She sat Indian yoga style on her bed, wearing an embroidered peasant blouse, silent, eyes rimmed with red. We hurried by. Once out in the crisp air, we talked about it in excited and frightened whispers.

"What'd they do?"

"I think it has to do with boys."

I could easily imagine Susie breaking every rule known to man with a boy, and what's more, I could easily imagine any boy being willing to risk everything for her. I sighed to myself.

"The seniors are acting the same way as Susie, I hear," Ann Drendel whispered harshly. "They all refuse to talk."

In a couple more hours, new rumors floated down.

"Drugs. It's drugs. They were caught doing drugs."

"ON CAMPUS?!" I was totally wide-eyed.

"No." Patty Hearst, the bearer of the latest news, looked at me with disdain. "Of course not on campus. They were doing drugs during summer vacation and at Christmas."

"Really? What kind of drugs?"

"Weed," spat out Patty Hearst. "*Someone must have told*," she hissed.

"What's going to happen?" Ann asked.

Patty leaned in closer to us, intensified her gaze and lowered her voice, "There's no telling. The nuns had them up all last night in the classrooms with all the lights on questioning them. None of them have said anything this morning. They went back in this afternoon when classes were over."

We didn't see those girls for five days. Some classes were canceled—Sister Aaron's English, Sister Jane Fox's American and European History sections, Sister Humpbert's English and Sister Clare's Ethics. The morning after their prolonged disappearance, the girls were all seen in their rooms, pale, frighteningly gaunt and red-eyed. Within hours they were gone, and all their belongings with them, leaving only a few dustballs in the corners under their stripped beds.

18

Kyle Tomkins was blond and the first time I noticed her she was wearing a short-sleeved, white-striped, poor-boy t-shirt and yellow plaid culottes. Her legs were very tan and muscular, like a tennis player's, and she wasn't wearing stockings with her white strap sandals. She was walking across the back parking lot with a load of books, on a Sunday evening, clearly coming back from the Study Hall. It was near Spring Break, and most of the students had eased off a bit on taking their studies seriously.

"Hi," I said cautiously. She replied in kind, but did not smile.

Later that week, I walked down to the sophomore end of Long Dorm to visit Kit, when I saw Kyle sitting quietly in the corner. There were six girls in Kit's room talking, some sitting cross-legged on one of the upper bunks. The room was strewn with paisley and flower print dresses, striped shirts, pink and blue pastel stockings, Lanz nightgowns, underwear and long wool skirts, and earrings, gold bracelets and chokers lay in tangled abandon on the tops of the dressers. I didn't think Kyle had noticed that I noticed her in amidst the girlish debris.

" . . . and there's nothing to do," Cindy Doyle was just finished saying.

"That's for sure. Less than nothing," I chimed in, suddenly enthusiastic about our plight. "Here we are—it's Friday night and we're sitting here waiting for what? TV? Probably there'll be nothing on but a Western. There's nowhere to go and there definitely aren't any boys . . . ," I moaned, restless. "Meanwhile . . . ," I drew the word out. I was giving a show now, talking fast and windmilling my arms around for emphasis. "What are other girls our age doing tonight?" I pretended to look to the heavens for an answer.

"They're going on dates with incredibly handsome guys with motorcycles. They're wearing tight jeans and the wind is whipping their hair back as they clutch the strong muscles of their boyfriend when he speeds just a little too fast down the California coast.

"Then, they park in a secluded cove, and his hand is warm as he helps her down the rocky path. When they get to the beach, they lie in the sand, the moonlight shines on her long hair and dark eyelashes, making her even more beautiful, and they drink a very good bottle of white wine, which he has been able to purchase legally because he just turned 21."

I was exaggerating a bit, pulling out all the stops, performing actually, for Kyle's benefit. She seemed so distracted, so apart from the rest of us that I figured I'd better make it good if I wanted to catch her attention.

"And us? . . . Here we sit . . . ." I shrugged. "Anybody got a box of licorice?" I knew someone had to have one, the question was whether they were in the mood to share.

After that, Kyle and I became friends of sorts, mainly due to my unaggressive pursuit. She had a small, square, exercise contraption in her room that was suspended on springs. She stood on it and twisted back and forth to exercise her waist and hips. Usually, when she wasn't studying she was on that square, tirelessly twisting; sometimes the number of twists she did in a day—all definitely counted—numbered in the thousands.

I took to lying on her bed and talking to her while she twisted; she was a good listener and didn't ever interrupt.

One free weekend she asked me if I wanted to come home with her to Hillsboro and visit. I sure did. I liked to go to new places.

"Be sure to bring your bathing suit," she told me. Almost everyone except the girls who lived in San Francisco had pools.

Her grandfather picked us up at the airport in a Mark IV Lincoln Continental, and I rode in the plush gray vastness of the backseat. He seemed very white-haired and grandfatherly, and it was quickly apparent that Kyle was just as reserved with him as she was with me. After twenty minutes of smooth and rather silent driving, we pulled into a driveway. The simple white frame exterior, glimpsed through high, dark-green hedges as we pulled into the garage, did not at all prepare me for the luxury that lay within.

Kyle's house was the first house I had ever been in that fit my idea of a mansion. I mean, it didn't seem that much bigger than the house I lived in or Joan's house, but it was built differently. As you entered through the large oak door, you immediately found yourself dwarfed by the huge front hall. Across a gleaming expanse of marble floor were two *Gone With the Wind* style staircases leading from the first floor to the second. Every room was lit by chandeliers, and the breakfast room had black-and-white checkerboard marble floors and oversized French doors that were thrown open to reveal a rolling vista of perfectly manicured lawn. Down at the end of the lawn, two box hedges were cut so immaculately they had only a tentative connection to nature. Between them was an exquisite turquoise swimming pool rimmed with white tile, and between the edges of the lawn and the pool were two immaculate lines of dark sycamores.

Every room took a day and a half to cross and every doorknob in the house was gold. The library was dark and wood-paneled, with hundreds of books and shelves so high you had to use an oak ladder which slid along on brass runners. The living room had three separate areas for people to gather, each with a couch and easy chairs handsomely upholstered in matte satin. Now this, in my opinion, was a mansion. Forget about that wood floor and chintz-covered window nook stuff.

The second day we were there, Kyle and I had breakfasted on raspberries and were both floating on air mattresses (hers yellow, mine orange) in the pool, when she started talking.

"Nice house, hunh?"

"Yes. Very nice," I replied enthusiastically.

"We haven't lived here long."

I thought she was referring to herself and her two little sisters, also blond, who were nine and six. I didn't say anything, yet the silence between us wasn't oppressive, laden as it was with insects, birds and the laziness of the heavy sun.

"We used to live with my mother. Did you know that?"

I didn't know. How could I? She'd never told me.

"We used to live with my mother. It was a lot different," she paused again. Her voice sounded flat, almost sing-songy. "The houses we lived in were small and dirty. Sometimes my mother was nice, sometimes she wasn't. She'd be drinking and she'd disappear for a long time. Like for days, a week, three weeks. I was the oldest, so of course I was the one who had to make sure the house was clean and we all went to school. I would try to make dinner, but if she was gone a long time, there wouldn't be any food. Once—no twice, the electricity got cut off. Then my sisters got scared."

We floated, one of my feet dangled off the air mattress into the warm water. She paused for a long time. The turquoise of the pool and the perfectly groomed surroundings took on a surreal aspect.

"One day when my mother was gone and hadn't been there for a week, my grandmother came over and saw us, and we've lived here ever since," she shrugged. "That was two and a half years ago."

19

After my experience with Horace, it was no wonder that I wasn't looking forward to the organized campfire mixer our school was having with Robert Louis Stevenson. Once again the fun was mandatory. I consoled myself, at least mildly, with the super good outfit I devised for the event.

"You're wearing that! To the beach?!"

I spun around and admired myself in the mirror. "These are my favorite clothes," I said. "What could be better for a party?"

"But June," Joan protested, "even besides the fashion side of it, don't you think you're wearing too *much* clothing?"

"What? Are you crazy? It's the beach—at *night*. It's cold."

The beautiful outfit began with my brown velvet dress with round gold buttons. I wore it a lot, as often as I could, but this time I wore underneath it a gold lace skirt that belonged to Cindy Doyle. On her it was ladylike, on me it was . . . unusual. Then of course, I had on the brown suede lace-up boots, and as the *piece de resistance*, a long purple coat my Aunt June had had made in Japan right before World War II. It was the single most beautiful piece of clothing I'd ever seen, purple silk with a fuschia silk lining, both sides delicately embroidered in the same color thread so as to be nearly invisible: vines on the outside, and on the inside, dragons. A row of tiny, purple silk buttons ran from the mandarin neckline to the cinched-in waist. The coat flared out from the waist and fell to the ground in extravagant folds.

"But June, that coat is dragging on the ground."

"So what?" I said defensively, my aunt had been quite a bit taller than me. "I think it looks good."

The sleeves were also long, and on the back of my hand came to sharp exquisite purple silk points. I loved that coat and could not believe I could be so lucky as to own it.

"Orange, brown, purple and fuschia, June," Joan said simply.

"Velvet, lace and silk," I answered. "Besides, it'll be pitch-black dark."

Nothing she or any of my other roommates said could dissuade me: I knew that something very special could happen to me in this very special outfit.

We were no sooner off the bus when the nuns herded us over to the fire and began distributing hot dogs and sticks. I found myself sitting next to a rather straight-looking, brown-skinned boy.

"How do you do?" I said politely.

"Fine," he smiled.

Good smile.

I was not quite so perfunctory. "Your name?"

"Les. Les Brown."

"Where're you from?"

"Chicago."

"Oh, my father's from the South Side of Chicago."

"So I am. From the South Side."

I laughed. "Are you Catholic? My father said all the neighbor-hoods are divided by parish and everyone knew them so if someone said . . . ," I made my voice tough, like how I imagined a big city kid would sound, 'where ya from?' you answered, like, 'St. Philip Neri.'

"I'm not Catholic," he said.

"Oh," I waited a second in case he wanted to tell me what religion he was, but I knew it would be rude to ask.

"Today is Earth Day," Les said.

"I know. Are you into that?"

"Very. You'd be surprised. It's easy to think it doesn't make any difference out here in California where the air is lovely and everywhere you look for miles is green, but in my neighborhood in Chicago, it's a different story . . . ." He talked fast and passionately, "There's garbage everywhere, bombed-out buildings and empty lots with nothing but broken glass, chunks of concrete and used . . . ." He stopped.

I held perfectly still, unbreathing, for fear he would say that word, that c word.

"Well anyway," He looked at me apologetically. He didn't say it.

"No, it's okay," I assured him. He was cute and smart. Maybe he would like to be the first boy I kissed. I giggled at the thought.

"What's so funny?" Of course he was immediately on the defensive.

"Nothing. You want to go for a walk?" I asked.

"Are you allowed?"

"No. But I bet if we act like we're just going down to the water and then we drift a bit that way and then it gets just a touch darker, we can go off behind those rocks."

He looked at me with respect. "You're devious."

I mock sighed. "Forced to be. Against my will."

We walked.

We walked and talked and talked and talked some more. I moved closer to him. Hours went by and I moved closer yet. Finally we were standing, sheltered by some large rocks and having one of the dumbest conversations *ever ever ever* with our faces about a half-an-inch apart.

"Do you like math?" he asked me, provocatively.

"It's okay. Why? Do you?"

I was getting kind of mad. Why was he taking so long to kiss me?

"I have a pretty good teacher this year. Math teacher I mean. Well, algebra really," He continued very seriously.

I couldn't believe this. What on earth was the problem? "Oh yeah. I'm into algebra myself. I kind of like the p's and q's."

"What do you mean?"

"You know, the logic stuff. Don't you guys have that? If p then q, and so on?"

I could see he was searching his memory. I took advantage of his distraction to move a bit closer. The next time he moved his head we would be kissing for sure, if only by accident.

It worked. Of course, it finally happened only about five minutes before the nuns started calling us to get back on the bus, but still I liked it. And I was really happy I was wearing such a superbly romantic outfit on the sexy dark beach for my first kiss.

20

I was daydreaming as I walked to English class, so it took a minute to notice that Teresa was running after me.

"Hey June, wait."

I stopped and turned to face her. "Okay."

She came up a bit out of breath. "June, listen. You know our Speech teacher, Mrs. Hauke? She's looking for some new people to be on the debate team and she asked me if I could think of anyone who would be good and I said you and Joan. She agreed you guys would be great if you want to do it."

"How does it work?" I cautiously asked. Being on the debate team sounded either scary or boring, and maybe both.

"The entire country is assigned one topic, which they have for a year. This year it will be: 'Should the powers of the Environmental Protection Agency be increased by Senate mandate?' You write a speech and read quotes from 3 x 5 cards."

"3 x 5 cards? Where do you get those?"

"Well, most people research the topic, but they send you a sample debate with cards in the beginning of the year and we can just split them up. One thing that is super great about it is—we get to leave campus on Saturdays a lot." She grinned wickedly.

"Okay, I'll do it," I answered.

What I did not know was that, sure, we got to go off campus, but where we got to go was not some kind of fabulous treat. We would drive one or two hours to a public high school, usually with puke green hallways and old smelly classrooms filled with fellow teen debaters who were inevitably the most obese, odiferous, boogers-dangling-from-their-nose, purple-sweater-with-holes-clad, annoying, right-wing dolts. Or worse, plaid-suited, super bony and pushing their painstakingly amassed 3 x 5 cards around in metal files stacked high in wire grocery carts.

When we would get to a classroom assigned to the debate we would often have to help our opponents unload the boxes and boxes of cards they had amassed to counter our arguments. Consequently, we developed a talent for the offbeat premise, making it our goal to come up with arguments that the geeks would find unfathomable, like the reason the Environmental Protection Agency should pass laws to protect the environment is that the jobs created by the extra work of controlling pollution would help the country economically.

I would get particularly annoyed at the "men" addressing me by name in an argumentative sentence so I took to writing fanciful pseudonyms on the blackboard, Brunhilda, Guinevere or Aspidistra so that when they pompously began a sentence "Well, as the *second defense*, Brunhilda, *claims* . . ." we would dissolve in badly disguised giggles.

Ann Politzer had coincidentally stored her share of the 3 x 5 cards in a Pappagallo shoe box with a decorative map of the world. She occasionally used the box to vehemently demonstrate a geographic point.

21

Cindy Doyle came running down the hall and slid into place in front of me like a big-league ballplayer stealing third.

"June, you got a phone call."

By the activity of her eyebrows I could tell it was from a boy.
"Who?"

She shrugged. "How should I know? But he has a *really* sexy voice."

I picked up the black receiver. The phone was actually in a

booth, surprising as it was, that our privacy had been thought of for even one second. Must have been an accident.

"Yes?" I tentatively inquired. It could have been one of my brothers, or at least the two older, John or Stephen, whose voices had already changed.

"It's me."

I recognized Les's voice immediately, and my heart gave a little thump.

"Oh, hello," I tried for cool sophistication mixed with warm welcome, instead I got a crazy cracked tremolo sounding like I had no idea who he was.

"Do you remember me?" He now sounded confused too.

"Yes, oh yes," I breathed. That was a little better. I sounded less like I was in imminent danger of hospitalization and more like I might be at least alert.

He laughed. "What're you doing?"

"The same old thing. Torturing my friends."

"Oh, is that all you do?"

"Sometimes I lie on my bed and think up new ways to torture them."

"No studying?" he asked.

"No. I have been blessed with a photographic memory."

"Really?!!"

I could tell he was actually excited. I would be too if *he* was the one who told *me* he had a photographic memory.

"I wish. No, quite the opposite. I have to write my name on a piece of paper each night before I go to bed and read it several times when I get up in the morning."

He laughed. A very, very deep, very sexy laugh. I did in fact feel my knees buckle just the tiniest bit.

I cleared my throat. "How about you, Mr. Brown? What have

you been doing with yourself?"

"I have been busy continuing to celebrate Earth Day."

Wow. Good answer. He was supercool. I sighed and it might have been just barely audible because now he cleared his throat.

"Well, my little caged princess, I actually am calling for a reason. I heard through the unerring grapevine that y'all are having a dance in two weeks, and I thought that rather than sitting here tearing my hair out with worry that you'd accidentally invite a lesser swain, I'd call up and invite myself as your date."

"Yes."

There was a long pause.

"Definitely, yes," I said.

"Alright then," he said. "Uh. I guess I better get back to studying—I mean, exercising my photographic memory."

"Yes."

"Good-bye."

I was a bit too weak to remove myself from the phone booth. I stood leaning there against the smooth wood wall.

The night of the dance came and I was nearly frozen with excitement. I'd actually been getting colder and colder all week in anticipation, but only on the day of the event itself did my molecular structure start to achieve a totally immobile, glacial state.

"What're you going to wear?" my roommate Cindy asked.

"I have no idea," my mouth barely moved. "It's going to be hard to beat that beach party outfit. What do you think?" I lay inert on top of the yellow corduroy bedspread.

"What's wrong with you?" she asked. "You look sick. Don't you want to go? I thought you liked this guy."

"I've got a crush on this guy so big my body can't contain it. Don't you see it leaking out of my pores and pouring over the sides of my bed?"

"That's disgusting," Cindy shrugged and turned to her closet. "I've got this green thing," and she pulled out the most beautiful shimmery mermaid-green dress with a halter neck and not that much top to it.

"Wow, you'd lend that to me?"

She frowned and looked intently at the dress for a minute as she held it up on the hanger. "Yes, and you know what, I don't even care if you ruin it."

She was referring to my rather notorious tendency to destroy clothes. Not on purpose, there was just something about me that made buttons fly off, seams pop open and pens break in my pocket.

"Wow."

"You're welcome."

Not an hour later I was waiting by the door to the dining hall with the other clean-haired teenage girls in brightly colored flowing dresses, expectantly craning our necks to catch the first glimpse of the bus from RLS. Behind us the golden light streamed out into the darkness from the line of French doors, and the air was heavy with the scent of honeysuckle.

The lights of the bus came around the corner and pulled into the parking lot. I saw Les get off the bus. He was beautiful. He broke into a grin, his teeth flashing brilliantly and his long, long eyelashes, seemingly brushing softly against his cheekbones.

"Hi," he said and took my bare arm.

I shivered.

We went in and stood around with the other awkward couples.

"How've you been?" he asked.

"Fine. How 'bout you?"

Strangely, the conversation was very exciting, even though I was dimly aware that we weren't saying much.

"Would you like some punch?" I asked.

"Sure," he smiled that devastating smile again.

I started to walk off, but he reached out and caught my arm.

"How 'bout if I come with you?"

Sipping our drinks, we looked around the dance floor. I grimaced.

"It's all a little strange, isn't it? Did you hear the dogs barking when you came in?"

"Oh yeah, what was that all about?"

"Men. They're trained to bark at men."

Les laughed, then asked me, "Would you like to dance?"

"The music's not that great, is it?"

"No."

Anyway, our interest did not really lie in dancing.

"Let's go out on the terrace," I finally said.

We strolled out the glass doors, leaned against the balcony and stared down at the oak-leaf strewn ground below, the heavy smell of humus wafting up.

"How's your math?" I teased him

"Never you mind, Earth girl," he replied.

"Listen . . . ." I said, then, remembering the last time, just moved closer—I'm sure I don't know where I got the guts—and closer, until we were kissing.

After a few minutes he paused. "You said 'listen' and I was listening mighty hard, but I didn't hear that much."

"How did you get here? I mean, how did you get to RLS?"

He looked at me seriously. "I got a scholarship. A wrestling scholarship."

"Oh."

I kissed him some more.

"Maybe we should go back in and dance," Les murmured.

"Maybe we should," I said, before making out with him for another ten minutes. I rubbed myself up against his body. I was having a good time. He was having a good time. We both together were having a really, really good time.

"You know, this is driving the nuns crazy. Look. Look in the windows." I pointed through the French doors to other couples twirling in gaily colored circles, the girls' shiny hair flying out. Sister Jane Fox was glaring quite ferociously across the room and out at us. Her puffy cheeks and wattles looked even more swollen and pale than usual.

"They can't break us up because they're afraid of looking prejudiced," I said.

We both laughed.

22

I voted quickly and looked around the Study Hall. Two hundred and forty girls in identical, striped cotton uniforms all had their heads down, circling names. The late afternoon sunlight came in and caught the highlights in the smooth glossy hair (most of the girls had long hair, as straight as they could make it) of the first few rows of heads. I could see Teresa Barger in the front row, head diligently bent taking her voting responsibility seriously.

It was an interesting way of voting, the electoral system we had. I wondered if Sister Carlotta had been the one to devise it, or was it Sister Mary Kieran, her saintly predecessor? We voted for class representatives: two freshmen, two sophomores, three juniors and four seniors, who together formed the electoral college. It was much like the American system of presidential elections, but with age substituted for population density.

After the class representatives were elected, a series of secret meetings began, attended by the representatives and the ten major nuns. In the meetings, the student body president would read a list of eligible candidates for each office, and if an elector thought some-one should be considered for an office, she would raise her hand when that name was called. For example, for sophomore president, the entire list of sophomores was read, and usually about fifteen people would have hands raised for them. During the hand-raising, the girls would have their heads down so they didn't know who sug-gested who, but the nuns kept their heads up. It was always clear to us that there would be repercussions should an elector choose to raise her hand for someone "unsuitable" or "immature."

*　　　　　　*　　　　　　*

It was with great surprise that I found out that afternoon that I had been elected a representative.

FRESHMAN SUMMER

Never for one second was I sorry that my new high school friends lived far away because I had been crazy to travel since I first found out from books that other places were different. I'd been out of school about ten days when I started to get restless.

"Hey mom," I walked into the kitchen where she was busy making spaghetti. Half of our house had burned down the year before, so she was in the new kitchen with its red tile floor, big white cabinets and miles of butcher-block counters. My mom was simultaneously boiling water for noodles, searing hamburger meat and cutting a long Italian loaf and spreading it with garlic butter. She was wearing white tennis shorts and her long tan legs moved quickly as she dashed back and forth between the counter and the stove.

"Joan called me today. She wants me to come down there," I

said.

It was easy to fly around California. Pacific Southwest Airlines (PSA) only charged $16.95 to fly from San Francisco to Los Angeles, and $8.95 to fly from Los Angeles to San Diego.

"Why doesn't she come up here?" My mom looked up at me. "Come finish this garlic bread for me. Where've you been?"

"Reading," I said defensively.

"I guess you can go. But I need you back in eight days. You have to baby-sit."

"What about the boys?"

"Stephen already told me he's going to Yosemite with the Leonards, and John might be here, he might not. Anyway, I'd rather you did it."

"Okay."

It came as a surprise to me that Los Angeles was a lot more humid and hot than Santa Cruz. I didn't have any sleeveless shirts so Joan lent me one of hers—a green and blue cotton madras. The space between the middle buttons popped open a little but I didn't care. I thought that was a bit sexy. Both of us wore blue jeans.

"Let's get out of the house quick before my mom sees what we're wearing."

Joan's mom was a very strict Catholic and she would try to get Joan to wear a plaid calf-length skirt if she could.

"C'mon, Michael's out with the dogs, he'll drive us to Scandia."

Since Joan's father, Mr. Frawley, thought that the alcohol industry was owned by the communists—who were going to try to take over the country and kill the Frawley family first—their house was surrounded by ten-foot wrought-iron gates, with spikes on top, that were always locked. When you pulled up to the gate at her house, you had to call up to the maids on the intercom before you could get in. At night, the dogs—German Shepherds, trained to kill—were let loose on the grounds. There were monitored videos in the upstairs and downstairs libraries that constantly scanned the 3.75 acre estate in Holmby Hills.

Joan's older brother Michael came around the corner of the house.

"Hi Michael," Joan waved.

Michael always looked sad. His face was scored with pain. I knew he had a crush on me but I tried to act like I didn't notice, although it was kind of useful for things like when we needed a ride.

Joan and I both sat in the front seat of the car; Michael had chosen the maroon Cadillac, so there was plenty of room. Joan rolled down her window and slouched with her feet up on the dashboard.

"You went to school back east, right?" I politely asked Michael.

"Portsmouth Priory," he grimaced.

"Didn't Catherine Crimmins' father teach there?" I turned slightly toward Joan. I knew already from whispered late night conversations that the brothers at Portsmouth Priory were brutal and that some of the boys *drank*.

She didn't pay any attention to me.

She was singing "Diamonds . . . I don't mean rhinestones . . . Diamonds are a girl's best friend."

Joan had Michael drop us off at Scandia. She kept singing, mostly old show tunes, all during lunch, but I didn't care, I was busy looking at the Los Angeles characters who were sitting in grottos in the large Viking-themed room. There was a woman in a leopard print body suit that bagged at the knees and chest. She was also sporting a matching turban and *gigantic* false eyelashes, which didn't look that good since she was at least sixty, judging by the wrinkles.

There was a family of Germans whose table was piled high with sliced meats, pickles, thick rye bread, herring, so many full plates that some of the round scalloped edges hung dangerously over the sides of the table. They didn't seem to notice. The thick, square-jawed, somber mother and father and the slightly less thick blond-haired son's and daughter's heads bobbed up and down as they industriously shoveled in the food. Actually, Joan's singing made kind of a nice backdrop in the Scandinavian restaurant, with its dark wood walls.

Emerging from the dark restaurant, we were stunned by the glare and heat.

"We have to find a place to call my brother," Joan murmured without much conviction as she led me into a small warren of shops and up a brief flight of stairs. The heavy musk of purple frangipani overwhelmed my senses.

"I feel sick," Joan said weakly. "I have to lie down."

At the top of the stairs to our left was a pink Dutch door in a purple bungalow. The top half was open and inside we could see what appeared to be a hair salon. Joan walked in, made a beeline for a window seat with a long, purple satin pillow and lay down with the back of her hand held delicately to her forehead. The interior was cool and dim. I sat in a dark straight-backed chair in front of a coffee table covered with thick French and German fashion magazines. I picked up a French *Vogue* and affected ennui.

"I feel slightly nauseous," Joan moaned to the room at large, maybe to explain our presence.

As my eyes adjusted to the light, I noticed that the dimly lit room held two occupants besides us. One was a very, very, wealthy-looking woman who was having her white-blond hair teased straight up. The person who was doing the teasing was dressed in a skintight purple jumpsuit, very high heels, and had purple glitter eye shadow extending in points into purple hair about three inches long that stuck straight out like a lion's mane.

I looked again. The person had no breasts to speak of, but no bulge *down there* either. The person, the hairdresser, leaned a tiny bit closer to client and hissed cattily, "I bet she's pregnant."

I was shocked. Was that a man or a woman? I couldn't believe she was talking about us! And didn't she know, wasn't it totally obvious that Joan and I had just barely been kissed and we were certainly still completely virgins?

24

Late that night, back at the Frawleys, I wanted some food, but I was afraid to go down to the huge kitchen by myself. Luckily, Michael was there, with his best friend, Dean Yardley, who was husky. I surmised that he might be talked into eating.

I walked down the hall and stuck my head around the door. "Hey, Dean. Hey, Michael. Are you guys hungry?" I was hoping to arouse hunger in them with auto-suggestion.

They looked interested, particularly Dean.

"Sure."

"Let's go downstairs and see if there's anything to eat," I said casually, as if it were no big deal. As if there could possibly not be something to eat in that brilliant cornucopia of every tasty delight known to man that the Frawley family called a kitchen.

"I'll stay here. I'm tired," Joan picked up her book, Destiny's Child. On the midnight blue cover was a lurid illustration of a girl with flowing raven tresses looking fearfully back at a castle on a hill while lightning struck the crenellated towers. From the direction of the castle, a handsome man on a charging steed raced toward the girl. I could guess the plot.

Dean, Michael and I went quietly down the carpeted stairs.

"Are the dogs around?" I asked fearfully.

"They're still locked up," Michael said. "I won't let Pavlov in the house until after Dean leaves."

I sighed in relief. Those dogs were vicious.

We walked through the pantry where the china and silver were stored. The celery walls and white trim showed off the glass-fronted cabinets stocked with Spode china and Baccarat crystal. On the central island, neatly arrayed, were small silver bowls of salt with minuscule silver spoons, enough for one at each place setting. I'd already done my reconnaissance work earlier in the day and knew I wasn't much interested in the refrigerator in that room, which contained fruits and beverages—that was the light-refreshment-for-a-summer-afternoon-snack refrigerator. I went through the swinging white doors, almost authoritatively; Dean and Michael followed behind me. In the refrigerator directly to the left of the door were leftovers, food odds and ends. But what absolutely positively *glorious* left-overs: caviar and a plate of prosciutto, a bowl of sliced cantaloupe, five or six different types of cheese, including an exquisitely ripened French triple creme, and half an apricot strudel, carefully wrapped in Saran, which had been delivered that morning from Jurgenson's.

"That's good," Michael said pointing helpfully to the strudel. *As if I needed direction.*

"Wait a second, let me just look over here," I scooted past him to the dry pantry.

The panty was a big room just about the size of my bedroom at home and held more delectable unperishables than I could previously have imagined existing. I desperately wanted to look over all the food carefully, first to make sure that I made the best selections and also to assure that I ate them in the best order, but if I took too long, Michael and Dean might figure out I was weird. I grabbed a tin of Danish butter cookies.

"Get that strudel," I ordered Michael, "and also some milk."

The three of us started toward the breakfast room, where the family ate all their informal meals. I wished I could make some cinnamon toast, but didn't think cooking would fall into the normal behavior category.

"Oh, oh, wait. I think we should have some of that veal cordon bleu, too." I had spotted the covered casserole dish and knew it was a dinner leftover. "Would either of you like some?" That was my excuse for bringing the whole dish.

"I would," Dean said. He'd already gotten himself a Coke from the beverage refrigerator.

We went into the oval breakfast room where the roman blinds were rolled down over all the windows against the midnight dark outside. I could tell Michael was a little nervous and not really as into the whole eating thing as Dean Yardley and me.

"I bet Joan told you the story about Ondine and the assassination," I said.

"No," Michael looked over at me, his attention distracted from the food I was carefully laying out on the table.

"But you must have heard at least a little bit when it happened last year?"

"No."

"*Really*? You didn't hear about . . . ? Well, you know Ondine, right?"

"No."

"Hmm. I thought she came to parties down here sometimes." I ate a Danish butter cookie. Wow. You could really taste the butter. "Well, she was in our class. She was a friend of mine and she was kind of friends with Joan too." I shrugged. "I mean, of course in one way we all know each other pretty well from living together."

Michael had gotten three forks and plates, the same white ivy-patterned Wedgwood we'd used earlier for our dinner, and I'd given myself a healthy serving of veal and strudel. Normally, I would just eat straight out of the containers, but not with Michael and Dean there. The cookies were open between Michael and me. I settled in, knowing that this story was plenty long enough for me to eat all I wanted.

"All right, let me see . . . if you haven't heard any of this, I'll go back to when Ondine first came to Santa Catalina at the beginning of last year. She was a very beautiful girl with long, straight, dark hair; possibly one of her grandparents was Spanish, I mean, we never asked her or anything, but she did have olive skin and almond eyes. Exotic looking, you know what I mean. She was part Austrian too, well no, I think someone told me she might have had Austrian citizenship and she had gone to boarding school in Switzerland for the three years before Catalina. It was hard to tell what she was: Spanish, Austrian, her father was a count. Anyway, can you believe she'd been in boarding school before high school? Her mother was a fashion model in England, and her father was definitely royalty or deposed royalty from some country behind the Iron Curtain, but evidently . . ." Here I lowered my voice and whispered in exactly the same way Nancy Holt had when she'd told me, "*they'd gotten out with plenty of money.*"

I took a deep breath, appreciating my memory of her beauty. "I mean she was beautiful *and* skinny. She came after the school year had already started. One morning we woke up and she had moved in, she was staying in the bunk room at the end of Long Dorm. There was an empty bed from when Susie Tucker got thrown out."

I quickly took two bites of veal. It was super delicious, the cheese was melting in my mouth even though it was cold, and the tomato sauce was about the best I'd ever had. For a moment I spaced out.

"Then what?" Michael asked.

"Ummf. Ummm. Then after about two months, maybe less, she got a phone call; it was after lights out and she woke us up with an ear-piercing scream. I looked out my door and saw her running down the hallway toward Cindy Doyle's room, weeping, her long, white lace nightgown billowing out behind her. We all stuck our heads out of our cubicles and watched. She was more emotional than the rest of us I think."

I took a bite of veal cordon bleu. The juices rolled sensuously down my throat.

"Later, we found out that her family didn't have as much money as they once had. But man, you should have seen her clothes. She would have on a white silk-gossamer dress with a white silk over-gown and petit-point white shoes with pointed toes. And that was just to lounge around in."

I was going to go on, but I could see I was losing Michael and Dean on the fashion tip.

Both of them were looking astonished, but I wasn't sure about what part.

Maybe drama would recapture their attention. "So the rest of us could hear her sobbing in Cindy's room. Not that we meant to listen, but you know, it was the middle of the night in the dorm and you can practically hear people breathing four rooms down. And Ondine was saying, 'It's the . . .'" I began imitating her with sobs in between parts of the sentence. "'It's the. . . .' Sob. 'Mafia.' Sob. 'I'm sure of it. Who else would want to harm Uncle Augustin? They sent him a letter . . .' but then she quieted down and was just crying. The next day she was very, very silent, but there were rumors flying around like crazy. What we heard was that there was someone out to kill the entire family, and we noticed that the Houston Patrol stayed the whole next day and usually they're only there at night."

Michael and Dean were really listening now.

"Then, about four hours later she packed up, and when we came back from Study Hall she had taken her trunks out of the storage space. She was sitting surrounded by Vuitton luggage in a long maroon overcoat, and it was obvious she was just waiting for a taxi to come and take her to airport. The only thing she kept saying was that she had to move to a safer place. The nuns made an announcement about the unfortunate circumstances under which Ondine had to withdraw and said we would all pray for her and hope she was happier in her new situation. It was weird because they kind of made it sound like she was crazy and had made the whole thing up. As if she were to *blame*."

"Then d'you hear any more?" Dean asked breathlessly.

I concentrated my attention on the flaky crust and thick sweet apples of the strudel, which was unbelievably good and well worth the effort.

"Umm. Yes." I took another sweet, scrumptious bite. "Uh, Diane got a letter from Ondine about a month before the end of the year, and she was in a boarding school in Ireland also run by nuns, and she said it was weird, they were quite strict and she missed all her friends. When she left Santa Catalina she'd been whisked in a limousine to the airport and she'd had to stay in the car with its darkened windows until minutes before the flight left. They took her to a South American country where she stayed with friends of her father's in a villa on a mountainside for a week, then she was whisked off in the middle of the night to Europe. Evidently, there was a period of time when the family had to move from house to house to make sure that the killers didn't get her. The FBI thought it might be a family vendetta, but it turned out it was just a crazy guy, an American, a Vietnam vet, who had been living in the hills up above her uncle's villa outside Florence and had decided her uncle was too rich."

I ate some triple creme cheese on Stoned Wheat Thins. Man, oh man. "I guess he'd killed not just the uncle, but also the uncle's step-daughter and four or five servants. We saw a piece in *Time* magazine about it. You know a 'violence worldwide' piece. And Ondine in her letter implied that her uncle had been tortured by the guy before he killed him."

"Oh my god. That's horrible," said Michael.

"Yes," I agreed, and folded a piece of paper-thin prosciutto sever-al times to fit easily in my mouth.

25

Ann Politzer and I were lying on her twin beds and looking at the ceiling. We could hear murmuring from the next room of her father, an Episcopal minister, and her mother (a lovely, well-behaved if occasionally acerbic, preacher's wife) talking while they ate break-fast.

"What shall we do today?" Ann asked.

"You know, I don't think I'll be able to get a boyfriend for many years," I replied.

"Why not?"

"Well, how will we get boyfriends when we don't know any boys?"

"Yeah, that's true. That's depressing."

"What about Les?" she asked.

"I dunno. We had finals and there weren't any more dances and then all of a sudden it was the end of the year. I guess I sort of for-got about him."

We both stared at the ceiling some more.

"Maybe we should go to the beach and try to get a tan."

"Sure, okay," said Ann, who had masses of kinky-curly red hair and almost blue-white skin. "The good thing about getting a tan is that you look thinner with a tan."

"Yeah, that's true."

"But you're not that fat right now anyway," Ann generously offered.

"Un-hunh. Yeah. I've been on a diet. You know the one. You can eat all the protein and vegetables you want, but no carbohydrates. Yesterday I had a hamburger, a package of sliced ham and a whole carton of cottage cheese. Today I might have some Swiss cheese. Man, I love that stuff."

"And you're never hungry on this diet?"

"No, you can eat all you want as long as it's protein," I reiterated.

We got up and put on our bikinis. Hers was red with big orange flowers, mine was a small blue and white print. Over the suits, we pulled on patched jeans and oversized white t-shirts.

"We're going to the beach, Mom." Ann yelled in the direction of the breakfast room as we tried to scoot out the door.

"Oh Ann, wait a minute. Your brother has band practice tonight and so I need you home to watch Mary around five."

"All right," Ann agreed *almost* graciously.

We let the door slam behind us.

SOPHOMORE YEAR

I stared idly as Penny McNichol walked her odd, lopsided gait down the hall of Long Dorm toward me. I had arrived for the beginning of sophomore year to find that I had been assigned Penny as my first roommate.

During freshman year, the nuns had never put Penny in a room with only one other person, probably because she was crippled, thin and misshapen, with one leg much shorter than the other, big hunched-forward football shoulders and a bulging mongoloid fore-head. The nuns probably figured that nice Catholic girlies with good upbringings would never be unkind to Penny if there were other girls to observe them.

As she lurched toward me, I noticed the pink- and white-striped skirt of her uniform was starched straight out, but had barely a hip to catch it on her skinny, skinny frame. I sighed.

"Hi, June," Penny boomed from down the hall.

"Hi, Penny," I quietly replied and slipped back through the canvas curtains of our room to sit cross-legged on the yellow corduroy bedspread that had returned for another year. Penny was not far behind me.

"What classes d'you have?" she bellowed from right behind me.

"Same old, pretty much. English with Sister Aaron again, Spanish with Mrs. Romero again, Latin with Mrs. Stahl again, Speech, English, Modern History, etc."

I didn't bother asking her what she had—I knew it would be exactly the same, probably arranged differently, probably not all honors. I lay back on my bed with my arms behind my head and must have taken a small nap, because the next thing I knew, Diane Hull was shaking me.

"June, June, c'mon, it's time for chapel singing."

Every Thursday night, we had to go to the chapel and practice the songs we would sing on Sunday. It was always cold in the chapel, with its tile floor and impossibly high ceilings, but Thursdays even more so, when the building seemed hollow without the sanctity of Sunday service. The girlish voices rose up in sweet clear song, strangely beautiful even though we all professed to hate the practice.

When we got back, Diane came into my room and sat on my bed with me.

"Tell me," she gently asked. "How was your summer?"

"Oh, wow, wild. At the very beginning of summer, my parents went on a trip and I got the bright idea to call all my old friends from eighth grade and invite them all for a big sleepover on the beach. Boys *and* girls. Unfortunately, my parents came home early and caught us."

"Oh no." Diane seemed genuinely concerned. Which was probably how she did feel.

Slender Dana Hees stuck her head through the door. "*Hey*, here you guys are." Dana was pretty, with a raspy voice and a small cute mouth. She moved her head rapidly from side to side, her straight blond Dutch boy cut swinging. "Everyone else has disappeared. The dorm is empty."

"Well, come on in. I was just telling Diane about this wild party I threw which my parents came home in the middle of."

Dana looked excited. "Okay." She hopped up on the low dresser and brought her feet up, resting her elbows on her knees. "So, what happened?"

"Well, my parents arrived home from their trip early in the morning. Luckily, I'd left the beach to sleep at home with Joni Tannenbaum. Right away, when my dad came in my room he knew everyone was there because their stuff was all over. I woke up to him shaking me, and he had a super serious look on his face and was asking me, 'June, June. Who else is here? Where are they?'

"'Uh, Lark, Dina,' I began to sleepily reply, then woke all the way up and realized we were in trouble. I began trying to figure out if there was some way I could get down to the beach before my dad found Lark snuggled in a sleeping bag with Jim Bargetto and Dina Delucchi with Tom Meadows and Nancy with Billy Ford. I jumped out of bed and started talking."

Teresa pulled the curtain back.

"Hey, there you are. Mind if I sit in?"

"No, not at all," I held my arms out in welcome. "Come in, make yourself at home."

"June is telling us the story of her parents coming home early from vacation and discovering that she has invited all her friends over to sleep with their boyfriends on the beach," Diane explained.

"Great," Teresa said and went to sit on the bureau with Dana. Dana scooted over.

"Okay, so there I am, my dad has just woken me up, seen everyone's stuff and is asking where are the people who belong to the stuff. I'm stalling. He hasn't figured out yet that there's boys involved.

"So I go. 'Uh Dad, yeah. Uh. They're all down at the beach. How 'bout you and I go downstairs and grab us some chow . . .'."

I saw Teresa and Dana looking at me in amazement.

"Yeah, I actually said 'grab us some chow before we trek down to the beach.' Can you believe it? Of course my father immediately knew something was up. So he's waiting patiently outside my room while I get dressed . . . ."

"Can I come in?" I heard a voice from outside the room, it was Juanita DeSanz.

"We," Cindy Doyle added.

"Sure."

They found a place to sit, but not on Penny's side. Usually people will sit anywhere in a room, in a sense we moved so much you never thought of any room as your personal property, but there was something about Penny that made you not feel like sprawling out on her bed.

"So I'm getting dressed and my dad is waiting for me and I know he knows something is going on, so of course I can't decide, should I wear the striped crewneck top or should I wear my gray hooded sweatshirt? I stall a bit longer by going and brushing my teeth. By now my father is looking ever more determined and I'm thinking 'How am I going to get out of this?' Man, he is going to kill me if he finds my friends in sleeping bags with their boyfriends. I am desperately sending ESP messages to them to get up but I figure that's unlikely to work. I mean—it *is* only eight a.m . . . ."

Penny burst through the door, pulled up short and peered around, breaking into a grin. 'Well, well, well, we've got a party goin' here. Hey, I know. How about a little sing-along?"

Everyone's eyes widened slightly in horror and disbelief.

"Hey, yeah, sure," someone murmured unenthusiastically.

And with that, Penny, very smoothly, reached under her bed and pulled out an acoustic guitar.

"Uh, Penny . . . ," I tried desperately to think of a way to stop her. "I don't think we want to sing right this minute."

She didn't pay any attention. "You all know 'On Top Of Old Smoky' don't you?" She played a couple of bars. "I know, how 'bout 'Down in the Valley'." She began playing it and singing. "C'mon, sing along . . . ," she cried to us on top of the guitar relentlessly playing.

Not knowing what else to do, we all sang along.

27

It was midnight. Every night for the past two weeks I'd listened to the crackling of hard plastic wrappers and the soft, subtle, squishy sound of Penny chewing some of the treats she kept stored in her bottom drawer. Now I was halfway between disgusted and ravenous.

I knew what she had in there. I'd looked over plenty of times during the day as she nested something in or wriggled some other goody out of her cache. She had a lot of trail mix, she had Stoned Wheat Thins and Ritz crackers, there was a bag of crunchy granola and a box of licorice. Oh yeah, and to complete the list—a bag of dried banana chips.

Lying there on my bed in the nearly impenetrable dark, I got hungrier and hungrier.

"Penny!" I said in a loud whisper but felt immediately chagrined because it accidentally sounded like I was going to get mad at her.

After a pause, she answered, "Yes?"

We both were whispering because of the partial walls of the dorm.

"Penny . . . ," I started again, softer, nicer, a hint of pleading. "I'm hungry. Do you think if I promised, absolutely promised I'd pay you back, I could have just a little of your food?"

I waited. There was a long pause pocked with the sound of girls turning in their sleep, Lanz nightgowns brushing against cotton sheets, a branch tapping a window far, far down at the other end of the dorm.

"Okay," she said, a little grudgingly.

I breathed a sigh of relief that my humiliation was not for naught. I saw the dark shape of her looming over in my direction, arm outstretched.

"But don't ask for anything more," she sternly warned. "I don't have that much." She handed me a crinkly package; I felt with my fingers that the paper top had already been torn open.

Anticipation flooded my pores, my taste buds began salivating: food was everything. I gently put my finger in through the stiff plastic package and felt . . . oh no . . . a suspicion . . . I knew it, but I had to put the round disks to my mouth to prove it—she'd given me the banana chips. I flopped back on my bed, letting the banana chips fall sloppily to the ground. Soon I was sound asleep.

28

I walked quietly down the hallway, feet padding on the linoleum floor, and into the bathroom. Clutching both my Spanish books in my arms, I pushed open the door to a small room containing a bathtub and felt the soft resistance of a body already stationed there.

"Oh, oh, I'm sorry," I said.

"It's okay." I recognized Joan's voice. "Come on in."

She was perched on the edge of the bathtub, wearing a long blue chenille bathrobe, holding the door open with her foot. I slipped in.

"I tried to get Sister Mary Ellen to give me an extra study hour, but she wouldn't."

"Yeah, me too," Joan said, although I noticed the book she was actually holding was <u>Incest in the American Family</u>.

"Um," I stood there. "Did you already study for the Spanish test?"

"Nope. Not yet. I'm going to as soon as I get through a few more pages in this book." She waved it around in the air for demonstration. "Then I'm studying."

"Psst! Is anyone there?" came from outside. I guessed it was Ann Drendel, just because her whisper was so much louder than anyone else's.

"Shh. Yes."

"WHAT'RE YOU GUYS DOING?" Ann really did have the yell of whispers.

I went out and stood close to her. "I have to study Spanish. How 'bout you?"

"French."

"Okay. I'm going into one of the stalls." I went and put one of the seat covers down, then sat on the cold plastic and began studying. I could hear Ann whispering loudly to Joan for a couple more minutes, then a squeak of the door as she went into the stall next to mine. I studied the conjugation of verbs (ayuda, ayudes, ayuda, ayudamos, ayudas, ayudan) uninterruptedly for half an hour.

"Psst."

"Yes, Ann?"

"Did you ask Sister Mary Ellen for a study hour?"

"Yes."

"It's funny. I've asked her every day this week and every day she said no. What am I going to do? I *have* to study."

"Yeah. I asked her Monday and Tuesday too. Seems like she always says no. I have six solids and I know for a fact it would be impossible for me to finish my homework in three hours because the Latin teacher actually let it slip that we're supposed to get an hour of homework from each class."

"From each?" Ann laughed. "Some of my teachers can't seem to keep it down to an hour."

We both heard a noise that was not Joan.

"Shh!"

Feet in soft shoes padded into the bathroom then looked around, then stopped. We weren't breathing. The silence was a bad sign.

Then: "GIRLS!"

We jumped. I heard Ann's softcover French book drop to the tiles with a dull thud.

"What in heaven's name do you think you're doing?"

"Studying," I said defensively.

Sister Mary Ellen pushed open the stall door and stared at me then opened the door to Ann's stall.

"And you?"

"Studying too."

"Is anyone else here?"

Ann and I remained anxiously silent, not wanting to tell a lie.

Joan emerged from the bathtub room, the expression on her face somewhere between shamefaced and defiant, her glasses pushed up on her head, wearing an over-size white t-shirt, the blue chenille bathrobe and bright blue plaid slippers, loosely holding the incest book.

"Me. I'm here," she said.

We watched Sister Mary Ellen's suddenly eagle eyes go straight to the title of Joan's book and acute distress suffused and reddened her round pink-cheeked face. Then she turned and fled.

We were surprised, waiting for a minute for her to come back with a spanking switch or something. After a few minutes, we realized that the path to punishment that had seemed so unswerving had reached an unexpected fork. Slowly, carefully, we tiptoed out of the bathroom, turned right and stood in front of her door. From inside we could hear what sounded like heartbroken weeping. That seemed strange to us. So strange we went immediately to bed.

29

"June. Tell us a story."

"Tell us another story, June," they harangued me.

This was worse than my sister Katy, at least there'd only been one of her.

"Mmmm," I murmured, but I wasn't going to sleep. Actually I had been contemplating whether I had the energy to go in the bathroom and read.

"Ple-e-e-ease," Juanita drew the word out to its most pleading, most guilt-inducing length. Even in the dark I could imagine her, a doelike girl, big-eyed, long legged and highly strung, smiling like she always did when she begged.

"Tell a story about what will happen to me when I grow up."

Two or three stories immediately crowded into my mind.

"Okay."

I could sense them settling back in the dark. I'd told them stories before of course, but this was the first time they'd demanded one.

"Okay, Juanita. You will remain thin, your hair will be the same,

straight and brown, but your boobs will get a little bigger. You'll go to the University of California at Davis and you will live in a house sheltered by three big trees . . ."

I was starting to get warmed up.

" . . . on the edge of miles of strawberry fields. You and your blond roommate Cary will go out and pick strawberries every morning for break-fast.

In your junior year, you will begin a highly passionate secret affair with a professor in the veterinarian school. The affair will be secret not because he's married but because he's so popular with women: he has thick straight blond hair, a square jaw and honest, deep blue eyes. If it gets out that he's dating someone it might cause a riot.

After you graduate, you buy a ranch with him up near Truckee and bear his blond-haired love child, Amalie. When your daughter is a year-old you have an outdoor wedding at which the guests are barefoot.

I stopped talking a little abruptly which left silence in the room, although I could tell Juanita, Carol and Cynthia were all still awake.

"Wow," Juanita finally breathed softly. "Thanks."

"Now me. Now me," Carol demanded.

"Okay, give me a sec." I had to think about what Carol was like. She was flashier than Juanita, but not super-confident. Her body was small and strongly muscled. She should have dressed in clean-lined sports clothes but she was from Fresno (her father was agribusiness money) so instead she wore stonewashed denim and ruffles.

At first you will experience difficulties, sadness. You will be going to UOP and the studies will seem hard and Southern California not really to your liking. The other girls from our class who are also there will be too busy to hang out with you much, and in the end of your freshman year, your father dies.

Carol gasped.

"Don't worry," I continued. "It gets better. Besides, I'm just making this stuff up." I paused for a minute, but got no response so I went on.

Within six months, your mother, heartbroken, follows him to the grave.

It was easy for me to picture Carol, with her tough, pert body, short hair and sly round face, holding up bravely at the funeral, one eye alert for handsome male mourners.

You have to spend the next six months putting their affairs in order, selling the house and dealing with lawyers. In January, just as you are about to go back to UOP, the lawyers inform you that, surprisingly, your father was heavily insured and there's quite a bit of money. You and your sisters inherit just a tad under a million dollars apiece.

As I took a deep breath, the rapt anticipation was palpable in the dark room. The furniture in the room was defined only as dark shapes, it was strange and also a bit scary that their belief was so strong. I could hear their deep breathing and wondered if they were asleep or bored. I waited.

"Please go on."

Okay. You go to a travel agent and ask for her most exotic trip. She suggests beach cabins in Jamaica or St. Thomas, but you aren't really interested until she, almost halfheartedly, in desperation, brings out a brochure describing a six-month tour of New Zealand.

Naturally, that's the trip you want and you go down there and love it. It turns out to be as beautiful as California but much less densely populated. Soon, you've fallen in with a group of slightly wild, wealthy horse-owners. Everyone takes private planes back and forth from each other's giant ranches, flying over magnificent canyons and spectacular forests to attend high-stakes races. This is the life you lead for two and a half years.

Finally, though, just as you are about to get bored with the high life, leaving a party to fly back to Auckland, you are standing on the tarmac in the midday sun, waiting for your hosts, when you begin a conversation with the pilot. You've lost interest in your companions so you press him, "What's your story?" He looks a bit taken aback but not unpleasantly so. "Same as the rest the blokes around here," he answers. "Not true," you reply, surprising yourself, and at that instant, you are absolutely sure you are right. He is special. "Where are you going after you drop off my friends at their destination?" you ask. You think you detect his eyes twinkling. "I'm going to the coast for some R & R. Why? Are you thinking of boldly forcing yourself on me?" "Very boldly," you reply. He turns out to be not just unbelievably good-looking but also well-educated. He's just a shade under six feet, has dark curly hair and a Roman nose with just a few freckles. He tells you about his house, which can best be described as a shack high on the side of a mountain. The two of you fall madly, deeply in love. It is only after you've been married to him for six months that his older brother dies and you find out that he's now going to be the next Earl of Viscount.

"Wait a minute," Carol said. "What about our wedding? What's it like?"

Oh my god. Your wedding was a truly raucous affair. It was in the biggest church in Melbourne because it turned out your husband knew almost everyone in the country. Your sisters flew over, and a lot of your friends from Catalina. I was there, and Juanita. Cynthia couldn't come for a reason that will be revealed later in her story.

Of course all the people from the wealthy horse-racing world came and all the pilots in New Zealand and Australia. Most of the guests were young and they got totally wild. The pilots were climbing onto the roof of the beautiful old hotel where you had the reception and singing at the top of their lungs. By halfway through the party, people were passionately making out with other people they shouldn't have been, and the band was totally far out so people were dancing everywhere. After about three days, you and Ethan took off in his plane and flew to the airport closest to his mountain and rode white horses with white saddles to his house.

"Oh. Ethan. I love that name."

Again there was silence; sound was deadened in Santa Inez dorm, with its thick, rounded, stucco walls. Carol and I were on the two top bunks and our clothes were in dressers against the opposite wall. There was not much actual room but there was a feeling of roominess because the ceilings were high, with dark beams. It was one of the old buildings, dating from when the property belonged to a wealthy landowner. It was heated just a little too well, and I always perspired lightly while I slept.

There were two windows, small, with thick sills and square iron gratings cutting the light that fell just barely into the room from the waning moon.

Heavy breathing seemed to indicate that at least one of my roommates was asleep. Maybe Cindy Nadai's story was going to wait until another night.

Then Cindy spoke up.

"I thought you were going to do one for me."

"Yeah," Carol seconded.

I sighed. It really did remind me of when my sister had the room next to mine and she'd always say, "June, June, tell me a story," and I'd always say, "Once there was a man and he lived and he died." Then she would wail, "No, June, tell me a real story, but not a scary one." And every night I'd use all my ingenuity to tell her a story that had every appearance of not being scary until right near the end.

I thought for a minute. *Cynthia. Umm. Okay. Cynthia goes to Georgetown University in Washington, D.C., which she only just barely has the grades or test scores for, but her interviewer is so impressed with her poise, he insists she be let in. The summer between junior and senior year of college, Cynthia gets a job teaching English to an assistant to the Kenyan ambassador. They become good friends; he's young, in his late twenties, very, very tall, jet-black. They go out to nightclubs occasionally and he delights in treating her to extremely luxurious restaurants. They're just friends, but Sadad is rich and needs someone to pal around with. He already has three wives back in Kenya.*

I paused. The faint possibility existed that they were asleep. No, I could feel them waiting. I think even Juanita was still listening.

When Cynthia graduated from college, Sadad asked her to come back to Kenya. He was being offered the job of Assistant Minister of the Interior and he wanted to hire Cynthia as an attache. Cynthia was unsure. Did she really want to leave the United States at the beginning of her working life, plus, the job didn't utilize her degree in education.

Her father yelled at her for her indecision. "You'd be a fool not to go," he said. "This is the opportunity of a lifetime." So she went.

In spite of the brilliant way Sadad had treated her in Washington, D.C., and the really nice dinners she'd had, she was in no way prepared for the life of kings they lived in Kenya.

Every night they went to someone else's palace, every night there was a twenty-course feast with a clear native alcohol called rezodo which tasted like licorice but was deadly, and every night after dinner there would be women dancing. The most beautiful exotic women Cynthia had ever seen, dancing with millions of multicolored transparent veils and accompanied by spine-tingling wailing singing.

But you know what? The most amazing thing? The men in Kenya and the princes who came to visit from surrounding countries thought that Cynthia was the most unbelievably exquisite creature they'd ever laid eyes on. They worshipped her. Her height 6'2" . . .

"I'm only 6'1"," Cynthia said, sleepily.

6'1"— drove them crazy, her white skin. Many of the servants particularly had never actually been around a white person and definitely not anyone with her color blond hair. Cynthia didn't realize that she had the status of a goddess, but whatever it was, she liked it.

It was strange for her, living there with the buildings all made of pink marble, set in endless expanses of sand. The sun beat down inexorably day after day, and the palm trees would move only slightly in the faint breezes. It took her a long time to get used to eating giant flat bread and oddly spiced vegetables while sitting cross-legged on ancient, priceless carpets.

One day, not quite a year after she got there, she was walking through the royal gardens on the way to her office when she spotted an incredibly handsome man who was a good five inches taller than she. That night at dinner, there he was again, sitting right next to her friend Sadad. She exchanged looks with him a couple of times and Cynthia felt an electrical current race between them, but they never spoke. The next day, he was gone.

How crazy should I go? I wondered to myself.

Cynthia waited a couple of days and then she asked Sadad. "Who was that eating dinner next to you the night before last?" She was trying to sound casual.

"Who? I don't know what you mean," Sadad answered.

Cynthia noticed that his normally serious face looked tired and somber. He was genuinely perplexed.

"The tall man, with skin blacker than yours and a djellaba on. He was sitting on your right."

Sadad's face relaxed into a grin. "My old friend Mohammed sur Ben Jihad. You best be careful, my friend, he has quite a reputation with the ladies. I heard his suite at Cannes this year was famous for containing the most stunning starlets at the festival."

So the way her heart jumped when she saw him turn his head in her direction, an unusual feeling for her, was just him using a practiced skill.

"Oh." Cynthia felt immediately disappointed. The feelings she'd gotten for this man were evidently common. "So he's just a playboy then?"

"No, oh no." Sadad was serious again. "Not just a playboy. He is the right hand man to the King of Kuwait. Some say it is actually he who is ruling the country."

Cynthia felt overwhelmed. She struggled to keep herself from asking more questions and instead forced herself off to bed. She didn't see Sadad smiling after her—because his good friend Mohammed sur Ben Jihad had called that very afternoon to ask who Cynthia was. But . . .

I left a long pause (tick, tick, tick, tick).

It was a year and a half before they met again. Cynthia's brother got into a terrible car accident from which it turned out he was going to recover, but she had some vacation time so she decided to go see her family.

By this time Cynthia had become incredibly sophisticated. She spoke Arabic, not fluently, but certainly serviceably and she had also become quite good in French. She'd had a couple of Chanel suits made, and had taken to wearing VERY EXPENSIVE low-heeled black suede pumps. She was definitely head and shoulders taller than everyone else and much more elegant. Her curly hair was swept back and looked very 1940's film star-ish.

Man, I was tired. For a couple of seconds it was silent in the room. The room was much darker, as the moonlight no longer shone in the windows.

"June, Ju-une, please go on," Carol's soft plea came out of the darkness.

"I can't," I said. "I'm too tired." And sure enough, I didn't even hear myself say the end of that sentence before I fell fast asleep.

The next morning I popped awake in my upper bunk a little early. Oh great, it was a Saturday. I quietly got my bathing suit and went down to the pool. Technically, we weren't allowed to go anywhere by ourselves, especially not swimming, but the pool wasn't that diligently monitored. Rather than watch us constantly, they counted on us to turn each other in for any serious infractions. I grabbed my striped beach bag and the tattered copy of <u>Dune</u> that I was reading.

It wasn't until I was actually getting into bed that night, exhausted by a day spent lying around in the sun and studying, that I realized the chances of my roommates forgetting to ask for more of Cynthia Nadai's future life were slim. Quickly I slipped under the cool white sheets and lay very quietly with my eyes closed.

Carol was standing by my bed first—I could smell her, a mixture of cinnamon, eucalyptus and almond (Pond's cold cream). Then Cynthia or Juanita was standing there too, both of them looking at me.

"Do you think she's really sleeping?" whispered Cynthia.

"No," Carol said, quite loudly.

"Yes, I am," I said clearly, without opening my eyes.

They both laughed.

"What time is it?" I asked.

"Ten. Or ten *to* ten."

"Okay. Sister Mary Ellen will be around in ten minutes to make sure the lights are out. After that, I might be able to tell you more of Cynthia's story."

"Yay! Yay!" They began jumping up and down.

Again, I felt amazement. I mean, after all, it was just a made-up story.

About half an hour later, I started.

"Okay, where were we? *Cynthia had been living in Kenya for over six years and she was flying back to see her family. She had grown quite elegant; I believe she was wearing a cream-colored Chanel suit with green trim and a silk blouse. She had on cream pumps and was carrying a small Vuitton bag. Her plane had landed in London and she was walking toward her connecting flight thinking of the slight foreign-ness of the airport, when who should she spot but . . .*

Now what name had I given that guy again?

. . . Mohammed sur Ben Jihad. Striding straight toward her with a great big happy grin on his face. He walked right up and warmly clasped her hand. Once again, Cynthia felt electricity. Mohammed smiled harder;

maybe he'd felt it too.

"You're even more beautiful here in England," he said.

Cynthia was overwhelmed. Speechless, but maybe that was the right reaction.

Mohammed looked straight into her eyes. "Are you staying in London?"

"No," she replied, surprised at how cool she sounded. "I'm flying to New York and then on to California."

"Please don't leave me."

Cynthia couldn't believe her ears. Who was this guy?

"It's been so long since I've seen you. I was a fool last time, too wrapped up in myself and Sadad to even make an opportunity to talk to you . . . ."

By now Cynthia remembered that he was an international playboy. She also noticed that he did have the longest eyelashes, and dark circles under his deep, dark eyes . . . no. She wrenched herself back to reality. He was practiced at the art of lovemaking. She had no desire to be just another notch in his belt.

"Yes! I do, I do." This was from the real Cynthia.

I ignored her.

So she pulled her hand out of his and resolutely said, "I believe you're mistaking me for someone else," quite firmly and walked off. She couldn't see the look of utter devastation on Mohammed's face as he stood and watched her. Neither, though, could he see the small tear that leaked out of the corner of her eye as she looked out the window of the plane at the fog shrouding the London airport.

Cynthia had a wonderful time with her family. They went to a cabin on the Russian River, which everyone agreed would be marvelous for her brother's recovery, but also, privately amongst themselves, they felt that Cynthia looked a bit drawn. They knew she had reached a position of high responsibility as an attache in Kenya and that her duties were exhausting.

The entire month of July, the family swam and lounged in the sun and at night they joked as they played cards in the huge living room of the extended log cabin her parents had rented. Cynthia went on many walks through the redwood forest with her brother and slowly both of them began to have pink cheeks and strong muscles again. But finally, it was time for Cynthia to return.

As she landed in London she couldn't help feeling a twinge of regret, but of course Mohammed did not run up behind her. Back in Kenya she found work piled almost to the ceiling—nothing had been done in her absence, it had all just waited for her return. Cynthia set about it.

Another six months went by. Suddenly, one day, the door to her office was flung open and Sadad burst in. He ran to her and grabbed her in a huge bear hug, lifting her off the ground in his excitement.

"I've been promoted. I've been promoted. I'm going to be the ambassador. We'll have a huge party!" and he grabbed Cynthia again and whirled her around.

So they planned and planned and planned. All the African royalty was coming and the three sexiest Italian princesses: Cosima de Bulgari, Anna Spolodetto and Guiliana alle Marchesa. Roman Polanski was coming, and Elizabeth Taylor. I mean, this was a star-studded event of the greatest magnitude, both socially and politically. Cynthia had her hands full, planning for months, which is why, one day when she was on her way to the royal kitchen, she was completely surprised to see ascending the white marble steps of the palace, Mohammed sur Ben Jihad, dressed in a uniform, regally erect. Cynthia knew that blushing was going to be obvious against her short, white satin Christian Dior sheath, but of course she couldn't stop herself. She hoped he would attribute it to the blazing red sun just now setting in the west and still barely visible over the minarets of the castle. She didn't know that bits of that sun were illuminating her figure and lighting up her long, tanned, bare legs. He walked up and took her hand as he had before, but this time the electricity was a thousand times more intense.

"You must allow me to explain myself," he pleaded, his sad dark eyes

looking right into hers and begging her to listen.

His deep, strong voice activated every nerve in her body. She was trem-bling.

There was no way she could say no. They spent the night wandering amidst the wildly fragrant jasmine and hibiscus blossoms while Mohammed pleaded his case to her. Describing how he felt about her, recounting the questions he'd asked about her from anyone who'd ever met her, and telling her all their answers and how each one had left him just a little more intrigued, a little more in love. He told her of his father's recent death and the sobering influence that had had on him, and Mohammed begged her to at least see him again, give him a chance to reveal his true character instead of simply believing rumor.

Within a month, they were married. Cynthia changed her religion to Muslim, her name to Noor sur Ben Mohammed, which means "Light of Mohammed," and became the Queen of Kuwait.

I gave the last sentence the ponderousness of a closing statement. Silence in the dorm room. More silence.

"Then what?" Juanita asked.

"I'm burnt out," I said and went to sleep.

The next night we all got in bed, exhausted, at about 3 a.m. We had a big geometry test Monday morning. It took a couple more nights before we recovered and didn't have any serious late-night studying.

"Tell me another story of when I grow up," Cynthia said.

"Hey, what about me?" Carol protested. She was sitting on the one chair, with a light forming a halo behind her tousled, short curly hair and her legs up inside her white nightgown with only her toes showing, curled over the oak edge of the wooden seat.

I was feeling perky.

"Okay."

Carol hopped down from the chair, turned off the light and got in her bunk.

In this story, Carol, you go to Arizona State University, and it is totally easy for you. You have a brief affair with a football player, he's very popular, but not really quick enough on the draw for you. Not dumb really, but you like boys who are clever. Unfortunately, two weeks after you break up with him, you discover you're pregnant. You don't want to marry him, and debate telling him about the pregnancy at all, but finally you break down and reveal all. You also tell him that you don't want to get married. It turns out that his father has made some serious money in used cars and since everything is on the up and up, let's-all-be-friends, the father offers to pay some big-time child support. Three years later, Manny, cuz that's the football player's name—Manfred the father of your child—gets a big deal NFL contract and he keeps you and Junior, Manny Junior, in some very nice clover.

"Oh, does the baby's name have to be Manny?" Carol protested. "I like Max better."

"It has to be Manny," I insisted. "That's one of the reasons Manny the football player gives you so much money. His family is Jewish. They love that name."

"Okay," Carol reluctantly agreed.

"Okay, it's my turn now again, right?" Juanita asked.

Juanita was very cute, she had a cute voice too with a bit of a burr in it and she was not pushy at all. She was a bit shy so I felt flattered that she liked the stories and was comfortable enough to ask for more.

"Hmmmm. Alternative future for Juanita." And one sprang into my mind. And then another one for Cynthia and a third round and I told them all until, finally, one night, about three weeks later, I began feeling devilish.

"Okay, it's Carol's turn tonight," I said.

"Okay."

"Okay."

I began.

Okay, Carol got into Reed College and since she'd gotten steadily more radical during the rest of her time at Santa Catalina, it seemed a good choice for her. After three years at college maintaining a 3.75 grade point average in political science and participating in many antiwar demonstrations, she met a boy with whom she fell madly in love. Jonathan was tall and handsome, with dark eyes, a straight nose and curly dark hair. His father was a senator in New York. At first the marriage seemed wonderful, but after less than a year, Jonathan began staying late at environmental concern meetings and offering weak excuses. It didn't take Carol long to find out he was having an affair with a beautiful blond protester named Rosalyn. Carol divorced him. Jonathan got a detective to lie in court and say that she, Carol, had been having many affairs so she didn't get any alimony.

Carol didn't really worry about it. She was young and they had saved enough money to buy a small clapboard house in Seattle where they lived. Luckily, through a glitch actually, they'd put the house in her name.

But one day, Carol got a hysterical phone call at work from one of her neighbors, an older woman living two doors down, who was sobbing as she talked.

"Your house is burning. Your house. Come quick."

Carol drove home as fast as she could, but the flames were leaping fifty feet in the sky. The fireman were hosing down the houses on either side in a desperate attempt to save them, but Carol's house was hopelessly engulfed. She could see the flames licking around the windows and the blackened shapes inside and how nothing could be saved. A sense of desperation so strong it overwhelmed her soul rocketed through her as she stood there helplessly, while the firemen yelled into walkie-talkies and rushed by with hoses amidst the red revolving lights.

"June, what are you doing? I don't like that story," Carol said.

"Do a different one."

"Umm. Okay." Suddenly I felt helpless—as if, against my will, I had to tell the story that had just sprung into my mind.

You graduate magna cum laude from San Francisco State with a degree in Business. One of the graduate teaching assistants is very handsome, Max (a little tip of my hat), and so after you graduate, the two of you marry. After a year, you realize you don't have much in common with him, and never did have much besides schoolwork, and so even though he doesn't beat you or cheat on you and you don't mind that his salary is very small, still—after a year, you have to admit when you get right down to it—he bores you.

"June," Carol said warningly.

"You divorce him," I quickly snuck in. "I'm sorry. I can't seem to help myself. None of it's true anyway. What does it matter?"

My three roommates remained banded together in accusatory silence.

"Alright. I'll try Cindy." I took a deep breath and began. *"Cindy Nadai gets a tennis scholarship to Stanford and indeed she is very, very good."*

This is an auspicious start because Cindy was a good tennis player.

She has to take a sabbatical from school her second semester freshman year to play at Wimbledon. Once there, for some reason, her tennis game gets better and better until finally—even though she's seeded 64th—she wins. It causes a big media sensation, Cynthia Nadai is a star. She gets a million sponsors and she's rich too.

For two or three years, Cynthia is totally on top of the world. Her photo is on the cover of many magazines, not just sports magazines, but popular magazines like Seventeen, fashion magazines and cereal boxes too. The rest of her family also gets a share of the attention. Then, the third year she goes to Wimbledon, she loses. In a flash, she's not so popular. She still wins occasionally, but less and less. Coca-Cola, her biggest sponsor, drops her and gives the money to a 16-year-old wunderkind from Missouri. Cynthia is horribly depressed. She wonders, has the best thing that's ever going to happen to me already happened? She had to admit, yes . . . it had . . . ."

"No!" Carol cried.

"No!" Cynthia and Juanita chimed in. "No, that can't happen! That's not what happens! Stop it."

I shrugged, unseen in my bed. I felt like I'd used up all the good stories. I was tired of good stories with brilliant romances with wealthy men, spectacularly fulfilling careers, giant mansions with gold flatware and fabulous vacations.

"Look, I'm sorry. Let's try tomorrow night."

The next night I went back to the good stories. Not great, not that elaborate, but the futures were rosy. A couple of weeks after that we changed roommates again.

30

"Okay, okay, okay." Joan pulled her pantyhose on quickly and slipped into navy blue flats. She didn't look at herself in the mirror. Joan was still thin, she hadn't gained more than the original 15 pounds. I think the five older sisters might have given her a casual disregard for appearances. I took one last fast look in the mirror, sure, yeah, the navy blue skirt looked good even if I did fill out the pleats a little too much. Joan was now sitting on my bed, reading.

"C'mon Joan, let's go. The taxi will leave and everyone's going to Del Monte Center today, it'll take hours to get another cab," I said.

"All right."

We slammed the door and raced full speed toward the front

parking lot. As we flew through the arched doorway, we saw Kim, Judy and Diane Hull all sitting on the wall, waiting for us, and the bulbous yellow taxicab pulling warily into the front parking lot. We piled in, me in the front seat.

"Where to?" the cab driver asked.

"Del Monte Shopping Center."

I was very excited about the outing, but I wasn't sure why. I only had $10, and $3 of that would go to cabs. Well, I could look, couldn't I, and besides, $7 was a lot of money to spend on candy—I'd go to See's.

After a brief drive through the deep green, oak-lined frontage roads of Monterey, the cab pulled round a traffic circle into the shopping center. Del Monte Center had been built when simply the novelty of going to a mall had been enough to attract people—there didn't have to be any interesting shops.

"Let's go to Macy's first."

"Okay," we all said after carefully pooling our money to give the driver the exact amount shown on the meter.

The troop of us walked quickly along the stone path leading to Macy's. Bringing up the rear, I had to admit my friends and I looked very similar—all with long hair, pantyhose, flats and skirts. All just a trifle more plump than high-school girls are usually. Obviously we were Santa Catalina girls, we knew everyone in town could easily identify us, particularly since one of the rules dictated that we had to travel in groups of at least four.

In Macy's, I looked at the stockings and hat departments. Stockings were a possible purchase. I fingered the cut-off sample legs longingly. Some of the nylons felt so smooth, and the teal blue tights looked incredibly nice. But I could only just barely afford one pair and I'd be sorry later when I arrived at See's with only 53 cents. I tore myself away from the stockings and went to the hats. They were totally out of my price range, but I liked to try them on anyway because round-faced girls like me look good in hats. I tried on a black felt hat with an exaggerated curve to the brim, like a bowler but bigger, and examined myself in a conveniently placed oval mirror with white plastic trim. The satin ribbon hung down the back. Nice. Then a straw hat with a big wide brim and a strawberry print ribbon. Too much hat. I put the hat back on its stalk and moved over to look in a glass display case. Inside were scarves, silky smooth bursts of color, red, green, blue and yellow, seeming to float in air as they rested on the transparent shelves. Everything was so unspoiled, so much cleaner than anything I owned. So neat and perfectly folded.

I wandered back over to where my girlfriends were buying clothes. Most of the girls at Santa Catalina had a lot of money, but even so, not many bought extravagantly. They came from families where frugality was thought to be a sign of class, and it was rare to see anyone but the South American girls come back from Carmel or Del Monte Center with more than a couple of bags.

Kim was debating whether to buy a blue and green striped skirt.

"It's a bit wild," she said as she frowned at herself in the mirror. "I accidentally shrunk my navy blue dirndl in the wash and I think this one looks good." She twisted back and forth in front of the mirror. "But it's not on sale."

I was thinking that a blue and green striped skirt made of some material that hugged your legs was not much of a replacement for a navy blue wool dirndl.

"Oh, I do wish it was on sale."

For a second she glanced longingly at the other end of the young women's sportswear section as if a saleslady might appear and rush over to attach a sales sticker, but it became clear that that wasn't going to happen. Instead, Kim held the skirt up against her body again.

"Do you think I should buy it?"

I was just about ready for some candy. That $7 was burning a hole in my pocket. Maybe a quick stop at a bookshop to do a little more fruitless longing, because otherwise the trip would be too short, the goal reached before I had entered the satisfactory level of anticipation.

"I'm going to the upper part of the mall," I announced. "Anyone want to join me?"

Joan and Judy looked over at me and frowned. There was nothing up there but a WalMart, a grocery store and the bookstore.

I shrugged. "Okay. Meet you at See's at . . ." I looked at my watch. "Four?"

"How about 4:15?" Joan said. "We don't want to rush back."

At four I was standing outside See's perusing the window display before I allowed myself to actually enter. Over to the right I could see the chocolate turtles. Those were very good. Next to them was a stand-up display, a little garden of candy actually, with milk chocolate and dark chocolate suckers (See's specialty) as the flowers. Between them was astro turf and a miniature white wooden bridge. I stared at the square-ish suckers. Man oh man, they were delicious. Just seeing them there, posed as blossoms, made my mouth water. Slowly I opened the heavy glass door. A bell went off in the back of the store.

"May I help you?" a plump, sloe-eyed teenage girl wearing a pink smock asked me immediately.

"*No!*" I said—too vehemently. I merely meant, "Not yet." It was *way* too soon for me to make a choice.

She looked shocked.

"Uh, I mean. In a minute I'll be ready."

She wasn't the least bit mollified.

I moved closer to the case and pressed myself up against the glass separating me from the candy (which was mainly chocolate-covered, my favorite). My eye slid smoothly past the fudge, bulging slightly in the middle with the weight of the heavy sweetness, and over to the chocolate-covered cherries, with one cut in half as a demonstration, the red syrup oozing out onto a white doily and pooling in a thick glob. Next to it, the mints were primly lined up and the next tray over held light milk chocolates embedded with almonds and walnuts, lumps that swelled out in fickle directions.

The milk chocolate sat next to the dark chocolate reminding me of the difference in flavor: the smooth, thick milk chocolate and the slightly bitter bite of the dark chocolate. The chocolate covered peanut crisps were next. I loved the crunch when you bit in, the peanut nougat sticking to your molars as the chocolate melted away.

One very important aspect of my decision was that I get enough candy so that even if I had to share, plenty would still be left over. It was difficult to eat in secret at Santa Catalina.

Finally, I spotted the perfect thing. Chocolate covered English toffee was on sale. A pound for $5.99.

"Umm." I tried to catch the girl's attention. "I'll have a pound of English toffee and two turtles."

"Do you want it in a box?" she asked, still a little sullen.

"Uh, no," I boldly declared. I didn't care one whit if she thought I was going to eat it all myself.

"What'd you get?" I heard Kim ask eagerly behind me.

I knew I was only going to have a little time after the taxi dropped us off to curl myself into an unnoticeable ball somewhere, hopefully with the really stupid but totally absorbing romance novel Joan had insisted I read, and slowly suck and chew some of my beautiful, delicious, totally satisfying chocolates.

31

"Sister Humpbert can speed read three books a day," freckle-faced Dorothy Thomas said to Hope Nordhoff.

"So?" said Hope.

I didn't reveal that I had been eavesdropping, but it did make me mad. So Sister Humpbert was a faster reader than me? I was pretty sure I could teach myself to speed read. When I was still in eighth grade, my father had bought us a spring-loaded instrument that flashed words on cards really fast. My brother John had been better at identifying the words, but I'd done okay.

Recently, I'd read that the key to speed-reading was to just pick up the most important words in a line as you trolled your index finger down the middle of the page. As I was drifting off to sleep that night, I determined to try it out with William Faulkner's <u>The Sound and the Fury</u> the next night in Study Hall.

Sure enough, I could read the whole thing in forty-five minutes. Afterward, it felt bad though, there wasn't enough time to savor the words. So I resolved never to do it again. Sister Humpbert could keep the record.

32

Joan and I had learned from some sophomores the year before that you could sneak over to the dining room—after Study Hall, but before 'lights out'—and possibly find one of the many glass French doors accidentally left unlocked. Joan and I would cross the back of the eerily empty dining room, staying away from streams of light coming in the French doors, and go through the stainless steel swinging doors to the huge stainless steel industrial kitchen. Then we would sneak into the kitchen and see what kind of food had been left out. Most of the good stuff was kept in locked refrigerators, but sometimes there was coffeecake from the morning or a couple of desserts from that night. Being totally bold, Joan had discovered that if you went through the small swinging door in the back, there was another small kitchen with the completely different, considerably better food that the nuns ate. You had to be careful when raiding the nuns' refrigerator, however, because if you got too greedy and were caught there, we knew without being told, you would be punished much more severely.

One evening in late autumn, Joan and I were both lying in bed, reading. She was in the next room, but I knew she was there because she called out to me occasionally, "Hey June, c'mere. I want to read you this really good part."

I would have been annoyed, because my book, Anna Karenina, was much better than her book, another romance novel, but I wasn't because it was Joan.

"Hey, June," she yelled.

I didn't answer.

"Hey June," she yelled louder.

"What?"

"Let's go raid the kitchen, I'm hungry."

"Sure, alright." I got heavily out of bed and pulled on a blue cotton skirt. By now all my clothes were a little tight.

I went into Joan's room and she was still lying in bed, reading.

"Oh brother," I sighed. "Do you want to go or don't you?"

We checked every glass door and then, in frustration, checked the ones on the far side, the balcony side, again.

"This is ridiculous." Joan stood with her hands on her hips—as if having free access to food was our God-given right.

I had an idea. "I know. Let's go look and see if, by some wild chance, they left that back door the servants use open."

Joan brightened.

We walked all the way around the dining room, down the scary unlit hill and then across the very small parking lot in the back used only by the workers, the sharp angle of the hill making us walk stiff-legged. There was a steep flight of stone steps leading up to a single, painted wood door. Joan and I mounted the stairs with difficulty. We turned the handle and it was instantly apparent that the door was firmly locked. Joan and I stood there in despair. It didn't seem possible we weren't going to get any food.

"Got any money for the vending machines?" I despondently asked.

"Course not," Joan snapped back. This whole thing had angered her.

I stared tragically off into space. Then I saw it. "Hey, wait a minute! Look there." I pointed at the window next to our stone perch. "The window is open a little."

Joan immediately leaned over and looked. "There's a screen. We'll need tools."

I leaned over too. I could just barely see that the handle to open the window was right there, on the other side of the screen. We sprang into action.

"I'm going to my room to get my Swiss Army knife," Joan said. "You stay here."

"What for?" I protested.

"All right. You can come with me."

Upon our return it was a simple matter to slip the sharp blade through the old wire screen and cut a small round hole through which we could slip our hand, open the window more, remove the screen completely—and crawl through. We ignored the 15-foot drop to the ground below should we happen to slip while climbing. Inside the storeroom, for that's where we found ourselves, was a wealth of delicious food items, far, far greater treasure than we had ever had access to before. There were *cases* of food in there.

"Look—raisins."

"And Saltine crackers. Millions of them."

"Hey, what's this covered with tin foil?" Joan lifted up the edge of aluminum foil from a cookie sheet and gave an involuntary whoop of joy. "You are not going to believe this!"

"What? What?"

"It's an entire sheet of just-baked chocolate chip cookies."

"Totally far-out!"

The cookies were piled up three and four deep, it was quite a haul. We took a box of raisins and a box of Saltines for later food emergencies but the cookies were the big snatch. We had to hurry out of there to be back in time for lights out with hopefully a few minutes to spread the word to the other girls that we had cookies.

That night, we had a lot of visitors in the Santa Inez kitchen. Even Seniors and Juniors came over. Joan and I earned great admiration for our feat and we basked in the glow, especially from the upperclassmen.

33

"C'mere." Judy stuck her head and arm through the canvas doorway and motioned me out of my Long Dorm cubicle. Judy came from Ysidro in Northern California. She had gotten chunky at Catalina, but she had a wide, square face anyway and her thick, square glasses made her look serious and studious. Actually, she was a bit of a troublemaker and she'd already read Marx, not for school.

"What is it?" I asked.

"Have you heard the stuff about Paul McCartney?"

"What?" Then I remembered. "Oh, you mean that he's dead?" I wasn't totally into the Beatles. I liked Spirit or the Rolling Stones better.

"There's more to it than that. Come with me. Patty's going to tell us a bunch of cool secret stuff."

I was lured.

Patty Hearst lived in the bunkroom on the far left. We padded down the length of Long Dorm. The curtains were closed and inside the only light was two candles flickering through the room making the usual assortment of print dresses, Indian bedspreads and cheap overflowing jewelry boxes look exotic and mysterious.

Magical Mystery Tour was playing softly in the background. Patty was sitting lotus style in the middle of the room, with her head lowered, the candlelight glinting off her blond hair. She raised her head slowly when we walked in.

"June wanted to hear about it too," Judy quickly explained.

"Yes," she whispered.

We sat cross-legged in a triangle.

"Paul is dead. I know for sure." She moved her hand up from the game board that was between us and I recognized an Oiuja board.

"Just a minute." Patty breathed secretively as she got up and went over to the stereo. I watched as details of her body—the smooth skin of her shoulder crossed by the strap of a black slip, the crooked line of her nose—were illuminated by the candle, then sunk back into darkness again.

"This is 'I Am a Walrus.' When I play it backward, you'll hear it." She moved her hand down to put the needle on the vinyl, then used her finger to rotate the turntable counterclockwise.

"Grumph blumph mish mirck umph," was the noise that

emerged from the speakers.

I listened intently. There! I could hear what sounded like "Paul is"—very muffled of course, but after those two words it was indistinguishable. If I'd had to translate it into some English word, absolutely HAD to, it would be more like "saddle" than "dead," making "Paul is saddle." But maybe she was right. She stopped the music and looked at us expectantly. "D'you hear it?"

Judy nodded.

"Okay." Patty smiled smugly. "Now look at this. See how on the cover of *Abbey Road* the other three Beatles are wearing shoes and only Paul is barefoot? That's because this is the suit he was buried in. The rest of them are wearing shoes indicating that they're alive, still connected to earthly things."

We peered intently at the album cover, no easy task in the flickering light, although the fact that Paul was the only one who was barefoot was plain enough to see.

"Why . . . I mean, what's the reason for keeping his death a secret?" I asked.

"Money," Patty Hearst triumphantly exclaimed. "If Paul is dead they won't make as much money and you know the Beatles don't own themselves anymore, they're owned by a corporation."

I was flabbergasted at the idea. A corporation? Own a person? Whoever heard of that?

34

I was slumped in my seat listening to Sister Jane Ferdinand lecture about the feudal system in Europe.

"Every feudal lord built a wall around the town, and in exchange for part of their crop, a tithe, the surrounding farmers would have the right to rush into the town behind the walls when there was an attack."

I wrote ATTACK on my notepad and sighed. I was hungry. It was too bad that European History had to be right during snack. I thought I might ask Joan what she thought of this almost irreconcilable schedule conflict. I glanced over at her, she was equally slumped and it was noticeable that the way her pen was moving bore a much more striking resemblance to doodling than note taking.

After class, I bemoaned the necessity of missing snack with her.

"Next time, let's not go to European History. Or no, better yet, let's be fair. Every other time we will go to snack. A fifty-fifty thing."

It was Friday before we had European History again. Just as we were about to enter the room I remembered our plan. I clutched Joan's uniform sleeve and whispered in her ear. "Joan, c'mon, let's cut this class and go to snack."

Snack was a meal, if you could stretch your imagination to call it that, which was served on the terrace behind the dining room between 10:15 and 11:00 a.m. It consisted of: the leftover coffee cake from breakfast—usually cake with cinnamon crumble on top (streusel), still on its heavy iron 18" x 24" baking tin; accompanied by bumpy plastic pitchers containing various warm drinks.

Joan and I made our way over to the dining room with only the faintest hint of sneak in our walk and wound our way to the oak-draped back terrace. It had to be admitted that the bedraggled coffee cake and faint glimpses of six-foot high barbed wire-topped fence through the heavy trees did not justify the great anticipation we had been feeling. I looked up. The trees would have been very romantic except that these particular California oaks had lately gotten some sort of worm infestation—worms with skins so thin and transparent you could actually see the entrails inside bulging out.

Joan and I headed straight for the food. It was very delicious, the cinnamon crunch topping being much the best part of course, so when it became clear that no one else was coming, we just ate off the tops.

After a few minutes, Joan broke the silence. "What's there to drink?"

I peered in the top of the closest bumpy green plastic pitcher. "Coffee's in this one." I could tell by the smell. Then I leaned over the next, "Uh, this seems to be tea, but it's kind of weak." The third one contained a thick light brown liquid; I took a small whiff to check it out. "Hot chocolate."

Joan had picked up the last pitcher—a green one—and peered in, disgusted. "This drink is yellow and has a grease slick on the top. It looks gross."

"Let me see." I took the pitcher from her and she readily gave it up. I sniffed it. "It's chicken bouillon."

I put it down and since it was a bit chilly, poured us both hot chocolate. A worm dropped down onto the topless coffee cake. Only a few feeble rays of sun forced their way through the trees as we drank.

35

Barbara Smith came through the wooden gate and around to the far side of the pool, fully dressed, and sat in the shade. "I was wondering where you guys were."

Joan looked up at her. "This is where we always are, hoping to disguise our bodily flaws by making them brown."

We all lay there quietly absorbing the white hot sun for a moment.

"Hey'd you hear Laura Knoop got asked to the RLS prom?"

"Oh yeah, who by?"

"Some guy I never heard of—Les Brown. She met him at a dance I guess."

Immediately my heart flopped in my chest and I felt nauseous. For once I did not welcome the possibility of vomiting.

"How'd you hear that?" Dana asked.

"Laura told me herself."

Again there was a silence, all the others too busy getting tan to focus their minds on conversation, me speechless in confusion.

"Well? Is she going to go?" Joan idly inquired.

"She said she wasn't sure. She liked him, but it's been a long time since she heard from him. I think they met at a dance freshman year. I betcha she's going to say no."

The next night at dinner everyone was talking. This guy, Les Brown, had asked Laura Knoop to the RLS senior prom and she'd said no, so then he'd asked Cynthia Briedenbach and she'd said no too, and then he asked Megan McDonnell.

None of my friends brought up the fact that the now infamous Les Brown was the very same one who'd given me my first kiss. Maybe they'd forgotten. Whatever the reason for their unprecedented silence on the matter, I was deeply grateful.

Anyway I might have been expecting it, maybe not, when the beginning of the next week, I got a call. I ignored the usual eyebrow waggling at the sound of a male voice by the freshman who'd answered the phone.

"Hello?"

"June, it's Les." I felt sick hearing his note of false cheer. "How're you doing?"

"I'm okay," I cautiously replied.

"Uh, I called for a reason."

I cringed. I would have given ten million dollars, no—the fortunes of everyone at Santa Catalina—not to have him ask me the next question. I longed to be able to stop him right there and say, "Don't even ask me. Don't you know this is a small school. I know who else you've already asked and they've all turned you down. Everyone's talking about it. Don't ask me and don't ask someone after me. This is breaking my heart. If you'd asked me first I would have been happy to go because I'm a sophomore and getting asked to the Junior Prom is a big deal, but it's too late—now I can't go." Instead, I didn't say anything.

"How would you like to go to the Prom with me?"

I could hear the defeat in his voice.

"Oh Les, I'm sorry. I can't. My parents have arranged for me to go home that weekend."

36

At dinner all the sophomores were whispering to each other that Sister Mary Ellen was getting ready to make an announcement. I fervently hoped that we were not going to have a meeting. I had both a math and a Latin test the next day and would prefer having the entire Study Hall period to actually study.

"After Study Hall tonight, there will be a special meeting of the girls who have just been moved to the infirmary. I don't need to enumerate who you are, the meeting will be in the infirmary, so simply return straight to your rooms at 9 p.m."

"Oof," I made a noise of annoyance. I hated all these constant meetings about the most minuscule concerns. It would probably be a meeting to find out who'd left the window open in the hall or who'd been seen walking from the bathroom in a suspicious manner after lights out or some equally banal concern with no connection to ninety percent of the girls attending the meeting.

After Study Hall I forgot about our meeting, but luckily went unthinkingly right to my room. The infirmary was on the second floor of a large building over the main dining room, the nun's dining room, and the secret passageway from the nun's quarters to the chapel, and had a total of eight rooms. At some point in the history of the school, the three end rooms had been changed into bedrooms with three girls apiece, the usual bunkbed and a single in each room, with a bathroom in-between. The rooms were small but cozy.

Six sophomores had been assigned there and we had moved in on Sunday.

After a few minutes, I remembered we were having the meeting and got my math homework ready while I waited. Everyone else slowly staggered in, and soon we were all waiting for Sister Mary Ellen.

"Do you think maybe she won't come?" Joan hopefully asked.

"Maybe she was just stretching her muscles. You know, testing out her power to see if we obey her."

Juanita frowned slightly at Joan.

Just then, Sister Mary Ellen's round, comic book face—shining with health emphasized by the almost artificial pink circles high on her cheeks and her big twinkly blue eyes—popped around the door.

"Good evening, Girls!" she trilled.

"Good evening, Sister Mary Ellen!" We responded in enthusiastic singsong synchronicity, trained one and all by Catholic grammar schools.

Her big, white-toothed, dimpled smile deepened.

"Now why don't you girls make yourself comfortable and I'll begin. You're not in trouble, I just want to have a small talk with you."

Joan, Juanita, Barbara Smith, Kay Covington, Ann Finnegan and

I made ourselves as comfortable as we could in a room that was now desperately crowded. Three of us sat, elbows on knees, hunched a little forward, on the bottom bunkbed.

Sister Mary Ellen smiled again, the pink cheeks glowing, another dimple forming in her chin. "Now girls, I just wanted to tell you that a really unusual situation has occurred up here with your residency. I'm sure you're aware that ordinarily there are three rooms of three girls each, making nine sophomores, but because of a slightly depleted student body (she meant because so many girls had left already this year—Alicia Dugan, who had astoundingly managed to talk her parents into sending her to the very experimental Green Valley; Catherine Mueller, who'd gone home after her hospital stay for anorexia, and Julie Tready, who'd seemed perfectly happy if a bit quiet until one day in the beginning of her senior year she'd run away) there are only six sophomores up here."

"Because there are fewer of you and because you are so very isolated from the rest of the student body, it is imperative that you all exert every effort to get along."

We all stared at her dumbstruck. When did we ever not get along? All the students were deeply bonded together as only those living, eating and sleeping the same subtle oppression can be.

She went cheerily on. "So I want you each to promise me that you will do your utmost to act in a mature and loving manner while you're up here so far away from the rest of the student body."

We gaped at her. I mean, we were right above the dining room. How far away was the rest of the student body? A thirty-second walk instead of actually living in the same room?

She sat there smiling, then a tiny flicker of impatience crossed her smooth countenance. "I'm waiting."

Joan raised her hand as if doing a Girl Scout salute, two fingers smartly pointing skyward. "I promise."

The rest of us followed suit.

"All right girls, that's fine." She had her big smile on again as her round little body swaddled in layers of black and white habit tripped gracefully out the door.

We sat there in shock.

Then Kay started laughing. Soon Joan and I were laughing and then all of us were in giggles. We imitated parts of her speech.

"So far far away from the rest of the student body . . ." Barbara Smith choked out. "She makes it sound like we're staying at the Mark Thomas."

We all fell over ourselves laughing.

"It is imperative that you get along." We laughed some more.

"Hey, I have a great idea." Ann Finnegan was jumping up and down. "Wouldn't it be great if the next time she came up here we staged a big huge *fight* and we pretended to get along worse than anyone in the history of Santa Catalina!"

"Yeah, yeah," We all started saying, "A Fight! A Big Fight. A Big Staged Fight."

"Okay, okay, that's a great idea."

We began planning immediately.

"How about if Kay and I start a pillow fight . . . . Like if we know she's coming, Joan you be the look-out, and we have a pillow fight but it soon becomes violent," said Ann.

"Yeah, yeah. And then you could lock yourself in the bathroom, Juanita, and pretend like you were crying."

"Right," said Juanita.

"I could knock on the bathroom door from our side yelling. "God damn it! I have to use the bathroom!" Joan said.

"*God damn it*? Joan are you *insane*?" I asked half seriously, "I think that might be going a little far for Sister Mary Ellen."

The plan worked perfectly. Less than a week later we put it into action. As soon as Joan signaled that Sister Mary Ellen was coming, Kay and Juanita began laughing wildly and hitting each other with pillows. Sister Mary Ellen looked confused until events escalated. Joan pounded on the bathroom, Juanita cried and Ann Finnegan accused Barbara of wearing her gym clothes while I yelled, "This is it, this is the final straw. I'm tired of pretending like I can tolerate you people." It only lasted for couple of minutes before Sister Mary Ellen turned and ran, tears already streaming down her face.

After a couple more seconds we stopped and stared at each other. The results were more than we could possibly have hoped, and at the same time strangely unsatisfying.

We stood around in various half-completed, mock fight actions. "Oh," Joan said.

"I know," Ann ruefully replied. "It seems anticlimactic."

"Do you think we should say something to her?" Barbara asked.

I shrugged. Just like cutting class for snack, the much-anticipated revolutionary act felt curiously flat.

37

To a certain extent, living in the infirmary seemed like freedom. I mean, after all, it was *far* from the other dorms. But maybe it wasn't just location; spring had come and the feeling of freedom was in the air.

One day, Joan was looking out the bathroom window, which was about shoulder height, and noticed that there was a broad enough expanse on the roof that we could sunbathe in a secret tanning spot, between two chimneys, hidden from the ground.

From then on, every Saturday, we would spread our towels out as close to the building as we could. The more modest girls like

Juanita and Cindy would wear their bathing suits, but even totally clothed what we were doing was highly illegal.

One Saturday we all were up there sunbathing when Susan Weyerhauser stuck her blond head through the window of the bathroom.

"What're you guys doing?"

"What's it look like we're doing?"

"Want to see what I got in the mail?" she asked.

"Sure," Joan said, slightly sarcastically. A lot of what Joan said sounded accidentally like she was making fun.

Sue didn't notice. She squeezed through the window holding a plastic bag. "Look." She held it up.

We all squinted as the bright sun glared off the transparent plastic.

"It's a sweat suit. I can lose weight. I ordered it in the mail," Sue's voice vibrated with excitement.

She ripped open the bag, unfolded the suit and put it on. There was a plastic straw sticking out from the shoulder where you were supposed to blow it up, which Sue began vigorously doing while we went back to reading and sunbathing.

A little while later, Sue stood up, triumphant. "Look!" She was encased from neck to ankle in a transparent, blown-up bag. Refracted through the plastic were glimpses of her white flesh in a hot pink and orange bikini. We all stared at her. She looked like a cross between the Michelin man and a piece of candy. She took off across the roof jogging.

"Look, look. I'm losing weight."

She jogged back and began to do push-ups.

Recovering slightly, Joan said, "See, look. Uh, Sue. Maybe you shouldn't make so much noise up here."

Sue looked disconcerted and a little hurt. "Yeah, okay." She stood there, arms held out from her body, fat-person-like, by the plastic. "You're right."

She deflated the suit far more quickly than she had blown it up and crawled back through the bathroom window.

We had no sooner returned to tanning than we heard a loud, hissing whisper spit out the window.

"WHAT DO YOU GIRLS THINK YOU'RE DOING?"

Uh oh. "You girls" was a dead give away. It was a nun!

"GET IN HERE RIGHT THIS MINUTE!"

We were deeply frightened. I was totally naked.

Joan went in first, then Carol. I felt my arms jerked through the window and I was flung across the room. It was only as I was flying through the air toward the bathtub that I realized it was SISTER JEAN! The biggest, fattest, meanest nun had caught us!

I hit my shoulder pretty hard on the white tiles of the shower and then crashed down into the tub.

Joan was standing to the side of the toilet, shaking, holding a towel to her small breasts, her freckles standing out in dark against her skin. Carol was clutching the straps of her bathing suit to her shoulders.

"THIS IS DISGUSTING," Sister Jean spat at us, her gigantic face turning red, her bulbous cheeks trembling.

"YOU'RE GOING DOWN TO TELL THE REST OF THE NUNS WHAT DISGUSTING REPULSIVE FILTHY SLUTS YOU ARE. YOU'RE GOING TO APOLOGIZE FOR THE NOISE."

She grabbed me by the ear; I was still nude. Then she led all three of us toward the stairs.

Oh God, I realized, Susan's jog must have been right across the top of the nun's dining room.

Halfway down the stairs, Sister Jean stopped. "THIS IS TERRI-

BLE. YOU GIRLS ARE A DISGRACE. BUT TAKING YOU
DOWN THERE LIKE THIS WOULD ONLY UPSET THE
OTHER SISTERS MORE. DO YOU REALIZE THE SERIOUS-
NESS OF WHAT YOU'VE DONE?"

"Yes, Sister," we all nodded quickly. Not for one second at Santa
Catalina did I ever consider my honor in the face of direct questioning by a nun. Plus, I was standing naked and goose-bumped on the
stairs on my way to the nun's dining room.

"WILL YOU EVER SUNBATHE NAKED AGAIN?"

"No, Sister," we happily lied again.

"YOU MUST WRITE A NOTE OF APOLOGY TO THE
ENTIRE COMMUNITY OF SISTERS BY TONIGHT. DO
YOU UNDERSTAND?"

"Yes, Sister."

She looked us all over again.

"Get upstairs and make yourself decent," she viciously spat out,
her arm held straight out, finger pointing indignantly back upstairs.

38

The alarm rang.

Okay, okay, I thought, then as my mind reluctantly returned to
consciousness, I groaned. Sunday morning. Mass. If it was not bad
enough that we had to wear our two-piece, white pique Sunday uniforms with the bows at each hip (the whole ensemble absolutely
guaranteed to make adolescent girls look twenty pounds heavier),
but now, on top of that, Tina Greene had somehow talked the nuns
into letting her play her guitar in a rather strange facsimile of a hippie mass. Instead of sitting in the old, polished oak pews, we would
gather round the altar, unsuccessfully struggling to look ladylike in

the straight skirts as we sang Catholic folk songs and Tina soulfully strummed.

It was a nightmare.

I rose and began dressing. Pantyhose first, of course, then my Lily of France sheer bra with its high-tech plastic front slide-in closure. I loved these bras and hoped that they would still be making them by the time I got a boyfriend.

One of the worst things about the modern ceremony was that my legs always fell asleep. Twisted into some impossible shape, calves folded underneath me and off to the side, trying desperately to look casual and yet not have my underwear show, the white pique would cut into my pudgy thighs and waist, and by the time communion was served, my legs would have fallen asleep. I would get that strange tingling sensation, have a hard time getting up, and finally limp to the altar. I could see the nuns frowning at me in disapproval as if I were mocking the mass. All the while, we would be singing "Raise High Your Love."

That morning as I was walking across the back quadrangle toward the chapel, I hit upon a solution. I would not sit up on the steps singing songs while my legs fell asleep. Instead, I would just stay quietly and reverently in the pews. That way I could avoid trouble.

"Hi Diane, hi Marion, hi Joan," I greeted my friends softly as we converged on the brick path leading to the chapel. As always, the Sunday uniforms made everybody look a bit like puffy upright ewes with pink faces. The sun was shining and I could smell the grass on the sides of the walkway. What a glorious day.

The inside of the high-ceilinged chapel was cool and hushed. On both sides of the altar were special seats reserved for nuns, and a few were already kneeling there praying. I strode determinedly to a pew near the front and took my place. I barely recognized the older nuns, nuns who would emerge from the secret passageway leading from the convent and then disappear after mass to rarely be seen again except to occasionally drift wraithlike across the campus, late at night, lit by a full winter moon. Out of deference, I left the first three pews empty.

"What're you doing?" Kim hissed out the side of her mouth at me, leaning slightly over on her way up the aisle.

"I'm sitting here today," I serenely responded.

Her attention was obviously piqued. She took two more steps toward the altar then stopped short and instead slid into the pew with me. Oh no, I thought.

Judy didn't even hesitate for a second when she came in later. She pushed Kim imperiously aside as she also slid in, just as if this is what the three of us did every Sunday.

The mass started. Soon 240 girls were all lustfully singing Catholic folk songs.

I couldn't help myself, I took advantage of the volume to make up some new words to the song "All That We Are."

With all that we are
All that we be
All that we ever have
We wish for more tv

All that we are
All that we be
All that we never have
Is because nuns are cree-py

Kim and Judy started giggling. I hadn't been thinking ahead. Now they'd called attention to me twice. I elbowed Kim very severely, but it seemed as though that only made them both laugh harder. By now I could see Sister Mary Ellen, Sister Humpbert and Sister Carlotta all looking over at me quite disapprovingly and I was going to get in trouble for doing practically nothing at all.

Sure enough, as I walked speedily out of the chapel after mass, Sister Mary Ellen caught up with me, her cheeks even more flushed than usual.

"June, I want to talk to you."

Her skin looked lovely. I couldn't help but notice how smooth and flawless it was. I followed her down the path beside Long Dorm and into the rec room. Inside was cool and green, all the windows shaded by thick bushes.

"June. Maybe you would like to explain to me exactly what was going on in mass today."

I sighed. "Sister Mary Ellen. I'm sorry. I just can't sit up on the altar to sing. My legs fall asleep and they feel like they might give out as I go to communion. It happens every Sunday and so today I decided to stay in the pews. But then Kim and Judy came and sat with me. What could I do? I couldn't exactly refuse to allow them in the pews during mass."

Usually you could get away with telling Sister Mary Ellen a small joke even when she was yelling at you.

She sighed. "I suppose not. But then why were they laughing so hard?"

I hung my head. Should I lie? She was so harmless it didn't seem worth the effort. Not like Sister Humpbert to whom I would prefer to tell a lie, just to get back at her for being intimidating.

"That was my fault. I said something funny."

Sister Mary Ellen sighed again. "June. You have a great deal of influence with the other girls in your class. Do you know we discuss you frequently at meals?"

The nuns discussed me at their nuns' dinners?!! I couldn't believe she had told me that.

"It's a shame that you use your energy to disrupt the order of the school. Has it ever occurred to you that if you worked *within* the system it might be possible to achieve some of your goals? For example, if the girls would follow the rules and then put together a reasonably worded petition to wear nice pants on Saturday and Sunday afternoons, I think that could be accomplished."

Wow! Pants on Saturday and Sunday! That would be the impossible made real, that would be super far-out! I thought what she said was maybe worth thinking about.

"Alright. You can go now."

She dismissed me, still looking a little worried as I dashed off.

39

"Tracy, would you like some more coffee cake?" I asked facetiously, bowing slightly at the waist, holding out the thick, white serving plate in her direction.

"Why June! Thank you very much. I do believe I will." She smiled as she served herself a piece. "Can I perhaps serve you a piece while I'm about it?" she asked, holding the flat silver serving spoon up.

"Why yes, Tracy. How kind of you. I'd like that very much."

Tracy and I laughed and giggled as we ate *all* the coffeecake, while the other girls, temporarily dieting, looked on in horror.

Naturally, after breakfast, I felt bloated and uncomfortable. Tracy McDonald and I had egged each other on, gone too far in the coffee cake direction again. I usually didn't like to throw up after breakfast, it didn't do any good because you'd just eat some other fattening meal later and it was also difficult to get privacy in the bathrooms near the classrooms. Even though it was against the rules, I decided to go back to the dorm. If I was caught, I would say I felt sick and needed my medicine, maybe I could get away with it. I wished I could pretend to have some bad disease, like diabetes, which would necessitate frequent trips to off-limits parts of the campus during school hours, but the nuns knew all that stuff about us. I'd just have to figure out something stupid, like I needed Sudafed. I knew if I looked both apologetic and deeply depressed my excuse would not have to be that strong.

I walked quickly past the Chapel Lawn and through the back door of Long Dorm. My brown-and-black saddle oxfords echoed a little too loudly in the empty dorm; a nun could be summoned by excess clatter.

Minutes later, I entered the first stall. I ignored the fact that I was afraid in the cold deserted bathroom with its row of reproachful sinks. I knelt down and put my fingers down my throat. I'd had a lot of coffee with breakfast to make throwing up easier. By now I'd learned the tricks. Never try to throw up just chocolate bars. Or peanut butter. That stuff will weld itself to the bottom of your stomach. Ice cream is easy to vomit, and cereal—anything with a lot of milk. If you must eat chocolate, eat it last so it's on top of the ice cream or cereal.

After I threw up, I was depressed. I washed up and rushed out of there quickly to be on time for English class, feeling a little weak.

40

Joan's voice carried clearly through the open bathroom doors, two rooms down. "We're having a secret class meeting in the rec room at nine."

"What about Sister Mary Ellen?" I heard Diane Hull ask.

"June told me she wasn't coming," Joan responded.

I smiled to myself. I was excited, it seemed as though finally maybe something would get done, finally we could make some headway against the immobile barrier of nun authority, nun rules. And Sister Mary Ellen had suggested the solution herself, even if maybe I wasn't going to implement her suggestion exactly as she meant it.

"Why don't you try changing the system from within," she'd asked. I'd been startled. But upon reflection, I saw she had a point. Couldn't hurt to try.

Quarter to nine came and I was there in the rec room, waiting. I figured everyone would attend simply because any other activity it was permissible for us to do at nine o'clock on a Saturday night was considerably more boring: doing homework or watching one of two local channels on tv.

Sure enough, everyone started arriving just after I did. Joan, Teresa and Diane Hull already knew what was going on. The rec room was big and square, but since recreation wasn't high on the list of activities, it wasn't used much and smelled slightly of dust. I waited, telling jokes.

At ten after, Marion Miller, Sarah Haskell and Pitts arrived. Good. I was interested in the people who were actually breaking the rules.

"Okay. Far-out. Everyone's here."

Even Suki Bryan came, sitting (not much of a talker, in fact she talked so little sometimes it was like she was going to school someplace else and had left only her body behind) in an easy chair pressed against a far wall. I hit a spoon against a coffee cup.

"The meeting will now come to order."

Everyone looked my way, some of them with raised eyebrows.

"Okay, let me start by saying that this is not an official meeting and I am not proposing myself as some kind of leader, it's just that Sister Mary Ellen gave me an idea and I wanted to see if possibly everyone would be interested in discussing it. First of all, let me see if we are all in agreement about certain things. The rules we now have are terrible?"

"YES!" Ann Drendel and Tracy McDonald yelled.

"Okay." I smiled. "I would like to be able to wear pants on Saturday. Any other suggestions?"

"Why can't we wear pants after school?" Cynthia Pitts said.

There was a chorus of yeah's.

"I'd like to be able to go to other places besides just the shopping centers. I'd like to be able to go to day student's homes," Pam said quietly. She was friends with the day students because she'd lived in Carmel and gone to lower school there.

"I'd like to go to the beach every now and then with only a few people, not the whole school frigging singing."

"I'd like to have a smoking room on campus," said Suzanne Murphy.

"Yeah," came from Susan Weyerhauser (who I thought didn't smoke).

I held my hand up. "Okay. Okay. That's why we're here. Maybe you guys remember that last Sunday, Sister Mary Ellen called me aside to talk because I was . . ." I cleared my throat significantly, "not giving the Catholic liturgy proper respect. Anyway, when she yelled at me she suggested that if I were unhappy with the set-up here I should try to change things from within."

I let that sink in. Marion Miller and Cynthia Pitts looked skeptical.

"I thought it was an interesting proposition. What do you all think?"

"It's bullshit!" yelled Kim Richardson.

I smiled. Kim was my good friend and a total pessimist.

"Anyway, what she said to me was that if we stopped breaking the rules and put a seriously worded petition before the nuns, we could get some reforms." I looked at my classmates. "Is it possible for you guys to stop sneaking off into the woods and smoking? Trying this out?"

"Yes," Marion agreed, rather amiably. Marion's grandfather had been one of the superwealthy railroad robber barons, along with Stanford. Her mother was deeply religious, and when she drove any-where with any of her ten children, she would insist they recite the rosary during the entire trip. If a rosary was incomplete when they returned home, Mrs. Miller would drive around the block until it was finished. Marion, the seventh or eighth child, was a natural rule breaker, but her personality was sunny and open with no hint of defiance or anger.

I took her as answering for the group. No sense pressing my luck.

"Okay. Let's try it."

41

Diane Hull, Kim Anderson and I were getting ready for bed.

"I don't feel like wearing a heavy nightgown," the ever crabby Kim complained.

I looked over at her. What was the big deal? I had on a t-shirt and a pair of cotton, boy's pajama bottoms, flannel with Christmas trees printed on a red- and green-striped background.

Kim threw her brush down on the carpeted floor. "The only nightgowns I have are all too *hot*."

The carved wooden outside door swung open and Sister Claire stepped through. The screen door creaked shut behind her. Her round, pretty face with dark eyebrows looked angry. I felt a jolt of apprehension. Sister Claire was the monitor for the downstairs Santa Inez dorm, but we rarely saw her because she usually walked through the dorm totally unconcerned with us. Even her wake-up calls were delivered in a tone that indicated that she herself didn't give a damn whether we ever woke up.

"What did you say?" She sounded almost neutral except for a touch of ominous over-enunciation.

Kim answered in a softer and much less whiny voice. "I said I wish I had a better nightgown to wear to bed."

Sister Claire exploded. "You little spoiled brat! How many night-gowns do you have? And what happened? You forgot to ask your mom...mee . . ." Every word was laden with sarcasm but most particularly the word "mommy." " . . . to get you something light on your last shopping expedition to I. Magnin? You girls make me sick. Anything you want and you just crook your little finger. Anything you need, someone does it for you! And you're pigs, filthy slobs, waiting for everyone else to pick up after you." Suddenly she crouched down and motioned at us with her crooked finger, "Here piggy wiggy wigs, here little piggies."

We were frozen in shock.

She straightened back up. "Well, I don't wish you well. I hope the whole lot of you filthy, disgusting sows suffer!" And she slammed out of the room.

We three stood there stock still, stunned into silence.

I slowly slid my eyes over to Diane. The lovely, quiet Diane Hull seemed an unlikely choice for Sister Claire's outburst.

"I don't think we're that big of slobs," I said cautiously, to see if I could break the heavy atmosphere.

"Maybe she wasn't really talking about us," Diane answered.

None of the three of us told anyone about what Sister Claire had said, but we were super, super, super neat for the rest of the time we lived under her unhappy aegis.

42

"June, I want you to know that if you win, I will be just as happy as you," Teresa said.

I turned in shock. That was an extraordinarily nice thing of her to say. "Wow, Teresa. Thanks."

"I think you're going to get junior class president anyway, because I was already class president," she said.

I agreed that was probably true.

"Hey Teresa," I whispered as we filed out of the dorm on our way to chapel singing. "Let's fake a fight."

She didn't answer, but I knew that no answer meant yes. When we got over near the chapel, she suddenly turned to me.

"You're nothing but an upstart." She had her hands firmly on her hips and an almost-real mad expression on her face.

"Oh yeah, well it's about time someone else got half a chance at the leadership of this class. You hog everything."

"Don't give me that! What? Like you're some kind of underdog? I doubt it. You write for the newspaper, the yearbook, you're on the debate team just like I am. If it's not me, why can't someone else be president?"

By now, a few of our classmates—Joan, who looked like she was eighty-five percent sure it was a joke; Diane Hull, who looked concerned; Marion Miller, who I'm sure was just happy to be in on some action whatever it was; and two upperclassmen, Janet Miller and Ann Taylor, both of whom were definitely concerned and looking about for help.

"You hussy," I yelled and pretended to hit her shoulder.

Instantly the crowd doubled. "Oh my god," I heard someone cry.

Teresa pretended to pull my hair. Well, actually she did pull it, but not that hard.

"I can't believe you," I said. "You'll pay for this."

"Girls, girls." Uh oh. Here came Sister Aaron running. We immediately stood apart.

"Yes."

"You can't fight like that. What's wrong with you? You have to be good sports."

"Oh, okay," Teresa said as if that was simply the first time the idea had occurred to her.

I put my hand out and we shook. Then I put my arm around her shoulders and we walked toward the chapel. No one could see the exact depth of the smiles we were wearing as we left the other students gap-mouthed behind us. For about two weeks afterwards I would hear snatches of conversation before people noticed I was there and shut up.

"I think it was a joke," one girl would say in a concerned voice.

"No, I heard they were really fighting. They pulled out each other's hair." The second girl's tone would have the strength of total conviction in which hearsay information is often delivered.

The conversations would trail off as I came up. Our class knew of course, and when I was elected by a small margin, the subject died down completely, replaced by the rumor that Ms. Berthold, the French teacher, and Mr. Stone, the chemistry teacher, were having an affair.

43

Dana and I were leaving Study Hall, our books hugged to our chests.

"So what'd you think?" Dana asked me.

I turned to look at her. "About what?"

"About the new officers."

"About the elections?" I asked. "About the fact that the entire radical intellectual clique has been elected and about how it's clear how our class is totally out of the nuns' control?" I was only kidding a *little*.

"I might not have put it so strongly," she said.

"What do you think?" I asked her.

"Maybe the new line-up means we'll be able to get some changes next year."

"Maybe," I laughed excitedly. "I hope so."

I caught a quick glimpse out of the corner of my eye that chilled me. "Don't look directly," I said to her, "but isn't that Sister Carlotta looking out the window of her office?"

I glanced again and sure enough, you could just barely see the mottled, pudding-white face of Sister Carlotta staring out between the slightly parted curtains of her office window directly at us. I tried to convince myself she wasn't watching us.

Dana shivered.

44

I was lying on the old green rug watching tv. One good thing about being in Sister Claire's dominion was that she disliked us so much she would never leave her room to check on us after lights out.

Everyone else was asleep and I had the tv on low while I read another Gothic romance novel Joan had given me. They all had the same plot. Girl of noble birth but reduced circumstances is forced to be a middle-level servant for a highborn man. When she arrives she sees from afar that he is very handsome, but there are dark whispered rumors of his ruthlessness. She performs her job brilliantly (nursemaid, nanny, head housekeeper) and he seems not to notice her until one day she is running in the fields (from a storm, from danger, out of high-spiritedness) and he rides a lively dark steed up from behind and whisks her up on the galloping stallion. She struggles, they have a brief but heated encounter and he releases her. She knows he is not the man for her, but then later something happens and she secretly discovers that he is heroic and good, they kiss passionately, pledge their eternal troth, and the book ends.

A black-and-white movie came on the tv in French with subtitles. Great, I could turn the sound all the way off. Immediately the movie mesmerized me. It was strangely filmed, the actors moved jerkily and often looked about themselves as if unsure where they were. The plot was that a man cannot get women to notice him so he dresses as St. Nicholas and gets his friend to take pictures as he poses with the women. While they are posing, he feels them up. This was the most graphic thing I had ever seen on tv, and I went to bed feeling a little uncomfortable.

SOPHOMORE SUMMER

Looking out the window of the plane, I saw an airport that looked like a giant nun's hat—like the one the Flying Nun wore—not our nuns. When the plane landed, I timidly got off.

Dominique and her mother waited at the gate. Dominique was jumping up and down, she was excited but her mother stood severely and unsmilingly beside her.

"Hi," I waved to Dominique from ten feet away, hoping that this would be considered a sufficiently affectionate greeting and luckily it was.

Dominique and I lagged behind, paying little attention to the process of traversing the airport, already eagerly exchanging information about our summers so far, while her mother strode efficiently through the clean, white, space-age architecture to the baggage claim.

We went out and a Rolls limousine was parked at the curb waiting for us. The chisel-featured driver had a dark blue cap and matching uniform, and he stared sternly straight ahead as he maneuvered the vehicle smoothly out of the parking space.

"Look, there's Manhattan."

Dominique pointed happily out the back window of the limo at some faint towers barely visible, wavering in the distant haze, and I gazed intently out the small back window at the fairy tale towers until they disappeared completely.

Hours later we pulled up in front of a light yellow, tree-shaded clapboard house. It was early, but I was so exhausted I barely made it up the stairs to Dominique's four poster bed before I crashed.

The next morning I was reading, still under the cool sheets, when Dominique jumped out of bed. My, she was energetic.

"Today we'll go to the Country Club and swim."

I didn't like that idea all that well. I would've liked it better if I hadn't eaten a million candy bars on the plane. With a couple days notice, I could manage to be pleasingly zaftig in a bathing suit instead of elephantine. Dominique did not have that problem, with her tall figure kept lean by a nervous temperament.

"C'mon." She grabbed her flowered bikini and got two towels from the cedar linen closet next to the bathroom.

We dashed out the door, barely waving to her father reading *The Wall Street Journal* in the breakfast room and rode bicycles over to the Southampton Beach Club. It didn't look that exclusive, the outside was all gray and built of battered wood, the girl's dressing room had gaps between the boards.

"Let's go to the dining room," Dominique suggested.

After we'd picked the best table overlooking the beach, a waiter approached and we ordered Cokes.

"I don't think we should get hamburgers, because my father always gets mad when he sees the bill," Dominique stated.

Suddenly I desperately desired a hamburger. "I'll pay for it."

"You can't," she primly replied. "They don't take money here. It's a Country Club. You have to sign the ticket and they send the bill later to your father."

"My father?"

"No. Not your father. He's not a member." She looked out toward the ocean. "Hey look, there's Ann Hearst. You know, Patty's sister."

I looked up dispiritedly. What was she doing here? They lived in Hillsborough. Although I guess she could come visit from California just like I did. Something about the possessive way she stood on the beach made me think she didn't have the same hamburger problem I did. Of course, she probably didn't even want a hamburger.

"I know," Dominique said brightly. "We can order one hamburger and split it."

46

When we got back from the beach that afternoon, Dominique and I went to her room and lay on the canopied beds and talked until the phone rang.

"Stay here," Dominique said. "Mummy said she wanted to talk to me for a moment in the library."

I moved to the window seat and sat quietly reading a John MacDonald detective novel. In a few minutes she was back, bounding into the room.

"Guess what? The most wonderful news. Mummy said we can stay in the guest cottage out back. Oh this will be so totally delightful!"

The guest cottage was heavily shaded by a stand of old elms. Inside was dark, paneled oak and hefty, square antiques. The single couch in our small living room was covered with dark red velvet, the armchair was a green and deep blue brocade. It didn't quite smell like dust, it was almost-dust and furniture polish. The bathroom was also paneled in dark wood and was quite small.

As we were going to sleep that night Dominique groggily announced, "I hope you don't mind. Tomorrow morning I'm starting work as a candy-striper, I'll be home by four."

What could I say?

She continued in a slightly defensive tone, "I didn't know I was going to get the job when we discussed your coming."

Of course she didn't, that had been back in April when we were still at school and she couldn't possibly have even had a chance to apply for the job.

In the morning I got up and gazed tragically out the window into the overgrown Southampton garden. What was there for me to do today? It seemed the only alternative was to ride my bike into town, buy some bubble gum and do a little work toward becoming a world champion bubble gum blower.

I walked the bike down the street looking in each of the stores. The white fronts, some pseudo-colonnaded, beckoned to the slim-hipped, rich women in their frosted lipstick, tan cigarette slacks and matching cotton twill shirts. I, instead, was wearing a purple velour sleeveless dress over heavily patched blue jeans. My blow-up baby doll figure strained the seams. The tops of my thighs rubbed thickly together as my sweaty hands clutched the blue rubber handlebars of the bike—a remnant from Dominique's pre-pubescent years.

I went into the gift shop; the smells of perfumed paper and sugar fought in the air.

"I'll have fifty pieces of bubble gum, please." I kept my eyes downcast as I paid the dollar sixty-three (dollar fifty plus tax).

I rode the bike back along the tree-lined roads and sat in the shaded cottage, chewing and blowing bubbles.

"Hi, hi." Dominique finally burst in through the door, practically tearing off her pink and white striped candy-striper uniform as she entered the cottage. She was glowing with happiness.

"I'm so happy. Don't I look happy?" She spun around in her white underwear, her thick red hair fanning out. She did look happy, but, even worse in my opinion, she also looked beautifully thin.

"Dr. Deerfield asked me out on a date."

Immediately I knew. "When?"

"For tonight, silly. He is the most handsome man. We're going to a movie."

Darn. A movie. There would be no point in asking if I was invited.

I smiled painfully. "That sounds like a lot of fun."

She looked at me and took both my hands in hers. "You don't mind, do you?" she said beseechingly. "I just don't know when I would ever get a chance like this again."

"Oh no. I don't mind," I answered quite untruthfully, but pretty convincingly I thought.

We went over to the main house for dinner. The butler silently served pork chops, rice and salad. We silently ate the food. I experimented with a new talent (never needed, never even crossed my mind really, at my house in California) for drinking my milk without making a sound.

After dinner Dominique's father gave a big "HO!"

I jumped about three feet in the air.

"Have I got a surprise for you. You two are going to love this!

Tonight we have my favorite dessert, grown by your mother . . ."

This part surprised me. Dominique's mother didn't look like a gardener to me.

" . . . in her garden. Rhubarb!" He looked around, smiling proudly at all of us. I noticed Dominique looked nervous. I guess she wasn't going to tell them that Dr. Deerfield was dating a 15-year-old later that evening.

"June! Have you ever had rhubarb?!"

I shook my head no.

"Are you ever in for a marvelous treat!"

Dominique had already surreptitiously left, dressed in black pants and a light pink silk shirt, by the time I threw up the rhubarb. I gazed moodily out the window, the entertainment prospects for the evening seemed limited. I read the last few pages of the detective novel by John MacDonald, then gazed mournfully out the window some more.

The DeGives had another cottage that supposedly had been rented to a writer from New York. I had glimpsed him earlier that day, slipping in the back door with a brown bag of groceries. He'd struck me as scrawny and a bit hairy. Now though, I was intrigued to see lights on in the downstairs windows, so I slipped quietly out our door and crouched down in the bushes beside the entrance walkway. Getting on my hands and knees, I cautiously crawled over toward the other cottage through the partially tended bushes. I got down on my stomach and wriggled forward a few feet. This was totally unnecessary I realized, got to my feet, brushed myself off and plastered myself to the side of the house beside the window. I slowly looked in.

Great! The window looked down a small passageway and straight into the living room where the writer was sitting *very, very* close to a woman with teased-up blond hair, lots of makeup, red stiletto-heeled shoes and a skintight red dress. They had glasses of amber-colored liquid on the coffee table in front of them, and I could see a square-shaped bottle with the words "Johnnie" written in white letters on the part of the label facing me. Liquor of some sort.

Things progressed rapidly. The writer and the red-dress woman (the fallen woman I named her in my mind, a term I had read but hadn't a hundred percent figured out the meaning of) talked, then he poured her more alcohol, they talked some more, then he kissed her. As he moved nervously away he didn't notice that she seemed to smile slyly to herself. He talked some more, rapidly, moving his hands a lot. Then, one second later, they were kissing passionately, the woman's red lipstick and red fingernails in sharp relief against his pale skin and dark beard. This was wonderful, better than a movie, better than bubble gum, it was as good as getting someone else's love letter accidentally delivered to your address.

He had her lying under him on the couch and he was frantically pushing up the red dress with one hand and caressing her breasts with the other. The white flesh of her thigh stood out against the dark blue velvet of the couch. I couldn't see her breasts, just the black bra pushed to the side. Too bad my vantage point was too far away for sound. She was wriggling wildly underneath him. Then—in a flash—the show was ending, he got off her, picked her up and carried her up the stairs (not without some difficulty I noticed).

I stood there for a minute disconsolate that such a high level of excitement would end so suddenly. I sure did want to have more fun. My eye fell on the half-full liquor bottle left behind. There was an idea. Dangerous too. I slowly and gently pushed on the window I had been looking through and discovered it was locked. Locked and too high up and small anyway. I wiggled sideways between the hedge and the living room window and pushed at the latch. Quite luckily, it was open and this window was big. I pushed it up and put one foot over the sill, then stopped and listened for noises. I could just barely hear sounds from upstairs that were consistent with what I knew about people going all the way. I inserted myself the rest of the way in and tiptoed over to the couch. What the heck, from everything I'd read so far I believed the activity they were engaged in—sex— took a long time, often the entire night. Definitely they would not be able to notice if World War Three occurred, much less a small, girl intruder.

I eased myself onto the velvet couch, spread my arms out, and allowed the excitement of the possiblity of drinking some of the liquor wash over me. I'd had wine before but never hard alcohol. I took a swig of Johnnie Walker.

"Oof." The alcohol slammed into my empty stomach. I sat still for a moment and the fire ran down my legs and arms and shot bits of liquid lightning into the skin on the edges of my fingers and toes. I took another sip. A couple of minutes after this I was emboldened to sneak around a mite further. I tiptoed into the kitchen to look through the drawers. Knorr's onion soup (maybe he made dip sometimes), Campbell's cream of mushroom soup and Hormel Chili. Not even any crackers.

I heard a loud noise from upstairs. Quickly I tiptoed back to the living room. Another similar loud noise, a bit like a scream, came from up there. I was paralyzed with fear. Then I heard him moaning. I laughed to myself, grabbed the liquor and snuck back out of the house.

It wasn't that hard to get rid of the still partially filled bottle the next day. I took it with me when Dominique and I rode our bikes to the club and it made a long arc through the clear air as I tossed it into a wire trash basket by the side of the road.

47

Joan and I agreed to meet at the bus station in San Francisco. She'd fly and then take the bus from the airport and I'd come up from Santa Cruz, then we'd go over to the O'Malley's together. Patricia and Helen O'Malley were in higher grades, but we had become friends with both sisters. They weren't pretty girls—they had squat, gnomish bodies and jowly, gray-skinned faces—but they were smart, very, very funny and completely self-assured. I thought that sometimes it happened that the squat, super-rich fathers married tall beautiful women and all the children looked like the dad. Actually, it happened more often than not, as if the industrialist genes were stronger.

When our yellow cab pulled up in front of their gray stone townhouse, we saw a note pinned to the mahogany front door. It instructed us to follow them to a Japanese restaurant a few blocks away on California Street. Joan and I shouldered our suitcases and trudged over. Through the bamboo slats of the sushi restaurant we spotted Helen and Patricia's heads in the back, with Mary Meyers and Vaughn Hills.

"Have some sake, you guys." Helen immediately signaled for the waiter to bring another of the small porcelain jugs and two more porcelain cups. "Menus too."

We ordered sushi, they ordered more and much laughter and talking ensued as the afternoon slipped away. Finally the bill came, delivered by a nervous Japanese host.

"Let's just split this six ways. It's easier," Helen jovially exclaimed.

Joan and I exchanged a stricken glance. Neither of us had much money and we'd refrained from ordering more than two pieces of sushi each in order to have some cash left over for the rest of the week, but what could we do? We ponied up our thirty dollar shares.

Late that night, we had a hurried consultation. No more restaurants with the O'Malleys. No more laugh-riot-laden meals with the rich juniors from San Francisco in frighteningly expensive eateries. Our funds had been reduced to the single digits. The next morning Joan, the two O'Malleys and I had a great time eating cereal with milk and watching cartoons.

"Hey, where're your parents?" Joan asked.

It was about time they should be making an appearance.

"Oh, they went up to the Russian River with the boys," Helen casually answered.

Both Joan's and my eyes widened with shock. Neither of our parents would have allowed us to be there if they'd known. In fact, we didn't like it that well ourselves; we'd never stayed in a house without parents.

"What are you guys up for today?" Helen asked. "Shopping in Union Square? How about we go eat in Sausalito?"

"Oh, no thank you," Joan and I blurted out simultaneously.

Helen looked at us strangely.

"We were thinking about just walking around."

Helen yawned. "Not me. I think I'll go shopping."

Patricia closed the newspaper. "I'm going over to Nonie's house on Nob Hill. We might go riding in the park. You two are welcome to join us."

I felt panicked. Horseback riding in the Golden Gate Park would surely cost my entire lifetime allowance.

"Thank you," Joan politely replied. "I believe we have our hearts set on aimlessly wandering."

Patricia shrugged. "Whatever."

Less than an hour later, Joan and I were sauntering past the three-story clapboard houses of California Street.

"It's not that interesting here. Let's go over by Union Square where at least there'll be shoppers to look at," Joan suggested.

"Okay. How do we get there?"

"Don't you know?"

"No." I took a totally wild guess. "I think it's off Fremont Street."

"Okay." Joan pointed in the general direction of where a street sign would be located. "What does it say? What street are we on?"

"How can I tell? I don't have my glasses on."

"Oh, brother." Joan's arm dropped leadenly. "I don't have my glasses on *either*. How are we going to be able to tell where we're going?"

We both started laughing. "Oh well, there goes any hope of ever getting anywhere."

So we just kept walking. Finally the street started looking a little worse—with houses in bad repair, paint peeling in strips from the front. There were foreign-looking men leaning against doorjambs leering at us in sickeningly appreciative ways. We kept stumbling and bumbling our way down the street, but in a much less carefree manner.

"Uh, Joan . . . ." And just as I said that a man made a lewd remark.

"He-ey girlies. He-ey girlies. You're pretty cute. I bet you got cute . . . ."

Joan and I both jumped and began to run desperately down the street. A couple of blocks later we were panting and sweating. We took advantage of the temporarily empty street to lean on a building whose single dusty window was a out-of-business pawn shop.

"What . . . gasp . . . shall . . . gasp . . . we . . . gasp . . . do?" Joan asked.

"Uh, I . . . gasp . . . think . . . gasp . . . we should try to take a bus back to the O'Malley's."

We walked further. Now the buildings had broken-out windows. One block had just a single cinder-block structure with no windows, and all around it was gray dirt strewn with concrete rubble. We crossed to the other side of the street to avoid it. The first bus we spotted we flagged down ferociously.

The bus driver made eye contact with me through the dirty windshield and pointed ahead of him. Joan and I began running, arms and legs flying in all directions. A block further the bus stopped, the doors wheezed open and we stood there, gasping for breath.

The bus driver looked out the opened door at us, patiently waiting.

After a few second's recovery, Joan said, "We're trying to get to Union Square."

"Wrong side," the bus driver barked and reached over to close the door. "You have to take the bus that comes on the other side of the street."

Both Joan and I looked over there fearfully. There was a bar with an already hopping business, and four bearded men lounging beneath a neon Budweiser sign, smoking cigarettes. The bus driver followed our terrified gazes.

"Get on," the bus driver said gruffly "I'll run you to the end of the line and you can come back. It's not that far anyway."

Joan and I gratefully hoisted ourselves up the steps.

Three or four hours later, safely back at the O'Malley's, we listlessly watched tv.

"What'll we do now?" I asked Joan.

"What can we do? How much money do you have?" she asked me.

"Five dollars."

Her shoulders slumped, we both stared at "Three's Company" playing lifelessly on the small screen. Then she visibly perked up. "I know! Let's call Teresa. I think Dana is down there too."

"How can we? It's long distance."

"Don't worry. I have my father's AT&T card. My mother gave it to me last semester." Joan was already dialing the phone. She hit the jackpot right off the bat.

"Teresa, hi!"

I jumped up and down beside the phone, overjoyed that Joan had reached her.

"What? It's beautiful?"

Joan talked to her, then handed the phone to me.

"Really? You saw Dana and Sarah at San Malo. Cool. Wow. I wish we were there."

"Yeah, me too," Teresa answered cheerfully.

After we got off we were glum. We both sat back on the cream silk couch in front of the 13" tv.

Finally Joan said it. "They're having a lot better time than us."

"Yeah," I replied.

"If we were down there, we'd be having fun." she said.

"Yeah, but we're not."

"Flying down there is cheap. Tomorrow morning we would just walk down to the beach and go swimming."

We sat there in silence a bit longer.

"How much money do you have?" I asked her.

"Eight dollars," she glumly replied. Then she brightened. "Yeah, but I have my return ticket to Los Angeles and there's part of the money right there."

We both had the same idea at the same time. It cost only $21.95 apiece to fly to San Diego on PSA.

"Okay, okay!" I jumped up. "We have your ticket for $16.95 and my five dollars, that covers your ticket. We have your $8, so we only need $13 for me."

"Change!!" We yelled simultaneously.

Joan and I were often in sync.

We scrambled through our suitcases and the pockets of the clothes we'd brought with us. Joan found three dollar bills and 68 cents. I found $2.75.

"That's $6.43."

We both sat back down. "We're still six dollars and 57 cents short. What can we do? We can't exactly go to the airport and ask them for a cut rate."

"Hey, I know," Joan said, "Where did we find that six dollars and change? Totally forgotten in our pockets. We didn't even know we had it."

"Yes."

"Okay, so I have an idea."

"Yes?"

"Maybe it's wrong. Maybe it wouldn't be all that nice of us." She lapsed into silence.

"What? What is it?" I demanded impatiently. Now that we'd thought of the plan to go to San Diego the city danced in front of me alluringly, the most perfect place on earth, the one place with the most amount of fun ever.

We looked first in the front hall closet which contained all the family's winter coats so we didn't have to feel guilty, they wouldn't have found the money again anyway for another six months. We persuaded ourselves there was plenty of time to mail it back anonymously before winter. We found four dollars and ten cents. It wasn't enough so we had to search the drawers. Joan and I had agreed that if we accidentally found a big stash of money that was clearly there on purpose we wouldn't take it because *that* would be stealing.

Surprisingly we didn't find anything like that. In fact, we were just about to give up completely when Joan discovered a piggy bank in a box in the back of Patricia's closet. It was perfect; it looked like it had been there for long time and it held $4.50 in nickels.

"Let's go."

We called Teresa, told her we were on our way, then wrote a note for the O'Malleys.

As we went out the door, with the straps of our suitcases once again slung over our shoulders, I felt deep excitement about the great adventure upon which we were embarking. We got merrily on the bus, which went straight downtown to the Greyhound station, where we could get another bus to the airport.

About halfway there Joan looked at me, stricken. "June. We're in trouble. We forgot to figure in the price of the bus to the airport."

"Oh no," I wailed. I really didn't want to back down now.

"We could panhandle," Joan said.

We knew all about panhandling because the newscasters on tv talked about hippies doing it and we always paid attention when they talked about hippies.

We looked around at the other passengers on the bus. One was a woman, sitting primly erect, with a pink shirt and a pink- and white-striped skirt. Her white cotton-candy hair was coiffed ever so precisely and her carefully applied rouge-brightened cheeks were scored with millions of wrinkles. A few seats up was a couple with unkempt hair and skin browned from outdoor living. The man had his hand up on the seat ahead of him, his fingernails were dirty; his shirt was torn and soiled. That was the entire human contents of the bus. Slim pickings.

"Maybe when we get to the Greyhound station," Joan said.

When we got to the Greyhound station, there were poor people running everywhere. It was a big and fascinating place, but without immediately obvious panhandling possibilities.

"C'mon Joan." I tugged at her white shirt. "Let's get in line for the tickets."

We were standing there, both of us bouncing up and down on the balls of our feet, twisting our hair, swinging our arms from side to side, looking around. Behind us was a balding man wearing knee-length, Hawaiian-touristy, flowered shorts.

"My my, you girls seem to be awfully nervous. Are you running away from home?"

Whew, there it was, our opening. We both turned all the way around to face him.

"No, no." I tried to look him straight in the eye in an honest, upstanding way. "We're nervous because we added up our money so carefully, we thought we had just enough money to get to San Diego and . . . ."

Joan broke in. "It's very important that we get there . . . ."

I interrupted her before she started in on anything too elaborate. "Yeah, we didn't add in our money to take this bus so . . . ."

"Oh girls, " he chuckled, his cheeks shaking in a jello-ish way, "Please. I'd be totally delighted to help two such lovely young girls as yourself. Damsels in distress and all. How much do you need? Ten? Twenty?" He was taking his wallet out of his back pocket as he spoke. I noticed that the fabric of his flowered shirt strained tightly over his protrusive belly.

"Twenty would be wonderful," Joan gushed and gazed at him with her most limpid expression.

He handed her the bill. Beautiful. Joan and I maintained our composure all the way through the line, on the bus (where he wanted to converse further, that was okay, Joan and I were both used to paying the piper) and into the airport, then we broke out into loud yells and crazy laughing.

"Wow! That was fun!" Joan jumped clumsily into the air, attempting to click her heels together like the twins in the Doublemint commercial.

I followed suit. We both were always trying moves we'd seen on tv commercials with generally miserable results.

"Let's do it some more." Joan turned to an old woman, bent nearly double, wearing a blond fur coat. "Excuse me, ma'am, spare change?"

The woman sniffed indignantly and crept on.

"Spare change?" she asked a frightened looking brown-skinned teenage boy in horn-rimmed glasses. He fished a dime out of high-water pants.

She spun around to me. "See? It's easy."

I hit her. "Stop it Joan, we have enough. We could get arrested."

She laughed. "Oh yes, imagine it: 'Shick Scion's and Prominent Doctor's Daughters Arrested in San Francisco Airport for Panhandling'." She hugged herself with delight at the thought. "Yes, yes."

"Let's run. We'll miss our flight." We dashed down the maroon carpeted corridor to Gate 3C.

*   *   *   *   *

Teresa was there to meet us in her father's gold Cadillac.

Along the curved road up to the Barger's house, modest homes (which turned out to be much larger inside) sat amidst abundant vegetation; each had a view of the waves of La Jolla rolling perfectly in big, fat curls onto the shining expanse of white sand. Off to the left was a luxury hotel with an open dining room and bar built on pylons out over the sand. The days here were almost always balmy and the ocean was warm, fed by the tropical Mexican current.

The Bargers had a four bedroom home, Teresa's bedroom, her parents', the guest room and another room for whichever of the grown-up kids was home visiting or living for a while.

The next morning we awoke to a lovely day with the sun streaming in through the patio doors. Teresa's father greeted us graciously at breakfast. "How wonderful my two golden girls are here. We're happy to see you."

Teresa's mother was glad to see us too, though she was always quieter than her husband.

"Do you have a plan for your stay?" she asked.

Joan and I glanced at each other guiltily. Part of the plan was to eventually tell our parents where we were, which was probably going to be trouble of some sort.

"We're thinking of going to the beach."

"I was just asking because I think Timmy and Janet are going to some rock concert tomorrow, you girls might want to join them."

Timmy, the second brother and third kid, was there for the summer with his wife Janet; they were both 22. I thought Timmy was the most perfect man and I hoped there would be someone like him for me when I grew up. He was tall and gangly and had dark brown corkscrew curls and thick, dark lashes. Better yet, he talked about the wildest things: his plan to open a drive-in movie theater in Kuwait, "Why not?" he would say, "They're rich, they all have American cars with nowhere to go and the nights are warm. I'd make a mint." Or the fly farm. He claimed there were areas with a dearth of flies, people who were *longing* for flies and he would ship the flies there to those deprived areas for a small price. Or his great bumper sticker idea: a package with a blank bumper sticker and thick felt tip pen.

Janet was, if anything, even cooler. She had straight, light brown hair and a round face with starry eyelashes. She was very pretty and didn't say much but what she did say was always totally far-out.

Going to a rock concert with Timmy and Janet was exactly the kind of fun we had been imagining would be going on down here, Joan and I smiled at each other in complicitious satisfaction. "Yes, we'd love to go." We went back to Teresa's room to change to our bathing suits.

That night Joan and I stayed up all night talking to Teresa's older sister Nora who had just come back from a year in France. Toward dawn, I realized she was more like us, not secretive like Teresa.

"Hey, how come Teresa is so reticent?" I asked.

"You tell me," she laughed. "I've often wondered and *I'm* her sister. Why don't you wake her up and ask her?" Nora suggested.

"Teresa, Teresa." I shook her.

She stirred and opened up only one eye, indicating that she was already awake enough to joke. "What is it? What time is it?"

"Listen, me and Joan were talking to Nora and we were wondering: How come we tell each other everything and you never tell us anything?"

"You never ask," she said and went back to sleep.

I was amazed. It was true I never asked. I thought if she wanted us to know, she would tell us. Now it turned out that she thought if we were interested, we would ask.

      *   *   *   *   *

"There's an elephant rampaging through the jungle, he's irate, deeply irate. Suddenly he screeches to a halt in front of a small mouse and he says, "What's wrong with you? How can you even be in the same jungle as me? You're so puny. The mouse looks up and says, "I've been sick."

Timmy finished telling us the punchline when he swerved sharply and pulled noisily into a gravel driveway at high speed. We piled out of Timmy's beat-up blue Volvo and we were all still laughing when I saw *him* there, standing bare-chested in front of the white framed doorway of his broken down house. A total man-god. Michael, Janet's brother, was the single most handsome man I'd ever seen in my life, I didn't even know men came this good-looking.

His long, light brown, sun-streaked hair, smooth and with no split ends, curled halfway down his back. He had big green eyes and dark eyebrows and eyelashes. I couldn't really look at his mouth, I just had a general idea that it was too beautiful and might make me feel out of control.

By the time I finished taking him in, everyone else was halfway toward his home and I was left conspicuously standing stock still by the car.

"June?" Teresa called. "Aren't you coming?"

I walked toward the house as if in a dream. We went inside, the square living room was covered with a cheap, beige wall-to-wall carpet and had two beat-up bean-bag chairs and a tile-topped coffee table. There was no tv, but a stereo of a quality far better than its surroundings and on the coffee-table quite an assortment of elaborate dope-smoking paraphernalia.

Michael sat down on the floor right away and began rolling a joint. "Make yourselves at home," he said with a wry grin. We all happily sat in various places.

I could see his toes from where I had my back against the white plaster wall. Even his toes were perfect, *frighteningly* perfect, very manly. They were square with blond hair and thick, horny toenails.

Through my overwhelming teenage lust I could vaguely hear

Timmy talking.

"What've you been doing for food?" Timmy asked Michael.

"Patrick's been giving me photography jobs for *Psych Today*." Michael smiled.

Janet was looking at her brother with pretty much the same degree of adoration as I was.

"This is the most unbelievable shit," Michael said. "One of my friends just brought it back from Nam, it's Indonesian."

Oh yeah, I remembered Nora had told me Michael'd been in Vietnam and he'd gotten a little weird because of it. You could be with him at a party or something and all the sudden he'd jump up and run out the door. He hadn't been drafted, the family had plenty of money, but he'd volunteered against his doctor-father's wishes. The fact that he was moody only intrigued me further. As I contemplated the world tragedy that underlay his moodiness, I felt even more deeply drawn to him. There was nothing acquisitive in my desire for him however. I could plainly see that he was far too good for me.

"Michael, you're a first-class gentlemen." Timmy tipped a pretend hat to his brother-in-law as Michael handed him a joint.

"And you sir . . . ," Michael paused "are an entertainer of the highest water and far more importantly, though I'm sure consequently, surrounded by beautiful women."

That joint made it's way around the room and another and another and another and we were all good and high by the time we reloaded ourselves into the car and roared out of Michael's driveway for the concert.

At the show, I lost track of everyone but Teresa for a long time. We found out we could wiggle our way right up to the front near the house-sized speakers and dance to every song. We smoked more pot with two boys with very straight, blond shoulder-length hair who looked like surfers and told us they went to UCSD. We didn't answer when they asked us where we went to school.

"We live in the area," Teresa charmingly replied.

We figured a possibility existed they would be reluctant to let us go after the show, so we slipped away during the second encore and found Timmy and Michael near the door.

"Here." Michael handed me a flat silver flask.

I took a swig. Whatever was in there was very strong. I took another swig.

"Let's go up to the beach," Timmy said.

"With wine," Michael answered.

I realized that they were old enough to buy alcohol legally and my heart skipped a beat. For a minute I felt weak and excited, overwhelmed by the fact of just standing next to the two of them. Was I ever lucky.

We drove down a hill to a beach I'd never been to before. We piled out of the car laughing again, high, but were soon quieted by the soft whoosh of the waves, the huge boulders on the side of the sandy path that led down to the sea, and the enormous, back-lit cumulous clouds sailing in front of the full moon. It was warm and windy.

I walked quietly down to the beach, watching where I put my feet on the cool sand, the path glowing white between the dark rocks and black bushes.

"Are you okay?" Nora whispered behind me.

"Yeah," I was having such a good time I didn't want to talk.

When we all arrived at the water's edge, there was more silence but now slightly uncomfortable.

"Should we build a fire?" Timmy asked.

"What for?" Michael flatly asked. "For heat? For light?"

It's true, the beach was now lit up by the ghostly brilliant light of the full moon, the clouds were making their swift way north.

"This is how the world always is for you Michael, isn't it?" Timmy suddenly asked, I think surprising even himself.

Michael nodded slowly and silently. He unscrewed the top of the big wine jug and upended it into his mouth, then handed it to Timmy.

"Blood brothers," he said, then took off, the phosphorescence he kicked up glowing in spurts ahead of him as he walked up the beach.

JUNIOR YEAR

For some reason I felt incredibly joyful starting the new year. The weather was beautiful, the sunlight so clear you could almost see the colors refract, the blue spectrum lighting up the undersides of row after row after row of purple-green artichokes on the drive down through Salinas Valley.

Even school looked beautiful, the flowering shrubs had shot up even higher, covering the white Spanish walls, increasing the illusion of California peace and beauty.

My dad parked the car.

"You guys want to come in while I find out where I'm living?"

I saw their eyes widen slightly in alarm.

"No thank you, we'll stay here," they said with calm voices, subtly contradicted by the still slightly enlarged whites of their eyes.

"Okay."

I got my room assignment. "UPSTAIRS AT SANTA RITA," I yelled in my parent's direction, a bit further from the Volkswagen bus than I should have been. My dad started up the car.

They unpacked me and left right away. Not that they weren't fond of me, but they had thousands of children and this was not the first time they'd moved a truckload of teenage possessions.

"By mom, bye dad." I waved to them as they drove off, still feeling ebullient. I eagerly unpacked, singing "Wake up, wake up you sleepyhead."

"Hi, hi, hi." I hugged my friends. Diane Hull had gotten a tan and she looked not just pretty but sexy too. Dana Hees smiled her crooked smile at me, she also seemed happy to be back. Even Julie Maldonado looked radiant.

"How was your summer?" I asked Julie.

When Julie was born her feet pointed in the wrong direction. This is no big deal, a lot of kids have this condition, some of my brothers and sisters had had it and were cured by simply wearing shoes that looked like they were on the wrong feet. But Julie's parents said she would disgrace the family with a deformity, hired a nurse, moved her to a small gatekeeper's house on the edge of the property and said they'd see her when she was fixed. Julie saw her parents for the first time when she was five.

"Hey Julie, what's happening?" I said, happily.

A flash of seriousness crossed behind her dark eyes. Julie was unusual-looking, with dark eyes and eyebrows and light, thick, straight hair. She was big-boned, healthy, and moved cautiously as if afraid of accidentally inflicting physical damage.

"Have you heard the rumor?" she asked.

"Rumor, what rumor? I've only been here five minutes. I just barely recall what school we're at."

She smiled grimly. "The nuns are changing the rules. They're going to announce it later today, maybe after dinner. We're going to get to wear pants and some other things. Maybe the seniors will be allowed to date."

"Really?!" I was totally flabbergasted, shocked, pleased and then taken aback. A suspicion began to surface.

"How'd you hear about this?"

Her eyes shifted. Julie never did anything dishonest but somehow she'd managed to develop a set of quirks that seemed to indicate she had. "I was hanging out by senior dorm. I went to say hello to Sheila Steiner and all the seniors were talking about it."

"Wow. I better go over and see Mary Pickering right away. Did you see if she was there yet?"

"I'm not sure."

"Wow, Julie thanks," I said and raced off in the direction of Senior Dorm.

Emotions churned inside me like the mixture of baking soda and vinegar my brothers and I used to use to make miniature rockets. The nuns were very clever. We'd assembled the strongest radical student body officers yet and we'd been determined to fight for our rights. All the students had been following the rules and it seemed like we had a healthy shot at getting a few concessions: wearing pants on Saturdays and Sundays, being able to go to Mark Thomas for supplies on weekday afternoons if we needed something and weren't in class, maybe even being given permission to leave campus without four chaperones. Now it looked as though the nuns had preempted us. Rather than being forced into a corner, they'd taken the most innocuous rule changes and made them their own, knowing that the pressure would be released enough that it would be unlikely the students would take the uncomfortable and unprecedented step of demanding more. Fuck them.

49

Sister Aaron poked her head into my room.

"June. When you get a minute, could you come tap on my door? I'm in charge of your class."

"Again?" I said, with genuine surprise.

She grinned wickedly. "I'm the only one that can handle you."

My my.

Her room was tucked into a niche over the stairs and looked out on a walled garden. I'd never caught even a token glimpse of the inside and today was no exception. I knocked. She was thin, but it was still amazing how small a crack she could slip out of.

"Sister Aaron!" I exclaimed involuntarily because one minute the door was closed and the next minute she was standing there outside it.

She just looked at me, not moving a muscle, her eyelids with those pale lashes blink, blinking. "Yes, June?"

"Nothing."

She looked at me for a couple more eyelash beats. "What I wanted to say was . . . you are the class president and we have ten new students in our class this year. I know I can count on you to be kind and look after them; that's part of your job."

She paused.

I waited, it sounded like the sentence had an unspoken but.

"After everyone has gotten a bit more settled in, maybe after dinner tonight, I'll take you around to meet them."

"Yes, Sister Aaron."

She blinked in such a way that I wondered if sometimes she wasn't almost winking. She dematerialized herself back through the door and I was left standing there alone again.

*   *   *   *   *

I dutifully knocked on Sister Aaron's door at 7:00 p.m.

"Sister Aaron. Sister Aaron."

There she was.

"I'm ready."

She smiled. "I'm sure you're going to like these girls quite a bit. They'll be a welcome addition to your, ahem, rather eclectic class."

'Rather eclectic class,' I repeated the phrase to myself. It sounded good, explained the wide variety, the lack of homogeneity which actually did set our class apart from the classes that had been above us, whose characters I could easily describe as a whole: sophisticated senior class; straight, ugly and religious junior class; cool, smart and a bit cynical sophomores.

She led me into the big upstairs room at Santa Inez. The leaded glass windows on three walls of the room were curved, set deep in old stucco. This building was part of the original main house.

"Gwen," Sister Aaron said.

A small red-headed girl with dark eyebrows jumped up from where she'd been lying on top of her bed, fully clothed in a green plaid corduroy jumper and darker green tights.

"Gwen is from Venezuela," Sister Aaron said, looking at me as I shook Gwen's hand.

"Nice to meet you. I'm June Smith, president of the class. If you need anything ask me."

I looked right in her eyes. I could tell I'd have to tell this girl a lot more times before she would actually ask for anything although she already looked like she could use some comforting. Sister Aaron took my elbow and steered me away. Gwen remained standing by the side of her bed in her stockinged feet.

In the smaller room next door, which had four beds, we met Ann Sewell, Sarah Haskell, and Bobbie Bon.

Sarah Haskell had blond, straight hair but with a wispy curl near the part on the right side of her forehead. She had a strong, straight nose and calm blue eyes, lovely shaped light lips. Her face was serene and she looked directly at you, unperturbed. I could tell she didn't talk much.

"Bobbie Bon doesn't live in this room. She's Joan Frawley's roommate," Sister Aaron said.

I laughed. "That'll keep you busy."

Bobbie cocked her head as if perplexed.

"No, no. In a good way. Joan is interested in her own pursuits and the rest of us just have to make way for her gothic romances and old show-tunes. You'll love Joan. I do," and surprised myself by realizing at that moment that I did. I usually thought of people as brief and amusing acquaintances, not lifelong friends.

Next we met Liz Darst.

"Hey listen," I said to her, sorry I hadn't had the idea earlier, "Why don't you come along with us on our journey of discovery? I'm meeting the new students and you might as well meet some people in the same boat."

So Liz followed us. Next room was Teresa and Juanita's room. It was jammed with girls. Besides the legal occupants were Cynthia Pitts, Joan, Sarah Haskell, Kay Covington, Katie Finnegan, Suzanne Murphy and even Stella Blackwell in a corner pretending to read the newspaper.

Sister Aaron spotted two more new students, "Lucy Butler and Abby Miller." She looked around at all of us, aware that her presence had dampened the conversation a bit. "I believe you have enough on your plate for now," she said to me and went back through the door.

I couldn't help but breathe a sigh of relief—I fervently hoped being Junior Class President would not mean I had to get all chummy with the nuns.

I slid down to sit on the floor, my back against the wall.

"Haven't seen *you* in awhile," I said teasingly to Teresa.

Everyone laughed.

"Listen, I have a great idea. Has anyone shown you new students where the vending machines are?"

The new girls shook their heads "No."

"Okay, this is very important information. Let's go."

We walked outside and down the rickety St. Rita stairs held snug against the side of the white hacienda building, frangipani wound in the railings. Lucy, Gwen, Kay and, most surprisingly, Teresa—who had few indulgences besides a moderate consumption of Junior Mints—traipsed down the steps.

We walked across the parking lot, between the dining hall and first row of classrooms, continued on past the Study Hall path and down a small hill to a little concrete bunker in the foundation of the Study Hall. The green steel door was open and we could see the glow of the vending machines before we got there. I'd made this trip more times that I could count and knew to take my time—considering each item carefully, then thinking it over again, because once the food was eaten, the fun would be over.

The soda machine was first and then next to it was the better candy machine (though Teresa would disagree because the Junior Mints were kept in the machine on the wall opposite). Then, furthest from the door—its short, strong, steel legs sitting firmly on the gray concrete—was my favorite, the variety-of-semi-real foods vending machines. This machine had little rotating plastic compartments and the whole front was transparent, lit by an unearthly green light which did nothing for the attractiveness of the ham sandwiches, apples and oranges spun within. Also rotating were cartons of chocolate and plain milk and different flavors of yogurt. The eerily glowing machine was cold to the touch, refrigerated. I pushed the black button on the side and the food spun slowly around.

I could tell Gwen Wiedepohl had never seen a vending machine like this before. Of course not, she was from Venezuela and even we had only had this one since the middle of the year before.

"What would you like?" Teresa politely asked Gwen.

"Oh nothing thank you, I'm full from dinner," she shyly replied. "I just wanted to see where they were."

Lucy, meanwhile, was checking for money in the return change slots and then trying to force open the plastic doors to obtain free food. I looked over, she was very busy and certainly not shy for a new girl.

"This is so great. I love this, I'm not sure what to get! I'd like to have a yogurt, but they're so expensive, I only have sixty-five cents and so if I get one . . . ."

We were all staring at her. This girl was an *event*. I could tell I was going to like her.

"I'm afraid if I get a yogurt, I won't have any money left over for candy . . . ." She darted back and forth from one machine to another, her freckles and aristocratic nose lit up by the unearthly glow of low-wattage lights trapped behind lurid pictures of candy (completely unlike that actually available in the machines). She had far too sophisticated a face for a 16-year-old. If you gave her a french twist and a pair of pumps you would have sworn she could spearhead a hostile business takeover.

I stopped paying attention to Lucy's rather astounding personality to focus on my vending choices. "I'm having blueberry yogurt." I hit the button and the yogurts whirled by: raspberry, plain, apple, then there was the blueberry. I pretended to have accidentally gone too far for the sheer pleasure of watching the food go round again. Ham and cheese sandwich, turkey and cheese sandwich, red apple, yellow apple, red apple, orange, orange.

I put my money in just before the blueberry yogurt came up, opened the door and then kept my finger on the button and FOR SOME REASON the door stayed open for the next yogurt. "Grab it!" I yelled.

Lucy roughly pulled it out, her arm going between mine, one of which was desperately holding the door, the other pushing the button. The next yogurt rolled in. Lucy got it too! And then the next one. She got the apple yogurt! And the next one. "Great, great, get 'em," everyone was yelling, even Teresa and Gwen. We got every yogurt on that row. Wow! I couldn't believe it, we'd hit the jackpot.

We lined up our ten yogurts. Three blueberries, four apples, two lemons and one vanilla. Everyone got one and there were still three left over. I ate another one, so did Lucy, then we took the last one back to the dorm for whoever would want it.

"That was totally magic." I sighed with deep satisfaction to Teresa on our way back up the path. I thought I was going to like being class president very much.

50

Later that week I was slipped a note by Lindsay Hayes, a deceptively wide-eyed sophomore who was becoming a hand-groomed pet of Sister Carlotta. The note said, "Come to a meeting in the main office at 3 p.m. on Tuesday." Of course I didn't have a class then (no accident I'm sure) and I had been planning to actually read some fiction in the library.

Sister Carlotta's secretary, Ms. Lord, a junkyard dog of a woman, led me in after a ten minute wait.

Sister Carlotta looked straight at me and said warningly, "You are going to have many important duties during your term as class president, including the Fashion Show, Father/Daughter Weekend and the Junior Dance. It's a big responsibility."

"But the Fashion Show is not until February," I pointed out.

Sister Carlotta turned her watery, expressionless blue eyes on me and Sister Jane Fox, who had been hiding on the shadowed couch, looked at me sternly.

"All the arrangements must be made in the first semester," Sister Aaron rapidly interjected as she smiled and batted her eyelashes.

I put my head down apologetically. "Yes, Sister."

I waited obsequiously for more.

"You will also be responsible for class meetings, you have to keep the other girls organized, spiritually confident, and impart a sense of well-being to everyone. If you stumble on a situation which is not within your capacity to handle you must report it to us immediately. You are facing a formidable challenge in a class as diverse as this, but we and your classmates clearly believe you are equal to the challenge. Don't disappoint us."

I hadn't known a "pep" talk from Sister Carlotta was part of being elected class president; now I'd learned.

"No Sister." I waited again, trying to make myself obedient and quiet all the way to the furthermost reaches of my being or at least as far as the nuns could see, but it appeared that that was all. I got up and smiled at each nun in turn. "Thank you, thank you, thank you. I know your confidence in me will not be misplaced."

51

"I can't Lucy," I wailed.

"Sure you can." Joan urged.

"But it's very dangerous to skip Study Hall. And besides it's not like it's not obvious, there your desk is—sitting empty. And I *am* the Class President."

Lucy made a dismissive gesture.

"No really, it'll be okay," Joan assured me. "Lucy and I did it last week and nothing happened."

"Are you sure?" I looked intensely at them to see if they were telling the truth because it sure was a tempting idea. Study Hall was intensely boring. At one o'clock each day, the entire student body assembled in the Study Hall, recited the "Pledge of Allegiance" and then a line of girls would form and go one by one up to the microphone and make an announcement, always tedious, usually unnecessary. Like, "Could all the members of the ski team meet on the terrace at 1:15." And the ski team would consist of only five girls. "Could all the sophomore day student Navahos with red hair please, please, please remember to bring canned chili for the Halloween food drive."

"Sure we're sure." Lucy was pulling at the puffy sleeve of my yellow down parka. "We'll go hide in the bathroom next to the day students' lounge. That way we can hear when everyone gets out and mingle right in."

"Okay."

We crouched in the bathroom between a row of old, heavy porcelain sinks facing old-fashioned, green-painted plywood stalls.

"Why don't blind people parachute?"

"That's a stupid joke."

"Not as stupid as we'll feel if we're caught here."

We all giggled even though the remark wasn't that funny.

"How long do we wait?" I asked.

"Don't worry, you'll know," Lucy assured me.

"I don't know about this. It's possible we could get more bored and more uncomfortable than if we'd gone to Assembly. Maybe if we do it again we can bring a deck of cards . . . ," I said. Although truthfully I had to admit that even this crouching between the sinks on the cold tile floor was far far preferable to attending Study Hall.

Unfortunately, cutting Study Hall turned out to be quite addictive, and even though it seemed like we were bound to be caught at some point, every day Lucy, Joan and I were willing to gamble that it wouldn't be *this* time. We'd tuck our striped summer uniforms around our knees and talk about the other girls, the nuns, what we were going to do on our vacations and, most importantly, what we were going to do when we finally got out of there.

52

Right about this time, I had figured out a totally brilliant dressing strategy or actually I had stumbled upon it accidentally with Lucy's help.

One day she said to a group of us, "Hey, you know what, if anyone wants some extra uniforms, I've got a ton, Leslie Redlich's mother and Susan Wood's mother are friends with my mom and I got all their old uniforms."

"Those are the ones before they made the stripes smaller on the summer uniforms, right?"

"I dunno, you can come over to my room and check it out. I

have a lot more than I need."

I rushed over there cuz I figured if I had fifty uniforms I only had to do my laundry twice a year. Pulling on one of the striped pink-and-white summer uniforms I remembered that both Leslie and Woody were several inches taller than me, which resulted in hemlines almost brushing the tops of my saddle oxfords.

"Oh my god," Lucy blurted out and laughed.

"This looks cool. I can wear them with bobby socks and then only a tiny strip of my skin will show."

"June, that looks weird."

"Listen. What's the rule about skirt length?"

"The skirts have to be less than two inches above the knee."

"Yes. And is there a rule about how long they can be?"

Lucy looked puzzled. "No. Why should there be?"

"Voila." I flung out my arms and modeled my new look with a twirl.

Another rule was that we had to wear the complete uniform, but in cases of extremely cold weather, we could make additions. So with my brand-new, ankle-length, wide-striped pink skirts I wore the entire uniform, then a red raincoat, and on top of that a yellow ski jacket. On rare days in California when it was very cold or when I felt particularly disgruntled, I also wore a Dr. Seuss type yellow and blue wool scarf.

53

Saturdays, which I had once spent studying or associating with the other girls, were more and more becoming an opportunity to lie down at the pool and sun myself. We were never bothered down there for some reason, probably because seeing the girls half-naked was more than the nuns could bear.

"Hey June." I could hear Teresa calling from the other side of the swimming pool fence.

Lucy, Pitts and I were all covered with baby oil, lying on our stomachs with the tops of our bathing suits untied. As I sat up, I held the small pieces of blue and white material to my breasts.

"I'm here."

The moment Teresa came around the edge of the pool house, the wind blew up her silk skirt at the bottom. She always looked so energetic, so supremely well tuned. It was ill-advised of me to chose her as a rival, she was such a clearly superior example of American girl teenager. As much as I loved her during the summer, it was a small but constant irritant to endure her well-meant worry about me during the school year.

"It's time to go to work on the Yearbook."

I groaned. "Can't we do it here?"

"You know we can't. We'll never get any work done. Lucy will extrapolate and the next thing I know you'll be telling her some fantastic story and . . . ."

"Okay, okay, you're right." I tied up the strings of my bikini top. "What're we doing today?"

"The pictures in the front."

"How about this: June, Lucy and Pitts bare their lovely bosoms to the camera, hoping against hope that someone will spot the provocative pose and offer them a job modeling."

Lucy and Pitts laughed. Teresa frowned slightly at my not-that-brilliant mockery.

54

Each of the ever-mounting responsibilities came with its own list of difficulties. We would no sooner get through the Christmas Play (in which we were unable to get rights to the play so I had to rewrite the entire thing from the book) than it was time for the tin can drive (imagine a tin can drive directed toward people who live in dorms and the only store they're ever in is Macy's). In math class I would amuse myself by averaging my hours of sleep for the week or month, and the figure usually hovered around two. Joan had remained imperturbable as I got more and more frantic. She stayed close to me but seemed unaffected by the conditions which I was undergoing, and went right on, as usual, reading her Gothic Romances long before she did her homework, and singing Broadway tunes.

"What am I going to do?" I wailed. I was upset about the Junior Dance. "I don't want that damn easy-listening band they've had every other year. This is 1971. I don't want to hear '16 Candles' or 'La Bamba'."

"Didn't you get some tapes?"

"I got four tapes, each more putrid than the one before. My only hope is Kathy Grant's boyfriend's band. They're supposed to be super-good hard rock."

Joan spread her hands. "So? There's your solution."

"They haven't sent a tape yet," I wailed, "And Sister Aaron insists we vote by tomorrow."

"Hmm." Joan went back to eating red licorice. "I don't think you've got a problem."

Then the answer came to me. Joan was right. I felt totally calm. "Okay. Alright. I'm alright now, I have the solution but I'm going to need everyone's help."

Joan shrugged. "No problem."

Late that night, I snuck around and visited everyone in their rooms. "Tomorrow we're going to vote on a band. I know you all heard the tapes of the four bands I've already played and they're terrible. We need a band we can really dance to. Kathy Grant's boyfriend has a great band, great. They're called "Ed." Even though we've never heard them, I know they're great."

The next day "Ed" was unanimously voted the first band to grace the Junior Dance besides "Bob Clingon's Swingers" in fifteen years. I was ecstatic.

55

Not that my problems were over.

"Oh my *god*, I don't have a date for the dance." I looked critically at myself in the mirror. I was trying on a possible outfit of my brown velvet dress with small, pearl-shaped buttons down the front and new brown suede, high-heeled lace-up boots. I looked good I thought, but of course I'd been on a three day coffee-only fast.

"What am I going to *do*?"

Lucy looked down her aquiline nose.

"We'll ask one of the day students. They'll know someone cool. Though I think you guys ought to think about what kind of dates you make. I mean, you guys are not exactly wild party girls. Look at you. It's Saturday afternoon and you're perfectly happy reading. *Reading* for god's sake. Can't you make an honest attempt to sneak out?"

"To where?" Joan asked.

Lucy was now beyond exasperated. "Where doesn't matter, dummy. It's the principle. Sneak out to the beach or a diner. First of all, it's appalling that you're all virgins. I bet the seniors aren't all virgins. I bet Juana Shurman isn't a virgin."

We all stared uncomprehendingly. I was pretty sure Juana was a virgin. I didn't think it was that easy to lose your virginity. After all, I was pretty sure that good Catholic boys wouldn't have sex with you until the two of you were married. I figured that since I probably wasn't getting married for quite a while, what I'd have to do was start dating someone and then after three or four years, when he really trusted me I could probably TALK him into sex before marriage. But of course I hadn't even started dating anyone yet. I sighed and put the idea out of my mind.

"You guys are hopeless," Lucy said.

56

Perla (a senior day student) strode manfully across the parking lot with my date. Bill, she'd told me his name was. William Faulkner. I could not have been more nervous.

"This is Bill. This is June. You guys can take it from here," Perla said with typical teenage grace, then turned to go back to her car, totally satisfied with the elaborateness of her introduction.

"How do you do?" I shook Bill's hand. "Oh. Nice handshake. That is a big thing in my family. We've been known to entertain each other for hours after dinner with imitations of bad ones."

Bill brightened. "I love families that invent their own parlor games."

I looked at him suspiciously. He didn't crack a smile, but just as I turned to lead him off in the direction of the dance he raised an eyebrow. Mmmm.

"This dance might be a little wild. I'm in charge and we got a band we'd never heard," I said.

"So I've been warned."

Hey maybe I was going to like this guy. I had developed a slight prejudice in his favor when Perla told me he'd painted his motorcycle gold. He wasn't bad looking either. Straight sandy brown hair, a broad face with very straight, dark eyebrows and a strong chin. Not skinny but on the other hand not fat. He was wearing a very slick green sharkskin suit and a cotton shirt with tiny toasters with wings and a small collar buttoned to the top, no tie.

"Nice look," I said.

"Likewise." he responded, nodding at my chocolate-brown velour dress and brown suede boots. I couldn't help myself, I smiled.

While the band was setting up, we sat on the side of Study Hall.

"So what are your goals, uh, I mean post-high school?" I politely asked.

"Ride my bike all around the county."

"Really?" I asked. At first I thought he meant bicycle, but then I remembered the gold motorcycle. He called it "bike" for short. Cool.

"Yeah, really. What are yours?"

"Live in a house with a bunch of cute, long-haired guys and take a lot of drugs."

Oh man, I couldn't believe he'd made me give him that answer. I felt a strong desire to kiss him. William Faulkner.

"What're you thinking about?" he asked.

I jumped. "WHAT?!!"

Now *he* looked startled.

"I come from a high-strung family." I tried to cover up.

"There they are again."

I sighed. "There's no avoiding them. My head is stuffed full of stories about them from my mother. It takes all my willpower to keep them from leaking out on tests. For example, there was my great great great great great great and so on uncle, who was one of the first pilgrims to come over. I believe he was on a ship headed for Georgia or South Carolina, one of those states where the English sent all their incorrigible criminals. Anyway the captain of the boat announced that when the people got off the boat they could have all the land they could see from where they were. As they approached the land my great great whatever cut off his hand and threw it on the land so he could have the harbor."

I snuck a look at William Faulkner. He was silent. Now I felt an even stronger desire to make-out with him. Although experience had already taught me that this wasn't that hard with boys—all you had to do was separate them from the crowd and then wait a thousand hours, I knew that tonight circumstance might be against me.

I jumped up. "Would you like a tour of the campus?" I asked.

"Sure." He jumped up too.

I led him down to the Hockey Field first.

"We're not really supposed to be down here," I warned.

"Got any other stories about your family?" he asked.

I felt acutely embarrassed. "Oh no." I just stood there, idiotically looking at the ground. "What about your family? Got any brothers and sisters?" I desperately struggled to recover.

"I'm an only child."

"Oh." I scrutinized him with increased interest. Hardly anyone I knew was an only child or even close. Rich Catholics tended toward whatever was the most amount of kids the mother could physically bear. Maybe he was too foreign to be a boyfriend for me. Staring at him I remembered again he was cute.

"Uh. Hey, it's making me nervous being here. C'mon, I'll show you some classrooms."

"Okay."

We climbed up the hill wordlessly and I led him over to the plainest building, which also happened to be the place where we would be the least likely to be interrupted. "This is mainly used for history." I took him in the classroom. "Though I had Latin class here my sophomore year and see—look over there, that wall can be unhooked and moved back to make the classroom bigger. Anyway, last year there was a big section of European History in here before the Latin class and so the wall would be open. Whenever I got here before the Latin teacher, Mrs. Ulrich, did, I would push all the desks back to the far far corner." I demonstrated with my arms. "All squished up, then I would write in neat letters on the board 'PLEASE DO NOT MOVE DESKS.' And Mrs. Ulrich would come in . . ." I began to speak in a poor imitation of her heavy Eastern European accent. "'Please class, moof ze desks to ze front.' No, no, we would shake our heads and solemnly point to the words on the blackboard and then, when she would disagreeably agree to obey the non-present authority who had written them, we would pretend we were too far away to hear her. 'Alright,' she would say. 'Zere vill be no quviz today.'"

William Faulkner laughed. Then he reached over and touched my cheek and kissed me. Crazy!

After a few minutes I got nervous.

"Let's move to another classroom."

He let me lead him. Once there we immediately returned to kissing.

Then I got nervous again and moved him to another classroom. He went over and sat on the window ledge looking out over the Hockey Field and I happily sat on his lap, my knees up facing him. Suddenly, after quite a bit of this, I realized I'd pretty much dumped my responsibilities vis a vis the band.

"Bill, oh Bill."

"Yes?" he murmured.

"I think I have to go back and check out what's going on with the dance. What time is it?"

He rolled his wrist so I could read the dial and he could continue kissing my neck.

"Oh my god!" It was 10:20 and the band had been playing for an hour and a half. Where did the time go?

I still felt a little bit trippy from the intense kissing as we walked across the lawn toward the Study Hall. I was holding William Faulkner's hand.

The Study Hall sure did look beautiful (if you could forget its usual use as a mental torture chamber); light was streaming from the windows and a red glow was directed on the long-haired musicians. A couple of figures broke from the darkness of the building and came running toward me.

"June, June, we looked everywhere for you. The nuns have even been searching the classrooms."

Luckily they hadn't been searching the classrooms where I'd actually been.

"What is it?" I asked.

"The band . . ." Cindy Doyle began, very panicky.

Susan Work continued in her dry way " . . . they're frightening us, Junie."

I got a little closer and saw that everyone was sitting on the floor while the band played hard, hard, hard rock.

I turned to William Faulkner. "Let's go back," I said, kiddingly, but I saw his eyes light up in a deeply gratifying way.

"No June, you can't." Susan said in a panic.

"Then we could dance."

He grinned and we did dance.

We were the only ones.

57

Since the first triumphant time I'd been elected a class representative, I'd gotten the job again each semester. The excitement I'd felt initially was now tempered with the depressing knowledge that we were mostly rubber stamping the nuns' favorite candidates. To be fair, their choices were usually the same as those the students would have made, but the exceptions, the competent girls who were just a little too feisty or uncontrollable and then tagged with that most-damaging of Catholic labels "immature," were blackballed often enough to make me sad.

"Kit Tobin."

I stared at the wood pattern on the formica desk—the one thing I could see with my head down—and grimaced. I raised my hand. Kit Tobin was sensible, well-liked, much more mature than the rest of her class, intelligent, clearly a leader and admittedly a bit wild. Listening carefully, I could hear the rustle of other hands besides my own going up. Thank god someone else was also voting for her.

Mary Pickering read the next names on the list. "Jinny Trent. Alice Walton, Linda York." She went fast through those names, knowing ahead of time that no-one would raise their hands. It was hard to vote for freshmen, they were so young, like grammar school kids.

"Oh sorry, I skipped a name. Frances Corcoran."

I raised my hand again. Frances was Kit's best friend and the only other possible candidate. A distant second, but certainly worth having on the ballot. I hadn't raised my hand for any other freshmen. The nuns seemed hyper-alert.

As Mary read through the lists the tension grew—nuns and students alike knew there was going to be a fight about Kit Tobin.

"Mary Ellen Fay." Mary Pickering read the first name of the reduced list and smiled around the circle without humor.

Teresa raised her hand. "Mary Ellen is my "little sister" (a role juniors were appointed to for incoming freshman) and I think she should be on the ballot because she has two qualities I believe a freshman class president should possess (no-one there missed the reference to the fact that Teresa had been freshman president of our class) which are forcefulness and responsibility. I have also seen her helping the other freshmen with homework and various other aspects of school life here."

There was a pause, suddenly the energy in the room dropped. Lily Poth, a platinum-blond sophomore who thought she knew a lot more than she did, a girl with an air of officiousness at the age of 15, raised her hand. "I second the motion that Mary Ellen be on the ballot."

Mary Pickering looked around the room. "Any objections?"

Suddenly nothing seemed worth the effort.

* * * *

Sister Carlotta turned. "Trish, could you please leave the room."

Trish had already gotten part way out of her chair anticipating the enforcement of the rule that a girl had to leave the room if her sister or cousin was discussed. Trish was possibly the smartest girl in the school, she aced every class and every test without seeming to pay any more attention than a rather casual disdain. She was blond and freckled, strong, square and sexy. We all waited quietly until the sliding glass door closed behind her.

"Kit Tobin is highly qualified to be the freshman class president. She is clearly a leader," I said.

A distinct wave of strong disapproval emanated from the nuns.

Mary Pickering spoke up calmly. "I agree. I've known both the Tobins since grammar school and Kit is very smart. And mature."

Sister Humpbert spoke up. We were all a little surprised that a nun would speak so early in the discussion. Their voices counted so much more heavily than ours that usually they waited until we were through commenting before they either confirmed that someone was acceptable or, in rare cases, put the strong kibosh on a choice they didn't want to see on the ballot.

"I'd like to point out that Kit has now been described as mature twice, yet she didn't come back after Christmas at the appointed time."

"She had a *concussion*," Katy Finnegan protested.

"Nevertheless," Sister Humpbert said coldly. She made it clear that anyone with moral fiber would refrain from getting a concussion until some more appropriate time, like the beginning of summer, when a convalescence would not disrupt things.

The tension in the room increased, suddenly it seemed to us students that every issue we'd backed down on as electors—assuming that the nuns were right and what the heck, they'd win anyway—had been a failure of courage on our part. The nuns, I sensed, were furious at not getting their way at once.

Sister Aaron broke in with her soft sibilant tone: "I believe that Sister Humpbert is trying to point out that while we understand the student body's respect for Kit Tobin's intelligence and drive, which we all share, perhaps it would be wise to consider the fact that she doesn't always meet her obligations."

At this point we should have stopped fighting. The nuns had made the eventual outcome perfectly clear.

Teresa raised her head. "Kit Tobin is roommates with Mary Ellen Fay so I see her frequently and I have to say that I would wholeheartedly support her candidacy. I find her thoughtful and conscientious. The other members of her class look up to her."

I felt shocked. Sister Humpbert actually had her *teeth* clenched. "I don't think she is an appropriate choice at this time." Each word was forcefully emphasized.

We all looked at her in amazement. This was terrifying.

I didn't notice, but I had raised my hand. "I believe that I would have to just as forcefully say that I (*oh my god, what was I? suicidal?*) believe that Kit Tobin is the best person for the job and to leave her name off the ballot would make this entire electoral committee a travesty; it would be revealed as a forum for us to exercise power instead of a fair and just process." I could not believe I'd said that. I might as well just walk right out the door and shoot myself. I felt as if my blood had drained from my body. I'm positive I was very, very pale.

"I agree with her," Sheila Steiner said.

Damn. She was suicidal too.

You could feel the nuns trying to intimidate us with mental force, the room had no air. But we also were unyielding.

Then, in an instant, the debate ended. "No," Sister Carlotta said and suddenly it was over.

A dead silence descended on the room, the girls all bowed their heads voluntarily.

"I think we should break until tomorrow," Mary Pickering suggested.

Without an okay, we all got up and filed out the sliding glass door and trudged helplessly back to our dorms. Trish was still waiting in the small garden. She didn't bother to ask what had happened, simply fell in with us on our way across the back of the classrooms, through a grey drizzle.

*   *   *   *

"I heard the electoral board today was hot." Lucy hinted rather
strongly that she'd like me to divulge a little information.

"You could say that."

"What about the Kit Tobin thing?"

I felt horrible all over again. "Oh Lucy, what's the point of all
this anyway? It's not as if the nuns relinquish one iota of real power.
Do you know that as class president, I looked down at my calendar
one day and saw that I had *nine meetings*: nine meetings at which we
would sit around for hours and discuss many issues of the most
minuscule importance like what color paper flowers to have as table
decorations at the Fashion Show or whether we're allowed to wear
kneesocks with dresses on Sunday while real things like Kathy
Taylor being thought of as dumb because she's only good in math
and then she gets 800 on her math SAT are left totally unaddressed.
I mean there's a lot of stuff going on in this school. For example:
Don't you think there's something wrong with the fact that Joan and
I have been assigned our THIRD YEAR of English with Sister
Aaron? We'll get her next year too, I'm sure. I mean there is nothing wrong with her as a teacher but still. Is this an institution of
learning or am I just vastly naive?" I snorted. "I guess a case for the
latter could be pretty easily made."

Lucy looked upset.

"Don't answer any of those questions," I said. "It's too depressing." I stalked off to my room, thinking already about whether I had
any money in my purse to get a Snickers bar from the vending
machines. One thing about eating candy was that for at least that
small piece of time that I was chewing I felt totally sheltered from

outside concerns.

58

"June, hey June." I heard Lucy yelling from down near the phones. "It's your mom."

I ran down. "Hi, mom."

"Hi, sweetie. How are you?"

"Tired mom. Deeply tired. I spend my math classes figuring out how many hours of sleep I've had per night and it's usually less than two."

"Have you had a chance to go to Saks and use the charge card?"

I snorted. "Mom. Why not a charge card to a bookstore?"

"It'd be too expensive for us," she primly replied "Plus I'd like to see you in something other than that yellow ski jacket."

I laughed. "What else is new?"

"We got your midterm comments from your teachers."

"Oh umm hmm. They weren't bad, right?"

"Junie, we're always happy with your grades."

I glowed interiorly.

"Except for one comment that struck me as a little weird."

"What's that?" I foolishly was not on the alert.

"Your American History Teacher. It looks like Sister Jean Fox."

"Jane Fox. Yeah, go ahead." How bad could it be? I'd gotten As and B+s on every test and every paper, and heaven knows I talked a blue streak in class.

"You got a C."

"A C!" How could I *possibly* have gotten a C? I was in shock.

"And her comment seems a little strange to me. Do you want me to read it?"

"Go ahead," I said through clenched teeth. The C did warn me that I wouldn't like it.

"It says, 'June is a very good student and I'm sure she'll do much better next semester when she is not spread too thin by her duties as class president.'"

"God damn it."

59

After Christmas vacation that year, I felt different, somehow better. A small thought waved desperately from the far far distance of my consciousness field that I was relieved not to be class president anymore, but I ignored it. I vowed to never slack off, never not do the right thing, particularly to always do my homework and study for tests before the last minute. Putting my suitcase down in my room in Santa Inez unmindful of the dresses that would wrinkle if I didn't unpack them immediately, I decided to wander around in the cool evening air and look for whoever else was back. I loved the fresh way the flowers and turgid evergreens smelled in the winter.

Going out the screen door and breathing in deeply, I saw Teresa coming from the direction of the classrooms. She was wearing a black and white print dress with a skirt that fell in delicate rounded folds and flipped up as she walked, showing off her good legs.

"How are you?" she smiled.

I remembered again that Teresa liked me, even though I was a bit of a thorn, a constant reminder that she had not yet gotten a rival of steady habits. She would like to be playing a more evenly matched game.

"Great, I'm great." And I did feel great.

She looked a little surprised. "Got a lot of sleep over Christmas, hunh?"

"Yep."

"Ready for the A.P.s?"

I frowned a bit. "Which ones are you taking?" I wondered if the nuns had thought Teresa capable of handling more Advanced Placement classes than I.

"English, Art History and American History," she said.

Good. Those were the same ones I had.

"What about your grades? What'd you get from Sister Jane Fox?" she asked casually.

"That witch. She gave me a C+ in History even though all my tests and papers INCLUDING an A- final were all As and Bs. She had the nerve to write on the comment sheet that I'd do better when I wasn't class president. I should just flunk all her tests and I'm sure I'd still get an A."

She looked at me seriously. "You're not going to do that, are you?"

"No, no, no. But I'll show her."

A week later we got our first paper assigned in American History.

I wrote a great paper, turned it in and when we got the papers back a week later was quite surprised by my grade. A over F. What? Then it turned out that everyone got that second F. She had decided, out of the clear blue sky, with no warning, to give us one grade for content and another for form.

On the way out of class, I walked over by Teresa and bumped her with my hip to indicate I wanted to talk to her. Joan came up too.

"So . . .?" I asked.

Teresa smiled resignedly with one side of her mouth.

"So outrageous." Joan said. "Out of the clear blue sky. I mean . . . , if she'd warned us, that would be one thing."

Dana came up. "The no warning was so totally typical of her."

I twirled, my ankle-length, red- and green-plaid winter uniform flying out around me as I sang. "Oh am I happy. So happy."

"What is it? How can you be so happy? Every single one of us got at least a partial F," Dana complained. "And to top it off, she assigned another one."

"Yeah," Joan said, "we're not even halfway through the first month. How many papers are we going to have to write for her class this semester? Fifty? At ten pages apiece, that's 500 pages. That's a friggin' book."

"No, no. Forget about that. I am planning the greatest thing," I crowed.

Everyone looked at me as if I'd finally lost it.

"I'm going to the library right this minute. I will be giving Sister Jane Fox the best, most perfect, most stunningly grammatically correct paper she has *ever* seen." I was chuckling gleefully.

Over at the library, nearly empty on an afternoon when the semester was not yet in full swing, I ran my finger down the spines of the plastic-encased books of the historical section. Keller, Kleinwort, King. Martin Luther King. Of course. The perfect subject! A radical leader who preached non-violence and was brutally assassinated. I pulled out the book and went with it over to a desk near a window. I bent to the task, absorbed in the possibilities for this term paper, thinking of how wonderful I could make a paper with three weeks to work on it and a burning interest in the subject.

Outside in the brilliant relentless sunshine I could see the other girls walking in twos and threes, gossiping and laughing. Most of them had already changed for the day out of their uniforms and into flower-print dresses. Here and there, a plaid-skirt-and-green-jacket clad girl would fly by, usually in a bigger hurry than the others. Between the brick walkways, geraniums and begonias bloomed in a riot of red, yellow and orange.

Martin Luther King, the words marched across my vision in thick, important black type, then I was lost in his life. The biography was like a novel. I'd read the whole thing by the next day, speeding through it, even with stops for abundant note-taking.

Sunday I went to the library again and read another biography. This one was a bit denser, in a drier academic style that would have curtailed my pleasure if I was not now ravenous for facts about my new hero. Reading that book took almost a week. By the time I finished the second book, I had pages and pages of notes.

"Two books, June? Isn't that excessive?" Joan asked. (This didn't surprise me; Joan had so little time left after reading Gothic Romances that she cruised through her own papers by using what she remembered of books in their Classics Comic format—conveniently, a company that her father owned.)

I boasted. "I'm going to read another book too. I found one in the library about events that were going on during his life and that will place him historically. You know, *the setting*."

Joan shook her head at my foolishness.

Three weeks before the paper was due, I began writing. It was surprising how pleasurable the process was when, for once, I actually had the facts at my command.

When I finished at three a.m. Saturday morning, I kissed the paper. I said, "I LOVE this."

The next day I approached Teresa.

"Hey, hey. Crazy cat."

She grimaced at me. I was high on accomplishment.

"Could you do me a favor and edit this paper before I type it?"

"For grammar?"

"If you see anything that sticks out sure, but I'm thinking more of mellifluousness."

"Is that a word?" she asked.

I grinned.

"Love to be part of your latest project, June," she said.

When she gave the paper back a few hours later, I looked over her changes, approved them and gloated, then danced with it through the cool night air over to Lucy's dorm to get her to do a second edit.

That night, I painstakingly typed the paper. Well, actually I started to painstakingly type but the sound of it annoyed Cynthia Nadai so much she got out of bed and typed it for me. I stood beside her and watched, under the theory that if someone is suffering while they do something for you, you should steadfastly suffer with them.

I put the paper in a safe place and exulted over my coming triumph all day Monday. On Monday night, I went humbly to Sister Aaron's door. I knocked. She opened it the usual sliver.

"Oh Sister Aaron," I said very, *very* politely. "I wanted to ask you a favor. I have here a paper I'm doing for Sister Jane Fox's American History class and, as you might have heard, she has a new rule that the papers must also be grammatically and stylistically correct. So I wondered if you could take a look at it for me?"

The door swung open. Sister Aaron, in her inimitable fashion, was still wearing her habit. I was shocked that I could see inside, a green, nubby fabric couch, a rag rug and a big-screen tv.

"When do you need it back?"

"Wha?"

"When do you want me to return your paper?" she asked more sharply.

I wrenched my attention back. "Friday would be good," I cautiously suggested.

"That will be fine." Sister Aaron smiled at me and took the paper. "Oh . . . it's typed. That's good."

I looked at the floor. "I thought it would be easier to read."

I spent the weekend in the library once again, this time reading books about form and structure for the footnotes and bibliography. I had amassed thirty-two footnotes, my all-time record, and it was not a huge struggle to do so either. Usually, I had to actually manufacture footnotes out of whole cloth at the last minute to give the illusion of having references. I was humming as I worked. Using the previous A over F paper and the books as a guide, I carefully wrote out the final pages. While doing so, I had a stroke of brilliance, the total trump card.

On Sunday night, I approached Sister Jane Fox.

"Sister Jane Fox, oh Sister Jane Fox." I ran up behind her as she walked across the lawn in front of the first classroom building.

She and I were the only two over near the classrooms.

She stopped and turned. "Yes?"

I was a bit breathless. "You can tell me if this is not allowed, but I have here my footnotes and bibliography for the paper due Friday and I wondered if I could ask you some questions."

She smiled, I believe triumphantly, although I couldn't imagine why. "You've gotten so far." Her voice was smooth, like creme caramel.

"Oh, I loved this assignment," I sweetly replied. "I've been having a *wonderful* time."

Moving over to stand beside her, I showed her the pages.

"First of all, in my last paper, you marked the periods at the end of each footnote as incorrect, but in <u>The Chicago Manual of Style,</u> <u>Thirteenth Edition</u>, which you recommended we use, it says the periods *should* be there. Should I use them a la the reference work or not?" In my voice was no hint of criticism or irony, but still her smile drooped slightly.

"Don't use the periods," she said sharply.

"Okay." I marked the page. "Now here, the volume number. Should that be in parenthesis or not?"

"Yes, I want the volumes enclosed."

"Okay." I made another mark. "Now what about this editor? Should he be included? He edited the speeches of Martin Luther King. Is the book alphabetized by his name or by King's name?"

"King's name. What does it say in the The Chicago Manual of Style?"

"It doesn't say. Or at least I couldn't find it."

"Do it by King's name then."

"Alright now. In general, how do these look? Do you see any problems?"

She took the two pages and looked them over. "No, I think you've got it right. Just fix the things you've asked me about."

"Okay." I grinned very, very big. "Thank you." And I meant it with all my heart.

That week I got the paper totally typed up and could have handed it in by Wednesday, but Joan convinced me that would be overkill. Friday, though, you can be sure I was the very first person waiting outside that classroom door, paper in hand, desperately eager to turn it in.

60

A week went by, a regular, boring winter week, not much sun, not much happening.

Joan and I were lying in the bunkbeds at Santa Inez. She was on the top, I was on the bottom with my bare feet against the cool, metal understructure of the upper bunk.

"Do you want to hear a story?"

"Yes," I said.

"When I was little, I didn't really see my mother and father. My brother Michael, my sisters and I stayed in the nursery with the nannies. On Sundays, we were allowed to come down for dinner and that was the only time I saw my parents. The rule was that if we didn't like any part of the meal we would be sent back to the nursery. And every Sunday, the second course was peas; I hated peas, so I would see the butler coming with the peas and I knew that when the silver platter with its silver spoon arrived at my place and I said 'no thank-you', I would be banished back upstairs. So, during my childhood, I would see my parents on Sunday until the peas were served."

I didn't know how to respond. "Do you want to go raid the kitchen?" I asked.

"Nah," she replied, "I'm at a good part in my book."

61

I was slowly walking to English class with Joan. I was a little wired from having only coffee for breakfast. As Joan walked beside me, I noticed how clean and crisp each blade of grass was on the raised lawn next to the path.

"June, you know it's been three weeks since we handed those History papers in. I can't believe we haven't gotten them back."

"Hey, look at me. I have no fingernails left. Or toenails." I held my foot up toward her.

"Ugh. Stay away from me." Joan feigned disgust.

We walked farther in companionable silence. Joan seemed to be humming to herself. I was concentrating on why the exact blue of the sky today seemed different than any other blue sky before.

"Maybe I might have to do something about finding out," she said.

62

The next night, I was lying in bed in Senior Dorm in the room to which I had just moved that morning.

Joan, wearing her pink chenille bathrobe tied up under her breasts, lounged carelessly against the door frame. She almost looked mad to me. I was lying on my back holding a book up and reading.

"Yes?" I rolled over in bed to see her better.

My roommate Juana ignored both of us. She was drawing in her notebook, probably something incredibly cool.

"What is it?" I asked again when Joan didn't say anything, just kept staring at me relentlessly.

"I broke into Sister Jane Fox's room," she snapped at me, "Do you want to hear or not? I'm going to tell you ahead of time that it's not good."

Oh my god. She knew the grade on my Martin Luther King paper.

"Let me put my clothes on." I began frantically searching for clothes. I pulled on my patched jeans (illegal clothing) under my Lanz nightgown before I peeled it off and snapped on my front-closing bra.

"Come out in the corridor," Joan said.

"Wait, wait, I'm still naked." I quickly pulled a white t-shirt over my head.

We walked out, no-one was in the hall of Senior Dorm that late Friday night. They were all studying or they'd already gone to sleep.

"Tell me. Tell me."

Joan's facial expression had changed from mad to some cross between apologetic and tortured. "I saw all the papers, June. Three weeks and no one's paper has been corrected but yours. I'm sorry.

You got an A over an F again."

"Oh god." In one second, I was heartbroken. How could what she had just told me be true? In that one second, I went from thinking how I looked kind of cute in my patched jeans to feeling my heart ripped painfully in two.

"Uh." An involuntary groan escaped and I turned away.

Joan came up and tried to put her arms around me but I pushed her away. I put my head down and bulled my way out the door of the dorm as tears of rage and frustration coursed down my cheeks.

Heedless of my dress code violation, I wandered across the front parking lot. I walked by the classrooms and took the stairs down to the lower school. Now I was sobbing loudly. Across the hockey field and through the tennis courts, I sat on the other side of the fence where a dirt hill led down to the barbed-wire fence through which I could see the headlights of cars speeding along, the people inside intently focused on their regular, everyday evenings. This was as far as I could get. I cried and cried and cried. Four hours of crying later, I trudged back up the hill and went to bed.

63

Mrs. Green smiled at all of us lounging in the sun on the green lawn in front of the classrooms. She taught Humanities and was actually pretty good; she taught us about Oscar Wilde, Mozart's life, Henrik Ibsen's affairs, and other facts made infinitely delectable by the nuns' sure disapproval. She loved Ann Politzer, Joan Frawley and Teresa, and they thought she was super cool. She was pretty, I'd give her that, but I'd noticed a few too many times that after a besotted student would confide in her, one of the student's friends or that girl herself would get in trouble from the nuns.

She stopped, flung back her pageboy hair and smiled her big-toothed grin again. She was tall with a thin, tan, broad-jawed, handsome face.

"How're you girls today?" she asked.

"Far-out," Ann answered.

"I'm happy to hear that. What're you talking about on this gloriously sunny day?"

She opened her arms as if to capture more of the pure California sun pouring down on her.

"June wants to get a Gold Card, that's what we were talking about."

I smiled at her, disarmed by her interest. A Gold Card was awarded to girls who got all As. I'd come pretty close but I always got one B+, in a different subject each grading period. She smiled back at me.

"Her dad says . . . you've seen her dad, right? He's handsome and he told June he'll grow a mustache if she gets one."

Mrs. Greene smiled at me again. "Well, I hope he gets to grow one."

We all laughed at the idea.

64

Speech Club meetings were sandwiched in the afternoons between gym and getting dressed for dinner, on Tuesdays and Thursdays. Consequently, we were all dressed in our gym uniforms with white bloomers and were a little sweaty. These meetings were just about the only thing I didn't mind attending, not because I loved speech, but Mrs. Hauke was nice, easy to tease and seemed just as baffled as to what the nuns were after as we were.

"Now, Sunday, we're going to go to the demonstration speeches at Seaside," Mrs. Hauke said.

We all looked at her.

"Do the nuns know?"

She slapped her hand to her forehead. Mrs. Hauke was the only person I knew who did the gestures described in books. She scratched her head when she was thinking, pulled her hair when frustrated, wrung her hands when distraught. "I forgot to ask. Darn. And I'm supposed to go out to dinner with my husband tonight."

A picture of Mrs. Hauke and her husband sprang immediately into my mind, the same one I got whenever she mentioned him. The mental picture I had of her husband was based on two rather flimsy pieces of information: first, that he worked at Ford Ord (so I always imagined him with a crewcut in an olive-drab uniform) and second, someone on our speech team (I could no longer remember who) had told me that he had a very small head. What I saw in my mind was Mrs. Hauke standing, smiling, with her big head next to her husband with his small head, also smiling.

"June? Do you think you could ask the nuns?" Mrs. Hauke asked.

"June doesn't get along with the nuns that well," Dominique piped up.

We all gazed at her, open-mouthed.

Mrs. Hauke got a sly look on her face. "I think it is the nuns who don't get along with June. Given a little material to work with, I believe June gets along well with anyone." Then she looked a bit shocked at her own words and we watched her try to backpedal. "Anyway, never mind, I don't know why I even asked. I'll call them tonight and have Sister Aaron tell you whether we're going or not. If not, it's no big deal—just a demonstration. Though I did want you girls to see it."

65

Cynthia Breidenbach, Marta Johnson and I were lying in our hotel room in Palo Alto, watching tv. We were bored. The excitement of leaving campus for debate competitions had worn off, even for overnight trips. The state championships held at Stanford were just more of the same, the same ugly, deformed debaters wheeling around the same grocery carts full of metal files containing thousands of 3 x 5 cards.

I jumped up and began dancing around the room, "Hey why don't we get dressed and go out? C'mon . . . ."

I tugged at Cynthia's arm.

"I'll betcha anything there are plenty of Stanford boys wandering around campus looking for someone to befriend."

I wiggled my eyebrows suggestively on the "befriend" bit.

"No way, no way. Besides, the campus is over a mile away and we don't even know in which direction," Marta pointed out.

"You're right. There's no sense in struggling. We're bored, we've been bored for years and we're probably still going to be bored after we graduate." I lay back down, spread-eagled on my bed.

Marta smiled. She was a beautiful girl, I always thought of her as looking like a high Egyptian princess, with a long, sinewy, cat body and an elongated, thin face with big lips, an aquiline nose and huge, almond-shaped eyes. Her hair was a little strange, it just stuck out stiffly from her head but in its way, it only seemed to add to her good looks.

Cynthia was an ethereal blonde with a perfectly proportioned, porcelain doll shape and a round face with a pointy chin, blue eyes, pink cheeks and a rosebud mouth.

I thought Marta much more beautiful, but there was no denying that Cynthia's version of the blond, blue-eyed, all-American girl was appealing. All three of us wore the long, flannel, Lanz nightgowns that were de rigeur bedtime attire for Catalina girls.

We searched around for something to watch on tv. The only choices were the news, a Western or a documentary about seals.

Cynthia told us about her brother Blake who'd gotten busted smoking pot at his college and spent the night in jail.

"What happened to him afterward?"

"Nothing," Cynthia said, slightly disgusted. "My dad hired a lawyer and Blake got a suspended sentence and a small fine, which my dad paid, and when he turns 21 he'll have to go up to Oregon to get his juvenile record erased."

"You can do that?" That didn't quite seem fair to me. Absolution was okay in the confession, but the law should be a bit more permanent.

"I think so, yes. I think it even applies to murder."

"Murder!"

We watched a bit more tv. The seals were falling in love and having seal sex (not that interesting, even for us virgins) on a rock. Then I got up and stretched.

"Listen, I'm hungry. I'm almost positive I saw a Jack-in-the-Box across the street when we drove here in the van."

"June! It's one o'clock in the morning."

"So? The Jack-in-the-Box is 24 hours."

Both Cynthia and Marta stared at me.

"What are you going to wear?"

"I'll tell you what: If you guys come with me and dare me to, I'll wear my nightgown."

They both gasped, then laughed.

"Okay."

"Okay, you guys have to wear your nightgowns too."

"Okay."

We were now all beside ourselves with excitement as we pulled on white socks and tennis shoes. It was a balmy night but Marta also put on a pink cashmere cardigan.

In a flash I was out the door of our hotel room and inhaling the fragrant scent of the night-flowering jasmine bushes that grew along the walkway of the motel. Light spilled out our half-opened door, making it stand out amid the row of perfectly spaced blue doors in the long, tan, stucco building.

"C'mon." I gestured for Cynthia and Marta to follow, as I saw them hesitating in the room. But follow they did, Cynthia carefully closing the door with the faintest click so as not to alert Mrs. Hauke or any of the other girls. The bright orange light of the Jack-in-the-Box could be clearly spotted across a tree-lined boulevard. I pushed through a gap in the jasmine bushes lining the walkway, then saw I was right in the middle of the hotel parking lot and possibly quite noticeable to the fat, bald man sitting in the brightly lit motel office writing something at his desk.

"Uh oh." I pushed back through the bushes and tiptoed, holding a finger to my mouth, back past our blue door and five more exactly like it, to the end of the hotel.

There, I pushed through the bushes and sure enough, on the other side of the thoroughfare, was the insistently beckoning Jack-in-the-Box sign.

Marta rushed ahead and I saw a white flash of her nightgown as she disappeared through the bushes lining the road, and then was gone. Cynthia and I quickly followed behind.

The road was a major thoroughfare, four lanes of dark new asphalt, separated in the middle by a tree island. The only reason it was possible to cross it was the lateness of the hour. Finally, the way was clear and we dashed across, our nightgowns flying out behind us, our shoes making scrunching noises.

Crouched in the island for a second, I could smell the mixture of sweet flower scent and car fumes. Cynthia and I were breathless. Then we ran across, giggling now, falling on each other, helpless with the sheer unbelieveableness of what we were doing. We squeezed through another bush barrier and were standing on the far side of a giant parking lot, in the middle of which the huge, happy, orange-and-white clown face for drive-in orders glowed luminously, sharply outlined by the dark.

We walked slowly forward. The fluorescent street lights occasionally pinged. Should we really be doing this? We could just go back. Surely crossing the road had been enough of an adventure. I stuck my nose up in the air and walked forward.

The inside of the Jack-in-the-Box was small—the smell of french fries flowed strongly out the door. The tile-lined room and stainless steel kitchen flashed so bright that we were unable to focus at first. Inside were three round orange tables, each supported by a single pedestal bolted to the floor, and similarly shaped yellow chairs like small group of evenly spaced, evilly colored mushrooms. We tittered and giggled our way to a table. Now what should we do?

Luckily, Cynthia had brought three dollars tucked into her sock.

"Coke?" she politely asked Marta and me.

We ceremoniously acquiesced. She went up to the counter, where we joined her. Hey, I thought excitedly. The guy waiting politely to take our order was cute.

"Three Cokes," Cynthia said.

"D' you work all night?" Marta asked at the same time, making both Cynthia's order and Marta's flirtatious question indecipherable.

"What?" the lanky boy at the counter asked, blinking at us in amazement.

"Three cokes," Cynthia said again.

We waited silently, there was no sound but the marching Muzak in the background. I thought I recognized John Phillips Sousa, who had, for some reason, been a favorite with my grammar school nuns.

When we got the Cokes we went back to a bright orange table. Our nightgowns exposed our tennis shoes and anklets when we sat down; my legs were the shortest, I swung one foot.

"What d'you think?" Cynthia whispered.

"He's nice," Marta said.

The boy in question had disappeared around a stainless steel corner.

"We can't stay for . . . ." Cynthia started to say, but another cute guy, with dark eyes and a round, brown face came out of an "Employees Only" doorway with a mop and bucket.

He saw us and said, "Well, I'll be . . . ." He paused and struggled to partially regain his aplomb. "How're you ladies tonight?"

I realized then that he was at least four years older than us.

A customer came in, a razor-thin man with greased-back hair, shiny suit pants and a green t-shirt. He too noticed us right away.

"Hey, hey, hey. What have we here?" He ran his eyes over the three of us.

The beautiful Hispanic boy worker began half-heartedly pushing the mop around. The three of us smiled because we didn't know what else to do; the situation was certainly far outside anything we'd previously experienced. Quite frankly, we were thrilled beyond belief.

"Wow." The customer had gotten an even closer look and probably begun to figure out how pretty Marta and Cynthia were.

"Crazy." He sauntered across the floor and rolled one leg over the yellow mushroom seat at the next table. "Mind if I pull up a chair? And may I be so bold as to inquire . . . where did you angels descend from?"

He was handsome in a kind of con-mannish way, but the questions seemed stupid to me. Complimentary of course, but how many places were there that angels descended from? I was disappointed at the disappearance of the first boy, the one who'd been at the counter. I wondered if we could afford some french fries, which would give me an excuse to go up to look for him. I peered at the price board, but I wasn't wearing my glasses because we were on an adventure and so reading the small print indicating the price of french fries was totally beyond my visual ability. I sighed.

The worker with the mop had given up the pretense of cleaning the floor and stood looking with total adoration at Marta, mopping the same spot directly in front of our table over and over again. The floor was quite shiny and wet.

I leaned forward. "What are we going to do?" I whispered to my two friends.

"Let's get some french fries," Cynthia said, with a quick, casual glance up at the price board.

She handed me a dollar-fifty and I went up. The cute guy was frying up some hamburgers—getting ready for the rush later I guessed. I smiled in his direction.

"Just a minute," he called out to me nervously.

"Oh, no hurry," I politely responded.

He was turning the hamburgers one by one over, and then over again. He had a giant, industrial-size spatula in his hand. I considered that he was probably using a special Jack-In-The-Box hamburger-flipping technique. I turned around for a minute. After all, it was impolite to stare. The other worker had gone back to mopping, particularly the table next to the table where the skinny whippet guy Jimmy (I knew his name because he announced it loudly to Marta just at that minute) sat.

"My name is Jimmy." He elaborately and cheesily tipped an imaginary hat. "Pleased to meet you. And what might you little ladies be called?"

He was wearing brand-new snakeskin cowboy boots. I giggled and turned back around. I saw the cute boy walking toward me with a shy smile on his face; my heart skipped a beat . . . .

BAM, CRASH, POW! Suddenly both Cynthia and Marta were standing, their hands to their mouths. I turned around just in time to catch a glimpse of Jimmy, legs higher in the air than his head, arms flailing wildly and an expression on his face that was anything but suave. A split second later, Jimmy was on the floor and the cute mop boy was holding his mop about three inches off the ground with a look of horror and open-mouthed astonishment on his face. An unfortunate unison of excess moping, brand-new boots and male interest had caused a calamity. Everyone was frozen for a split second. Then Cynthia and Marta were up and out the door. I had no choice but to follow them. I could see their nightgowns disappearing through the thick hedge then wafting across the deserted street while faint traffic sounds from far away drifted toward me. I caught up with them just as they reached the blue hotel door, and we all entered breathless, collapsing on our beds in fits of laughter.

66

February of junior year was boring. The weather was rainier than usual, and we knew pretty soon the nuns were going to give us a lot more homework to keep us from sluffing off during the last quarter of the school year—at least that was the word the seniors passed down.

One Monday, Sister Clare announced that Evelyn Wood was going to be giving everyone speed reading tests—to be administered in our regular English classes. Sure enough, we got the test the next day.

"Are you nervous?" Dominique whispered as we went in the classroom.

"Nah."

I like tests, particularly the reading portions. It seemed to go well, I had plenty of time to read the small stories and answer the accompanying questions in the three sections before Sister Aaron said, "Put down your pencils, girls."

As soon as they were over, I forgot the tests. There was no reason to think about them, heaven knows we took enough intelligence tests of every sort each year.

One Friday, a couple weeks later, Joan, Lucy and I were playing Spades in the bathroom near the day students' lounge when we heard the usual noises outside indicating that Study Hall was over. Lucy put the well-worn cards back in the Bicycle pack and we were all smoothing down our plaid uniform skirts when the door banged open. It was Diane Hull.

"June!" she said breathlessly, "I'm just warning you! You're in BIG BIG trouble! Today at Study Hall Evelyn Wood herself came to present an award to you because *you* can read faster than they can teach anyone to read. You should have seen. She called out your name, then called it again. Sister Carlotta was smiling, then her face turned all mad and ugly. You better do something quick!"

Oh God, it was worse than I expected. I raced over toward Study Hall right away.

I spotted her. "Sister Carlotta, I . . . ."

"You better have a flawless excuse, young lady," she said in a very angry tone.

That's when I realized—I didn't have one. I'd forgotten to think one up before the mad dash over to Study Hall, and as a matter of fact, I didn't feel like lying. I held my head up. "I don't have one."

"Come with me." She led me into her office. "Sit down. Close the door."

In that order? I thought silently to myself as I closed the door and sat down. I remembered that it would be bad to get thrown out and so I hung my head penitently.

"You have disgraced the school, young lady. Do you realize how selfishly you have behaved?"

There was a silence. I was having a very difficult time convincing myself to fill it. Instead I worried a nub of wool my fingers had discovered on the ugly, white-, brown- and green-plaid couch.

Her tone was noticeably angrier. "Well! Do you? Answer me!"

I wasn't sure which answer was better. "I'm sorry, Sister." That seemed good, particularly since I didn't specify what I was sorry for.

"You are uncontrollable! Incorrigible! You are headed for a life filled with problems. You think that it is some unimportant WHIM of mine that you all attend Study Hall! You have no idea. And you can see what has resulted."

There was another silence. I knew she was looking at me in a way it would be best for me not to see.

"It might be impossible for us to continue to nurture you as a student," she sharply threatened. "We'll discuss it. In the meantime, you have four "2s." The detention will start this afternoon."

I was dismissed. I knew the "we" who would discuss whether I got kicked out or not did not include me. I spent that afternoon scraping bubble gum off the asphalt with a white plastic knife—several plastic knives, since they broke easily. I was going to spend every Friday and Saturday for the rest of the school year engaged in various unpleasant jobs—like de-blocking sewage drains and cleaning out chimneys. While we worked, Pam Phillips told me about the time Laura Knoop had to clean out the barbecue pit and there was a dead and only partially decayed squirrel in there. At first, they had noticed that it smelled funny. When they told Sister Jane Fox it might make them throw-up, she told them that if it did, they'd have to clean that up too.

67

"June, June, get up." The voice was like a sharp crack on the head. I was positive I'd only just gone to sleep about ten minutes earlier. I dragged myself up. My arm was caught in the big rip that ran crookedly from the seam in the underarm of my flannel night-gown down to the side of my breast.

"Oh my god, Joan. Why'd we stay up so late?"

"You wanted to work on that English paper. I was reading my book."

She grinned lasciviously and held up the infamous <u>Everything You Always Wanted to Know About Sex But Were Afraid to Ask</u>.

"Only you," I said, too tired to finish the imprecation.

"I have to write an article for the newspaper today." It was only as the sentence was coming out of my mouth that it hit me: I wrote an article for the school newspaper every issue—I had to, the nuns had put me on staff a few months into my freshman year—but they were never published.

"Hey Joan. When was the last time you saw an article I wrote for the paper actually *in* the paper?"

"You showed me that one you wrote last time about the new speeches for student body meetings."

"No, no. I mean: When was the last time you saw one actually *printed* in the paper?"

Joan thought for a second. She started singing, "A long, long time ago, my mother told me . . . ."

68

"C'mon." I prodded Joan to answer my question.

"I'm thinking." she said, petulant, but cute. Cutely petulant.

"Okay," I tapped my foot. "One-one thousand, two-one thousand, three one-thousand, four-one thousand . . . ."

"You wrote that article about the basketball game with Teresa freshman year."

"Right. Right. Bingo. And *that* was the last time I had an article published."

"But you've been writing articles for the newspaper every month, right?"

"Yes," I said. I felt like an idiot, taking two and a half years to get outraged, but it definitely had hit me and I definitely was now outraged. A plan was already hatching in my mind.

That night I wrote an article for the newspaper, just like I always had once a month for two and a half years now, but this time I did not feel restrained to the usual falsely buoyant tone since I had finally figured out that no article I wrote would ever be published.

On the eve of the end of another year, it is natural to look back soberly on the mistakes and triumphs of the year past, while hopefully planning for the year to come. Traditionally, here at Catalina, the good sisters have done this for us, relieving us of the headache of unwanted decision-making, and we do send them a great big thank-you for that. However, perhaps a few heart-felt suggestions from the bosom of the student body would not be remiss. It behooves us to point out that the leniency of certain rules in the last year did nobody any good.

A noble experiment, indeed, but one that, in the final analysis, must be counted a failure. All that laxity, all that freedom - a terrible mistake and an unwanted and undesirable burden for the students to carry.

What the student body of Santa Catalina calls for is order. Here's hoping order will be given to us. Moral standards should be upheld, signals of decency flown high. As a suggestion for the kickoff to a new and more blissful Santa Catalina, we would like to ask the timely question: What could be more lovely than to see white gloves added as a constant accessory with all the uniforms? In fact, white gloves should be required at all times, off campus and on. Naturally this would necessitate rescinding the "pants on Saturday" rule, but it would not be exaggeration to say that universal applause would greet the repeal of the latter and installment of the former suggestion.

Secondly, talking between classes is distracting to students and teachers both. Wouldn't the campus be far lovelier if only the relaxing sounds of nature filled our young and tender ears? Also, of course, the students would absorb their lessons so much more thoroughly without a miasma of ceaseless chatter constantly interrupting their gentle thoughts.

Then, when the students had arrived in blessed silence at the next class, what a lovely sight it would make if they were to line up in order of height, an exact arm's distance between each girl, before entering the room. Envisioning the sight brings tears of joy to our eyes.

These are just a few examples of changes that could number in the hundreds. These proposals should merely serve as examples of a direction that all the lovely, eager, upstanding students at Catalina would oh-so-much love to see their beloved school head toward.

69

I was lying on my bed reading <u>The Importance of Being Earnest</u> again because I was too lazy to get up and see if Juana had something new on her shelves and my familiarity with the text of the Oscar Wilde play left plenty of brain room to ponder once again whether indeed I would ever get out of high school. After all, we had already been in for a million years, and there were certainly no outward signs that things would ever be different. Other classes had graduated, sure, but it was a far cry from that to actually graduating ourselves. At the earliest it would be a year and that was pretty darned close to forever.

Juana came in the room.

"Hey June. Whyn't cha come with me? I've got something to show you."

Oh wow, I was turned on immediately. The beautiful and incomparably sullen Juana Schurman had something to show me. I dressed in a magically short period of time.

"Yes?"

She looked me over. When she looked at you it wasn't exactly that you were found wanting, it was more that she didn't see any compelling reason to be any friendlier. I deeply, deeply, deeply admired her.

We went down the hallway and out the back door of Senior Dorm in a casual but studied manner. Her attitude made me suspect that we were headed in the direction of breaking some rules and if we'd seen a nun or an untrustworthy classmate we'd have reversed our direction immediately. It was only minutes before the nuns locked the back door of Senior Dorm. After 8 p.m., an alarm rang in Sister Jane Fox's room if anyone tried to get out that way.

We walked quickly toward the back fence, making our way through the huge oaks. The ground was covered with spongy humus, and the damp Spanish moss trailed along our faces in the dark. There was a path along the edge of the fence where the underbrush was less dense. As we walked by, the whippoorwills stopped singing. I snapped a twig loud; like in a bad horror film.

"Shhhhh!" whispered Juana.

After a few minutes the sound of other whispers floated through the thick undergrowth, seeming to come from many directions because of the dark. Then I recognized Joan's throaty: "What?"

We came out in a clearing near Othello the head gardener's house. Here, a street light from the access road ahead illuminated the silhouettes of six of our friends.

Joan, Teresa, Lucy, Mary Pickering, Trish Tobin and Mary Meyers were there waiting on the path.

"What's going on?" asked Joan.

"We're showing you something," Trish said. "It's our duty as your junior/senior roommates."

I was surprised to see Juana grin for a second. Mary Pickering snickered. I loved Mary Pickering. She got straight As, was the head of everything, beautiful, competent and yet so innocent it was impossible for her to get a joke. But these were not the reasons I loved her. I loved her because she always acted like she was happy I was a part of things; in some essential way she took me seriously.

"Okay now. Be quiet, this is very dangerous," Trish said, and she slipped around the side of Othello's house. A little too close I thought, his light was on, surely he was home at this time of night. But around we went, and in a minute we were no longer walking on pine needles but instead the hard asphalt of a road, down the back driveway, single file beside the chain-link fence.

I saw Trish squeeze though the small space between the gate and the fence, the chain and padlock pulled tight, then Mary Pickering was right behind her. My heart began pounding desperately in fear. Once on the other side of that fence no excuse would get us out of trouble. Then it was my turn—I hesitated and a split second later was through. The other side was even scarier.

We marched down the rest of the driveway, our feet hurtling ahead because of the steep angle of the road. Our footsteps clip-clopped heavily on the asphalt. "Shhhh!" someone whispered. The heavy old oaks loomed above us, making long shadows on the hill, contrasting with an eerie, fluorescent glow from the freeway lights. When we got to the bottom of the driveway we bunched up in a deep shadow and surveyed the landscape ahead.

The access road—gray and deserted, glowing surreally—looked very spooky, the clouds in the turbulent moon-lit sky throwing fast-moving shadows on the opaque ribbon of highway and steel guard rails. Looming over it was the overpass—a huge concrete buttress topped by a chain-link fence to keep you from throwing rocks (or yourself) down onto the racing traffic below. I felt small and easily smashed. But there we went, the seniors confidently leading the way, out into the world of inhuman man-made speedways. We crossed over the highway and then started down Garcia Street to Alvaraz. Safer, we were amongst slightly seedy apartment buildings, cheap hotels and gas stations. A block later, I spotted, looming out of the night sky, the big, orange and brown lit-up Denny's beacon.

We walked into the sound-deadened, beige, white and dark brown interior, with its fake-wood, Formica-topped tables and orange, quilted-plastic booths. Next to the glass counter, with its dried-out cheap cigars and selection of chewing gum, was a brown sign on a pedestal, aggressively proclaiming "Please Wait for Hostess to Seat You."

A blond hostess—with hair teased halfway to Sunday, and blue eyeshadow—came up. "Eight for dinner?" she asked.

Trish turned and looked at us, then back at her, and smiled. "Eight for dinner and coffee."

The hostess carefully counted eight brightly colored plastic menus from a wooden holder on the wall. "Follow me," she said.

And we sat around and laughed, SMOKED CIGARETTES and drank coffee. That was the first of many times that I went to the lovely, beautiful restaurant that is called Denny's and that was situated so fortuitously close to our school.

70

I half paid attention as Cynthia Breidenbach gave her speech on dreams. It seemed like a million years ago that we'd had such fun together at the Jack-in-the-Box. This speech was no improvement on the old way. Maybe the whole idea of speeches was what I was against. How annoying to have to come to Study Hall once every three months and listen to between two and three hours of speeches.

And if that weren't enough, each year was almost an exact replica of the year before. For example, someone would be assigned the topic of Father/Daughter Weekend every year. Every year we heard a speech about Father/Daughter Weekend.

This year, along with all the other "radical" changes, we were now allowed to give speeches of general interest, and Cynthia's was the first example of a "radical" speech. Its only advantage over a speech about the annual Christmas Drive or the Spring Fashion Show was that I hadn't heard it three times. Not that big an advantage.

My mind wandered. I could give a speech. Hey! I could give a speech about German concentration camps. I thought about it! Ho, ho! That would be really funny. Well, anyway, I'd suggest it to Mary Pickering, she'd get a good laugh out of the idea. My foot tapped impatiently as I waited for the Student Body Meeting to end. Finally, we were singing the Santa Catalina anthem, a song whose words remained resolutely hazy in my mind.

As everyone rushed hither and yon, I pushed my way though the girls to where Mary Pickering was standing at the far side of the front of Study Hall. Cynthia Breidenbach was there.

"Good, it was good." Mary was patting Cynthia on the back.

Teresa was also there as were a couple of senior day students, Maryanne Giottonini and Donna Moniz. I leaned against a desk and waited until everyone had wandered off but Teresa.

I sauntered up. "Hey, Mary, listen. I was thinking: I'd like to give a speech of general interest on German concentration camps."

After the briefest pause, both Teresa and Mary got it. I saw a bright flicker of interest in their eyes then a burst of laughter came from Mary. She always looked innocent, because she was Mary, but she knew exactly what I was getting at.

"The next Student Body Meeting is April 12th. How about

then?" She was already marking it down in the little schedule book she kept. "Great, great." She laughed. "I'll be looking forward to that." She spotted Lucy and Trish. "Hey Lucy, hey Trish, c'mere and listen to what June's going to do."

The next thing I knew, Lucy and Trish were carrying on, patting me on the back and congratulating me.

"That's brilliant. That's brilliant. You're unbelievable. When you give that speech it will be the greatest day in Catalina history," Trish crowed.

"Oh yeah. Oh June, when you write it, I'll edit. No, don't protest, I'd love to." Lucy avidly offered.

"Me too," Teresa chimed in.

Mary Pickering stood there, smiling happily. I felt a little backed into a corner. I hadn't really wanted to do anything but make a joke, and heaven knows I did *not* want to be even a tiny bit involved with the greatest day in Catalina history. But somehow I found myself at the library that Saturday doing research, instead of just having a little laugh with Mary and forgetting it. My idea at this point was that the speech itself would never get written. I was sure there wouldn't be enough material or motivation. Still, I kept running across shockingly apt phrases.

"Although the prison camps often looked quite lovely to the outside observer, with hedges and vines covering the fences, there was razor-sharp barbed wire at the top of the six-foot-high barriers, and men with guns who constantly drove the edges of the property to prevent escape."

Oh my god. The Houston Patrol. I copied the phrase down just in case I actually wrote the speech. Well, I thought, what I could do was write the speech for the amusement of my friends but then of course not give it. I also copied down the name of the source book. A few pages later, I ran into another astounding bit: "Children and very good friends were encouraged to turn others over to the authorities, in fact, the whole society was brainwashed into thinking that turning 'subversives' in was 'for their own good,' even though it had become evident very quickly that the punishments were dire."

Off I went.

The speech project took on its own momentum. Lucy and Teresa did a brilliant job editing, so the speech was deeply pointed yet subtle, and in spite of the fact that I kept meaning to tell Mary Pickering to take me off the schedule, that it was a hoax, April got closer and closer and then somehow April 12th was the next day and it was too late; I was going to have to do the speech for real. I didn't sleep that night at all.

April 12th was a Friday and the zero hour was one p.m. I was paralyzed with fear. I attended my classes zombielike, and then suddenly it was 12:30 p.m. and the whole school was marching ominously toward the Study Hall, then portentously taking their seats. It was a terrible nightmare.

Mary Pickering stood at the podium with a big, friendly smile on her face. "And now, June Smith has kindly decided to give a speech of general interest on German concentration camps."

It was at this point that I began to shake uncontrollably. Everyone was clapping and had turned their heads to look at me. I walked up to the podium, the neatly handwritten speech clutched in my hands. I started out smoothly, my voice clear despite what I was feeling, which could only be described as abject terror.

"It was Sister Jane Fox's American History class that initially interested me in this monumental topic, which I believe still affects us today."

Out of the corner of my eye, I could see Sister Jane Fox sitting on the bench that ran along the left side of Study Hall, smiling proudly.

"I hope this speech will help us all learn something about the universality of experience." I paused. My hands, which were holding the sides of the podium, had now begun to shake so badly that the pages were sliding off. I clasped them behind my back.

"In the nineteen-thirties in war-torn Germany, after the Weimar Republic, when the German people were experiencing runaway inflation so extreme you needed a grocery cart full of money to buy a loaf of bread, and unemployment was worse than during the Great Depression, no one suspected that much worse horrors were to come. It started innocently enough: The economy was recovering, and the leader who had helped implement the upswing convinced everyone, mostly simple souls who were afraid of anything different, that certain people had to be separated for the good of all."

My knees actually made a noise as they knocked together.

"Small children and good friends were brainwashed into thinking that . . ." As I started into the line I could see that I had captured everyone's attention. The nuns were sitting at various points around the edges of the Study Hall. Sister Carlotta was in the back, sitting at a missing student's desk in the last row.

" . . . turning in subversives was 'for their own good,' even though it became evident very quickly that the punishments were dire."

The entire student body broke into wild, uncontrolled, raucous laughter. I was totally horrified. Oh god, I hadn't even considered this possibility. Of course. With a grapevine as efficient as ours—*they all knew*. I didn't know how to react. I was petrified. I frowned as if totally perplexed, then went on reading from my prepared script.

"As the war went on, more and more people were sent off to the camps. The prisoners wore striped uniforms that distinguished them from the surrounding populace, and they were not given the respect usually shown to a dog."

Again, I paused for the wild laughter. From my vantage point, I could see Sister Humpbert get up from her seat and stride dead-seriously across the back of Study Hall to consult with Sister Carlotta. They both looked strongly displeased. No, it was a bit more extreme than that, they both looked *very* angry. I went on.

"Although the camps often looked quite lovely to the outside observer—with hedges and lovely flowering vines covering the fences, there was razor-sharp barbed wire at the top of the six-foot-high barriers, and men with guns constantly patrolled the edges of the property to prevent escape."

All the girls laughed and laughed, bent over, holding their sides, tears running down their faces. They couldn't see Sister Humpbert angrily striding across the back of the Study Hall and then, as if in slow motion, up the side aisle.

"Inside the camps, the moral and physical degradation got worse and worse. Some of the prisoners tried to starve themselves to death . . . ."

Sister Humpbert was mounting the steps of the stage, and she held up her hand for me to stop.

"June. Please."

I stood to the side as she leaned close to the microphone. She waited like that for the noise to die down.

"I am appalled to even have to tell you that this is no laughing matter. Perhaps you have become confused as to June's meaning in this speech, but I assure you she is talking about a deadly serious event that resulted in the death of millions of people. If you look around, you may see people whose own relatives suffered and died, and I *know* that you did not mean to add to their pain."

She stepped aside, gave me a flash of warning, and I resumed my speech. I rambled on, carefully cutting out some of the more obvious parallels, but I had no other ending for the speech than the one already written.

"One of the greatest mysteries is why the German people allowed this horrible tragedy to continue; rumors abounded, guards were in contact with their families, and information about these heinous war crimes was spreading. Worse, however, is the mounting evidence that American leaders suspected what was going on and did nothing to stop it. When American soldiers came to liberate the camps, they were shocked at the fact that concentration camp prisoners were in fact abandoned by the world and that millions had died. The few who escaped were emotionally and psychologically damaged for the rest of their lives.

"We can only hope, should similar events occur once more, that the common people will have learned their lesson and will not allow human degradation to continue—that this time, they will stand up and speak against it."

Everyone clapped, but not too enthusiastically after the reprimand. I was still shaking. I was so frightened of being expelled that I did a rather cowardly thing. I walked down the steps of the stage, followed exactly the same route Sister Humpbert had taken back from the stage and, while the other students were getting up and milling about, I approached her and said, "Thank you Sister Humpbert, for your help. I didn't know how to handle that situation up there."

She steely-eyed me. "Alright June. I think the whole thing is over now."

I knew then I wasn't going to get in trouble. I walked dazed and stiff-legged out into the sunshine, and my friends gathered around me in a circle.

71

I was taking a shower.

"June, June, where are you?" I heard Joan's plaintive cry.

"I'm in here taking a shower," I yelled.

Joan put her head though the curtain and stared at me for a minute. "You've gotten really fat now."

I laughed, but then saw the serious expression on her face. I sighed.

"I know."

I didn't feel shocked or hurt. Joan never meant me any harm. I was just going to have to go on an actual long-term diet. As soon as I got out of the shower, I walked, illegally clothed only in a towel, to Cindy Doyle's room and weighed myself. "One hundred, forty one pounds." For dinner that night I served myself only a single helping of green beans.

72

It seemed that the second half of junior year was going to trail on forever. Although I was no longer class president, apparently the job of talking to my classmates in the middle of the night still fell to me, and I was still class representative, which meant that I still went to about fifteen meaningless meetings a week.

I trudged back to the dorm, scuffing my feet on the gravel-strewn drive. It was Friday afternoon. Semi-hooray. I still felt terrible.

What should I wear to the Mark Thomas drug store? The green turtleneck and brown velvet skirt? Nah. It would be better to be totally inconspicuous. I changed into a blue skirt and yellow sweater, my blue serge jacket that had all the money in the pockets anyway, and left on my knee socks and brown oxfords.

I went over and signed out on the sign-out sheet and put my

hand into the jacket pocket to check out how much money was in there. Seven dollars and thirty-five cents. Not that much. The Mark Thomas seemed a million-mile walk.

The entry to the drug store was a small glass door with a steel bar across the middle. Chimes supposedly alerted the clerk to your arrival, but he actually appeared only after you had stood at the counter with your purchases lined up on the white Formica counter for a couple of minutes. The claustrophobic aisles of the hotel drug store were perfect for checking out all the items without anyone noticing you were there and getting annoyed at you for looking too long at the candy or sodas.

I fingered a blue box of Ex-Lax and thought about it. Did I want to do it? Did I want to gain weight today or lose weight? I put the box down and walked back to the candy rack. There were several boxes of licorice there and my imagination conjured the chewy texture and sweet taste of black licorice in my mouth. My gaze wandered over to a Milky Way.

I could go back to the empty dorm and curl up under my bedspread reading <u>Henderson the Rain King</u> and feeling the smooth chocolate melt in my mouth. Then I remembered Joan looking in at my over-inflated body as I showered.

No. I wrenched myself away and walked back to the Ex-Lax. Quickly, before I could change my mind again, I bought the small, cruelly cheerful blue box.

I unwrapped the silver foil. Chocolate, hah. Looking at it the first few times you saw only the visual promise of thick rich dark cream. But by now I'd taken enough Ex-Lax to know that by the time I'd swallowed twenty-four of those little squares, the bitter chemical aftertaste would dominate.

73

Cleo was the most beautiful creature ever. I had noticed this sophomore year when she was in my English class (taught by Sister Aaron of course) and I had often drifted away and simply contemplated the exquisite planes of her face and unusual, almost flat color of her blond hair. But now, with the starvation diet, she'd gotten even more stunning. Exquisite. Overwhelming luminescent. I was distracted briefly by a pang of regret that I myself couldn't seem to launch into a starvation diet. I desperately longed to starve myself for twenty or thirty days. I could tell from watching Irene, Kim and Cleo that it was easy after the first three days, but my father the doctor had already inculcated me with enough medical knowledge that I was frightened of the long term effects.

I went back to my contemplation of Cleo's beauty.

During the summer, the nuns must have had the opportunity to admit a few more paying students than they actually had room for, so four trailers were installed in the fallow ground behind Senior Dorm. I had finally gotten one as a room during the end-of-the-year roommate change.

The three of us lived in one half of a trailer, Cleo in a room barely big enough for a bed and dresser, Dominique and I in the bunk bed.

I was watching from the top bunk of our room as Cleo did leg lifts, her long ivory leg raising, then lowering. I counted—a hundred and twenty-five times—then the other leg began raising and lowering in the tiny space between the beds and the door.

In the bathroom the shower was running—Dominique liked to wash her hair every night.

Dominique was 5' 11" and had a thick hank of red hair reaching halfway down her back. She was not exactly pretty, her square face and full lips were her outstanding features, but her looks were unusual; she could have been a runway model. I contemplated her healthy handsomeness. No wonder the young doctors had been so interested.

I was still almost at my roundest, a little puff-ball of a girl with fly-away hair perched on the top bunk, gazing sadly down or trying to read as the two of them fought for exercise space. One night, during this argument, I was lying in bed reading Malcolm X, assigned by myself for American History.

"Hey Cleo, listen to this." I read to her from the book.

"I first got high in Charleston on nutmeg. My cellmate was among at least a hundred nutmeg men who, for money or cigarettes, bought from kitchen-worker inmates penny matchboxes full of stolen nutmeg. I grabbed a box as though it were a pound of heavy drugs. Stirred into a glass of cold water, a penny matchbox full of nutmeg had the kick of three or four reefers."

"Uh-hmm. That's very interesting," she murmured.

"I think I'll try it," I said.

"Sure, that's a great idea." Cleo was leaning over the tan Formica bathroom counter to look in the mirror as she plucked her eyebrows. Dominique was doing sit-ups.

I hopped down from my bunk, stepped over Dominique and went outside, slamming the flimsy door of the trailer. The field where the trailers had been set up was way on the far end of the school, so I had to walk past the senior dorms, the annex, Santa Inez and then upstairs to find Joan. She was lounging in her bed, leafing through a Barbara Cartland novel and talking to Lucy.

"I just don't think it's all that important," she was saying.

"What?" I asked.

"To lose your virginity before 16. Lucy says all the girls at Stone Ridge were non-virgins."

I laughed. "Who the heck are we going to lose our virginity to? Othello? The Houston Patrol?"

Othello was the 90-year-old gardener. He was quite nice and did a beautiful job gardening and, now that I thought of it, it was true that some of the more nature-minded girls did have a tendency to get a crush on him. But still—90?

Lucy and Joan both laughed.

Teresa interrupted. "Hey did you hear that thing about the Houston Patrol? Mary Meyers and Laurie Colwin were out walking, standing right outside Senior Dorm after curfew, and the Houston Patrol drove up, their lights flashing of course, and told them they had to get back inside. Mary said she was feeling kind of 'frisky' so she decided to ask them some questions. And one of the things she asked them was whether their job was really to keep people *out* or to keep us *in*. I mean after all, let's face it, there's not that many people trying to get in here. And they said, when they were trained, they were told that of course they were supposed to keep people out, but their main job was to keep the girls in. And then Mary said, 'So what are the guns for—if you see us escaping, you shoot us in the legs?' Mary's voice got a tiny bit hysterical during the 'shoot us in the legs' part."

"Damn." Joan evidently was hearing this for the first time too.

"Joan, listen," I said. "I want to go raid the kitchen."

Joan rolled sideways on the bed and looked at me with her heavy-lidded eyes, her thick straight eyelashes almost obscuring her pupils completely.

"Looking for anything in particular?"

I raised an eyebrow. "Yes." They listened as I read the passage from Malcolm X again.

"See, we'll get some nutmeg."

Teresa was standing, leaning against the door frame, one foot up balletically, shaking her head. "June, June, June, June, June. You're a better girl than all of us. What spirit leads you to always look for trouble?"

I protested. "How can this be trouble? I can't get in trouble for nutmeg for god's sake."

*   *   *   *

Joan and I circled the dining room, pushing at each of the glass French doors.

Finally, I whispered to Joan, "I found one."

We slipped in and padded quickly across the dark-red tile of the dining room floor. Joan quietly opened the swinging door, we slid through and she slowly closed it, holding on until it went silently back into place.

We knew exactly where the row of giant-sized, red- and white-checked Saga spice cans were, on one of the long steel shelves atop a stainless steel counter. I ran my finger in the air along the row, located the nutmeg and emptied a small spice jar's worth onto a piece of Saran wrap, which I then wrapped into a cylindrical shape.

"Okay, let's go."

"Don't you want anything else? Maybe there're chocolate chip cookies in the back."

Back at the trailer in the brightly lit bathroom, Teresa watched me as I took a heaping teaspoon of gritty nutmeg, emptied it as far back in my throat as I could and quickly washed it down with Lipton's Ice Tea pre-sweetened with Sweet'n Low. I repeated the procedure twice.

"You're crazy," Teresa said.

We waited for half an hour, but nothing happened.

"How do you feel?" she asked.

"I have a slight stomach ache."

"Ahf. Khara." She swore in Arabic and made a moue of impatience. "You deserve it. I'm going to bed."

"Yeah. I guess I will too."

I climbed despondently up into my top bunk. Cleo and Dominique were already sound asleep, Cleo in curlers, Dominique wearing a black-out mask.

The next morning, I heard someone calling my name from far, far away. "June. Oh Ju-une." I tried to open my eyes, but the dream I was having wouldn't stop. Cleo was there but she was attended by a coterie of rats in tennis shoes. I pointed and laughed. Dominique was there too, with a million pinwheels coming out of her head. The walls of the trailer had been cleverly redone in moving, psychedelic wallpaper that changed patterns from tie-dye neon, to paisley to monkeys to clovers, and then I had to reconcentrate on Cleo. It seemed like she wanted something.

"Hey," I managed.

"Oh my god," Cleo said.

A thousand years later, I felt my toe (which existed in an entirely different universe) being shaken comically. I felt the motion of myself giggling, but it didn't feel exactly the same as giggling usually felt.

"Cleo, Cleo, it's time to get up for Mass."

I could feel Sister Aaron's colorless eyelashes brushing my knees. I opened my eyes and again a riot of pink assailed me, a background of pink palm trees with a cardboard cut-out in black and white of Sister Aaron. It looked so very, very beautiful.

"I'm not Cleo," I said, as clear as a bell.

"Do you need to go to the infirmary?" Sister Aaron asked.

Suddenly we were walking on the walkway beside the chapel, and Mass was letting out. I seemed to be dressed in something blue and crinkly, like shiny blue foil wrapping paper. The ivy on the brick walls was growing so rapidly I could watch it curl around the brick, and Polaroids of my friends' faces were blowing by us, looming out of a blindingly white background, becoming frighteningly large and then disappearing again. Crazy, man. I was on drugs.

Three highly hallucinatory days later, I came to. Sister Jean, who now only looked slightly more surreal than usual, was carrying a blue plastic tray, upon which breakfast was sitting, greasy hills of bacon, hash browns and scrambled eggs. She sweetly trilled, "I'll bet you have the munchies today!"

I snorted, then choked, tried to hold back my laughter, almost succeeded but then heard the word "munchies" in my mind again and lost control, laughing and laughing and laughing. That day, several of my friends came to visit, but their every chastisement about the stupidity of my actions led me to gales of laughter. Finally they figured out that for the last three days, the nutmeg had not just been making me feel sick.

74

Between Chemistry class and English class, Joan and I had to walk up four flights of stairs, from the basement of the new science building to the third floor of the classroom next door. We felt the five minutes allotted between classes was far too short for such a strenuous journey.

"Up ya go," Joan said, leaning heavily on me, her arm around my shoulder. We both had our greasy hair tied back in buns, and she had also adopted my ankle-length fashion in the pink uniform, the just-brushing-the-tops-of-your-bobby-socks style that I'd concocted to thwart the "no more than two inches above your knee" skirt rule.

"I don't think I can make it today," I moaned.

"Let's sit down for a moment on the steps and rest," she suggested.

We simultaneously swept the miles of pink- and white-striped fabric of our skirts off to the side and perched ourselves on the cement steps. I inhaled the sweet-smelling air.

"Do you think we'll ever get out of here?" Joan asked mournfully. "Or do you think that this is actually some other type of more permanent institution and we are actually being punished for some crime we don't even remember committing that will cause us to be locked up forever, with graduation held out as a promise to keep us calm?"

I didn't answer.

75

The weather was warm again and the signs of spring were everywhere.

I sat slumped in my seat, wishing Study Hall were over, wishing it were over for good, no more, wishing it had never been invented, wishing "study" and "hall" had each never been thought of so they could never have been put together. Janice Reilly stood up at the microphone, managing somehow to look pert in her pink and white summer uniform.

"This Saturday, the boarders will be getting a special treat from the Sisters." With the sugary-sweet statement oozing from her lips, she turned and actually smiled smugly in the direction of Sister Jane

Fox. "So everyone will assemble in the front parking lot at four on Saturday afternoon."

A special treat from the nuns, that was a very bad sign. I'm sure it involved all of us having to gather in some friendly and idiotic way. Even worse there might be singing. By now, we had had so much singing practice, and of course we all knew all the words to the same songs, that occasionally (too often) all the girls would burst into spontaneous singing, say, while boarding a bus, which made it feel like we were living in some totally perverse religious musical.

Clearly looking at the idea of a special treat differently than I, or maybe just being natural masochists, the rest of the students started to clap enthusiastically. They clapped and clapped and clapped, they clapped like this for everything, every day was some sort of clapping contest. Clap, clap, clap, clap, clap, clap, clap. I vowed right that minute to never clap again.

That Saturday afternoon at four, I was in the parking lot with everyone else because, of course, special surprises were mandatory.

"Are you excited, June?" Shelly (a very naive sophomore) asked me.

"I brought a book," I replied and, blank-faced, pulled the corner of a trashy novel called <u>Tory</u> out of my pocket so she could see the lurid pink-and-purple cover. She scowled and turned to someone less cynical and I felt guilty. But only for a second.

We were eventually loaded onto buses which trundled in formation to 17-Mile-Drive, then down toward Carmel. Oh no, this could be a nightmare—not only were we going to have to spend our Saturday night doing something unspeakably queer, but normal people were going to see us doing it. Sure enough, the buses pulled into the parking lot of the Carmel beach.

"Everybody off!" Sister Aaron cheerfully called.

On outings she had taken to wearing, instead of her habit, crisp new blue jeans, an ivory cable-knit sweater and no hat. Her wiry red hair was boyishly short and stood straight up from her head. She had a tidy figure, but the outfit still didn't solve her eyelash problem the way a little mascara would. I thought she looked sexier in her nun's outfit, and that was a stretch. What is wrong with me, I wondered.

"What is wrong, June?" I heard Cindy Nadai behind me.

"Somehow I'm dreading this," I answered. "I'm 16 years old. I can think of ways I'd rather spend Saturday night than singing Catholic songs on the beach with a bunch of other girls."

Cindy grinned. "C'mon, it'll be fun. At least we'll be able to identify the meat we have for dinner."

"If you can call recognizing a hot dog identification."

We went down near the waves and actually frolicked for a minute, then were called back by the nuns.

"Come on girls, come on," Sister Jean yelled across the sand. "Time to eat."

"Now there's a good reason to dash for the food," I said to Cindy and Joan, indicating with a wave Sister Jean's voluminous folds of flesh swathed in acres of black cotton.

"You don't seem that happy tonight, June," Joan said. She did have a gift for understatement.

"I think I've got a year's worth of patience for a year and a half's worth of time. Do you think we're ever going to . . . ?" I pretended to ask her the question.

She pretended to think. "No, not really," was her serious reply.

I sighed.

Kicking sand ahead of me with my high-top Keds, I sullenly walked up the beach behind Cindy and Joan. The nuns had already opened the plastic packages of hot dogs and stacked them on wire hangers, and were distributing them one at a time to the girls as they lined up. Soon we were gathered around the campfire, singing the folk songs we'd learned in the dining room sessions and eating s'mores. After about half an hour of this, I happened to look up to the cliffs above us. There were about twenty truly cool—clearly detectable by their patched jeans, tie-dyed shirts and billowing Indian dresses, and by the lovely long hair on both sexes—people staring down at us. How deeply painful was it for me to be one of the people they were staring at in disbelief. I made another promise to myself—never to eat hot dogs and s'mores again. Never.

76

We were at the end of the year. Only finals and elections were left. I still had the feeling, which so far in my life I'd always had, that I was holding my breath.

77

"June, you'll have to leave," Sister Aaron said gently.
I'd been daydreaming. "What? Oh yeah."
They were going to discuss my candidacy for student body president. I was barely out the glass door when Trish stuck her head out and grinned as she called me back in. I knew I was on the list.
A few minutes earlier, they had sent Teresa out of the room. Then we discussed senior class president candidates. Again both Teresa and I were sent into the small garden on the other side of the curtained glass doors.
Then we did the nomination list for student body vice-president and junior class president.

"Marion Miller."

I whimsically raised my hand and was surprised to hear by the rustle that Mary Meyers, sitting beside me, had raised her hand too.

"Okay, Marion Miller," Mary Pickering said tentatively, looking for comments on my unusual nomination. Marion was not in Honors classes and had never shown much drive toward anything but clowning around.

What the heck, I thought, it's not like any of the offices represented even the smallest smidgen of real power anyway. I raised my hand to speak. Mary nodded in my direction.

"Marion is well-liked by everyone and has a fine sense of fair play," I stated, as firmly as I could.

"But do we consider Marion leadership material?" Sister Carlotta pointedly asked.

Trish raised her hand. "I believe that, if appointed to this position, Marion would rise to the occasion."

It seemed that I was not the only one who'd figured out that to be a student officer the only talent needed was the ability to attend many pointless meetings, and even that required less talent than it might seem on the surface since the only alternative activity was sitting silently in a room, studying.

Everyone looked at everyone else and decided to say nothing. This point was not worth a fight.

"Alright, we'll vote."

We put our heads down, and a couple of seconds later, to my surprise, I heard Mary Pickering read Marion Miller's name on the list of candidates for student body vice-president. I put my head up in time to see her give the tiniest shrug as she put a mark by Marion's name.

Then we finished the list in the totally expected way. Up for student body vice-president were Teresa Barger (who would be

removed if she won student body president as everyone expected)
Dana Hees, Diane Hull, Marion Miller, Barbara Smith and me.

Later that day, at the end of Assembly, Mary Pickering walked to
the stage and spoke: "Alright everyone, pay attention. This afternoon we'll be starting the voting." Her voice faded in and out. Mary
tapped the microphone a couple of times, it echoed loudly in the
Study Hall. "We'll be voting for student body president and junior
class president. As most of you know, the winner must get 50 percent of the vote. Failing that, there will be a runoff. Let's try to do
this quickly and efficiently."

The next day the results were announced. Sally Fay was junior
president and there was a run-off between Teresa Barger and June
Smith for student body president.

I smiled slightly when I heard it announced. In a way I was flattered that it hadn't just automatically gone to Teresa. But at the
same time, for some reason, it made me sadder to be part of the
run-off. It was strange to find myself caring when I knew that I'd be
expected to maintain a facade that I was no longer interested in. But
if you were student body president, for the rest of your life it would
remain a fact about you that could not be changed: You had been
elected student body president your senior year. I despised myself
for the depth of how much I wanted it. I ferociously reminded
myself that tomorrow Teresa would be the winner, although I did
have just the teeniest, tiniest chance.

78

"There's going to be a big meeting after Study Hall tonight,"
Katie Finnegan said to Katie Budge and me as we walked to dinner.

Katie Budge raised her eyebrows to me. "What about?"

I shrugged. "Must have something to do with rules."

That night we had pork chops (which I hate unless they are so well done they're crunchy) in a disgusting, light-gray gravy, yellow-instead-of-green peas and mashed potatoes. After I'd served myself, I passed the food to Frances Corcoran on my left. I'd carefully made sure to take small helpings, then smashed them around my plate in an artful way that deceived the eye into thinking I had eaten, and instead had six cups of coffee. After dinner I felt a bit shaky and definitely not in the mood for a meeting, but what choice did I have?

During announcements, Katie Finnegan stood up and said, "Could everyone please stay after dinner? We'll be having a brief meeting for all the boarders."

Damn, there wasn't even going to be a chance to go to the bathroom. I hated sitting through meetings when I had to pee. Right after dinner, everyone stood up as if they'd forgotten. I took a chance and quickly dashed out and used the bathrooms near the first classrooms, then walked along the French doors to the back of the dining room before I came in. The room was silent, Sister Carlotta, square, solid, and mean, was standing on the stage talking. She stopped when I entered and waited for me to take a seat. Luckily, there was a place right there at Mary Doughtery's table.

" . . .To continue, it has come to my attention that some of the students are evidencing confusion in certain delicate situations. For the benefit of all, this seems a good time to remind you of the appropriate behavior.

"Lately there has been a certain laxity in the rules governing your time off-campus. This laxity is intentional; it has been felt that greater responsibility could be accorded to the student body without fear of abuse and, in the main, this trust has not been misplaced.

"At this time, no fingers are being pointed, and in fact, such misunderstandings as have arisen have been reported to me, and as such, the best recourse seemed to be to merely outline procedure in order to prevent any further unhappy mistakes."

She took a breath and directed her gimlet-eyed stare around a bit. I wondered what could possibly be coming. I hadn't known that we'd come up with a new genre of misbehavior. I hoped it was not me who'd broken the new rule unknowingly.

"As you know, occasion has permitted that far more of you are acquainted with the fine student body at our fellow private school, Robert Louis Stevenson. We welcome the more frequent congress between the two schools and have done everything we can to promote it with dances and supervised social outings.

"Unfortunately, because of the acquaintanceships many of you young ladies have struck up with the gentlemen of Robert Louis Stevenson, and also because it coincidentally happens that far more of you have relatives enrolled there—brothers and cousins—it has been happening that groups of you are running into the Robert Louis Stevenson gentlemen off-campus in situations where you are there for another purpose.

"I'm sure no harm has been meant when you have socialized with these gentlemen upon encountering them in Carmel or Monterey during your permitted off-campus time. I'm sure in many cases, you have spent more time than you wanted simply out of an awkward inability to know how to terminate the meeting. You will welcome, then, this clarification of the matter."

Her tone became a bit harder—indicating that the rule was going to be defined.

"When you run into someone you know in an off-campus situation, you are permitted to talk to them for *two* to *five* minutes. That is enough time to be sociable. If you think more time is needed, you must call me here at school and explain the situation and I will judge the appropriateness of continued contact."

She smiled fixedly.

"I know this will clear things up for everyone. Thank you."

We all stood up. I dashed out the first French door and ran to the bathroom again.

When I came back, everyone was on their way toward Study Hall. I caught up with Mary Biaggi.

"What'd you think of that?" I asked.

She looked at her watch. "We've only got one hour left of Study Hall and I'm sure Mr. Lynch is giving us an algebra test tomorrow."

"Hey, so what? You could study for the next fifty years and you still won't pass one of his tests," I said. Joan and I, as always measuring consequence, had been discussing how cataclysmic would it be if we cut algebra on a day there was a test. Since every single person got an F on every single test, how much worse could not going at all be? Mr. Lynch had been hired away from a position teaching advanced bio-physical mathematics at the Naval Post-Graduate School. In the transition, he'd gotten lost somewhere in the vast gray area between that and our two-year algebra program. He'd flunked everyone the year before, but strangely there seemed to be no uproar.

Joan and I had never heard of anyone ever cutting classes but us, so the precedent was terrifically unset.

I went up to my desk in Study Hall and rather lugubriously took out my Spanish book. I stared out the glass window and watched the big, old oaks, dusty green, fluttering in a small breeze. "Tu dices diferente. Tu dices rebellious," I said to myself. Hell, I could speak Spanish. I put the book back and took out a pack of cards and began to play solitaire. I knew seven different types of solitaire, which was good because then I didn't need to shuffle that well between hands. I looked at the clock. 8:15 a.m., only forty-five minutes of Study Hall to go. Forty-five minutes later, I finished up my last hand before taking my Algebra and Spanish books out of my desk to study later that night.

I caught up with Joan.

"Hey Joan, what'd you think of the new rules?"

"Good idea," Joan said sarcastically. "Keep us from getting out of hand and having sex with our relatives in the streets of Carmel. Five minutes is hardly time to get to the French kissing." She laughed. "Can you imagine actually calling. I should." She did a super sweet-voiced imitation of herself. "Hello. Sister Carlotta? This is Joan Frawley. I just ran into my cousin Bert who I haven't seen in five years. He has been telling me how my father was bombing their house. He's only gotten to the part about when they moved to the hotel in Santa Ana. Is it okay if we talk longer?"

(It was in fact true that one of Joan's aunts, her father's sister, every so often developed the idea that Mr. Frawley was attempting to bomb their home. She would make her whole family move from motel to motel in the greater Los Angeles area.)

Lucy caught up with us.

"Hey'd you catch that?" she asked.

"Yeah, I know," Joan and I answered together.

"It's ridiculous," Lucy exclaimed. "No one with any balls will obey that rule. I'm sure if I ran into my cousin Bobby I'll only talk to him for two to five minutes."

Joan and I looked at her. Lucy didn't seem to be getting it about the seriousness of obeying the rules.

79

"Here we go again," Mary Pickering announced. "We're passing out the run-off vote for student body president and for junior vice-president." The process was repeated.

The next day she announced that Teresa Barger was the new student body president.

"Now we're voting for student body vice-president and the junior electors."

The next day the electors were announced as Lisa Early, Frances McNamara and Leelee Hanna. The student body vice-president was a run-off between Diane Hull and me, June Smith. I didn't really want to be student body vice-president.

80

The day after it was announced that Diane Hull won. Then it was senior president. The run-off was between me and Dana Hees.

81

That was okay. I'd already been class president and she hadn't. I wasn't surprised when I lost.

82

I lost again. Senior vice-president. The run-off between Barbara Smith and me. Lost. My natural emotional withdrawal was no longer protecting me from the fact that losing elections hurt.

83

Next we voted for religious coordinator. Again I was on the ballot. I pleaded with my friends, pleaded, pleaded, pleaded, and told them to pass the word along. "Please, I beg you. Don't vote for me for religious coordinator. It's not even appropriate for me to be religious coordinator. Can't you see that this is killing me?"

No one responded.

The next evening it was announced that the run-off for religious coordinator was between Cleo Schmidt and June Smith. I walked out of Study Hall and back to my room. I wasn't alone there, of course. Gwen Wiedepohl was already sleeping and Cindy Nadai was reading a book. I turned and went back outside.

I walked along the road to the senior dorm, noticing the shadows of the trees on the sides of the dorm, thinking about going and talking to Joan, then I changed my mind and walked back, almost to the classrooms. The night air was filled with the smell of honeysuckle, dahlias, daffodils and cut grass. I lay down on the lawn. I felt so horrible, so lonely. Surely this wouldn't keep going on. But already it had continued, all of it, for longer than I could actually stand.

I thought I'd go back to bed. I walked slowly upstairs, running my hands across the stuccoed brick. I heard people talking in Teresa's room. For a minute I felt happy. Hey, maybe there was some kind of group. My friends. I could go in and just listen and have a good time.

When I entered, everyone stopped talking and looked at me. Joan, Teresa, Ann Drendel, Tracy McDonald, Sarah Haskell, Ann Finnegan, Robin Kohler. They were sitting everywhere, some lying on the beds, heads propped on their hands, some sitting on the floor, backs against the wall, Teresa sitting backward in a chair. They looked sorry.

"Oh June . . . ," Teresa started, but I held my hand up.
"No, no."
I went back to my room and went to bed.

84

The vote for the captain of the Navajos was a run off between
me and Ann Drendel. I felt like someone had stuck a huge sword in
my stomach and everything tasted of metal.

I tried everything to get people to stop voting for me. I couldn't
understand. It was such a simple thing I was asking, the school was
small enough that everyone knew I didn't want them to vote for me,
but it happened again. I was in the run off for treasurer. I was starting to hate them.

85

I sat frozen at my desk in Study Hall. I could feel a draft cool my
calves. What was I even doing here? Why didn't I fling myself
through the glass at the front of Study Hall, as I'd been so afraid
Sister Humpbert would do to me during the German concentration-
camp speech? Suddenly I had a vision of throwing myself dramati-
cally at the glass and just bouncing off. I laughed and bleakly opened
my desk to get my cards. I dealt out a hand of regular solitaire,
turned over a black seven and saw the red six right next to it. Maybe
after I lost the class representative vote tomorrow that would be the
end of it.

86

On Monday, I lost another run off.

87

I didn't really decide, but after dinner, instead of heading in the direction of the junior class meeting like I was supposed to, I walked across the darkened parking lot and through the seldom-used front door of Santa Inez. I went upstairs and then down the back stairs toward the trailers. It was very quiet in the back drive, no one was around and from far away a few faint girl voices wafted on the wind. I kept walking. After I quietly closed the flimsy door of the trailer, I took off my pleated skirt and slightly itchy brown sweater and climbed into the top bunk. I lay stiffly on the single bed, stared up at the ceiling and hoped against hope that no one would come in to ask me questions. I determined that if they did, I would pretend to be asleep. I hoped no one would try to tell me something stupid like how much trouble I was in for missing the meeting.

I knew that after the meeting, everyone was going to watch a James Bond movie on tv in the Long Dorm rec room. What was this whole school thing about? It was clear by now what the deal with the nuns was—"charitable" was an adjective that should not be spoken within a thousand miles of them. It was difficult not to sneer at myself for having thought that things would be changed at Santa Catalina by us following the rules. How long had that kept me distracted? It wasn't really about wearing pants on Saturdays. I imagined the nuns in the nun dining room laughing their asses off. And how stupid was I to think I would ever get a Gold Card? That B+ I'd gotten in Spanish last quarter when I'd gotten As on all the papers and tests? Duh. Duh, duh, duh.

It seemed amazing to be 16 years old and exhausted. What would happen to me? I could marry Michael Frawley and have his children, drive a Mercedes station wagon to the private schools in Los Angeles or I could . . . ? What? What other possibilities were there?

"What's going to happen to you, June?" I heard in my head, mockingly. What could happen to me? I certainly wasn't ever going to win. What if everything everywhere was like this? I knew I wouldn't be able to be like them. Maybe there was nothing wrong with the way the nuns did things; it was me who was at fault, ranting and railing against imaginary enemies while the rest of the world, the rational one where the people all got it, scoffed at me. I wanted to cry now, a thousand times more than when I'd had my heart broken by the A over an F, but I couldn't. I lay there and thought all the exact same things again.

88

The noise of the dining room faded in my consciousness. Two more days to go, it was easy now for me to space it all out. The server boy moved in slow motion, taking the plates of chocolate cake off the rolling tray-holder and passing them one by one to us. He glanced up and met my eye. I knew that at least four of the girls at my table were on a serious diet. That chocolate cake was really good, one of the ingredients was chocolate pudding so the cake was extra moist. As a piece passed in front of me I could see the dark, spongy square glisten. The icing was thick, and seeing the slightly hardened swirls made by the flat spatula reminded my tongue of the small crunch before the rush of sweetness. The plates with the dark, moist cakes were put on the table and moved to their places in front of the other girls.

Sure enough, Teresa, Mary Myers, Tracy McDonald and Sue Pettit's cakes were just sitting there unheeded. I could ask for them. I didn't yet. A few seconds went by.

" . . . I'm sure she didn't know what she was saying," Sue said, a little sanctimoniously, to Teresa.

Teresa grimaced slightly. "What is it, June?" She was being solicitous of me these days.

"Nothing."

"June. June."

The cakes called to me. I steadfastly turned my head and looked out the window. I rubbed my hand along the outside of my thigh, where I could feel a new slimness, much less flesh than had once been there.

Nothing changed, but I knew I would stay on my diet. I poured myself another cup of coffee. After a few more minutes, the server boys came and cleared away the uneaten cakes.

89

I lost another election run-off.

90

Friday, a week before the year ended, Ann Politzer and I were lying on the grass with our knees up, long uniform skirts draped over our legs, the sun warming our fronts as we waited for humanities class to begin.

"How'd you like to come to a party tonight?" Ann casually asked me.

Unbelievable. The day students never asked us to parties, it was impossible, we could no more go to a party than I could fly up onto the roof or lose thirty pounds in a second.

"How?" I quickly said.

"We'd come pick you up at the gate at some arranged time," she said.

"Okay."

This was crazy. I'd never heard of anyone sneaking off campus to go further than Denny's. My "sure" was more the answer to a dare than any actual expectation that she would come pick me up or that I would actually be waiting there. And to sneak off alone, I'd never heard of anyone in the history of the school doing it.

Later in the day, Susan Work came up to me, in even more of a whirlwind of perturbation, disapproval and sly awareness than usual.

"Did you tell Ann that you were going to come to the party tonight?" she asked disbelievingly.

"Yep," I said, partly in pure delight at upsetting Susan.

"Yeah right!" she said and marched off in the direction of the typing classrooms.

I shrugged. I didn't have much to lose by speculation at this point.

Not that I spent time considering the idea, it was too far-fetched.

At about four, I saw Ann hurrying across the parking lot, obviously looking for someone. I stepped out from the shadow of a column in front of the first classrooms, whereupon she spotted me and came straight over. We were both wearing long pink- and white-striped uniforms, I had on my yellow ski parka and thick, round glasses.

"Are you really going to try and meet us tonight?"

"Yep," I said again.

"What time shall we be there?"

"I dunno, what's good?" I had no idea what time was normal for a teenager to go out.

"Uh, ten-fifteen would be possible."

"Alright."

Ann narrowed her eyes and peered intently at me.

I couldn't blame her for being skeptical. Quite frankly, if our positions were reversed, I would be pretty positive she was bluffing. In actual fact, I was totally positive that I was bluffing and, consequently, simply went about my normal Friday, taking a drugstore trip to the Mark Thomas; idly watching everyone eat a dinner of mystery meat and thick asparagus; and, as usual, playing a few rousing hands of solitaire during Study Hall. Not until about 9:15 did I remember the possibility and then it was as a twinge of fear in the pit of my stomach. Oh no. I groaned; now that I was afraid, I would have to make myself go, on principle. But why would I want to go to a party anyway? I had no idea how to act. I certainly didn't know how to talk to boys at a party. I'd basically never been to a party with people of both sexes my own age, only concerts.

"Alright." I tried to act casually to myself. "I better get ready."

Back at the trailer I decided to wear my jeans, my beautiful jeans now more patch than denim, my striped blue-and-white sailor shirt, and over it, for disguise, a Lanz nightgown. I got in bed and waited. Waited, waited, waited.

Cleo came in and made a lot of tiny, getting-ready-for-bed noises—teeth brushing, bobby pins being dropped on a Formica counter, the whisper of pants being removed, the responding whisper of a nightgown falling down over her head. Then Dominique came in and made the same small, teenage girl, bed-preparation noises.

"Hey, Cleo?" Dominique whispered.

"Yes?"

"Is June already asleep?"

"Yeah, I think so," Cleo replied.

The lights went out and I lay there waiting for another ten-million years then, finally, to the sound of their heavy breathing, I snuck down the ladder and carefully, so carefully, opened the door.

"June?" Cleo questioned sleepily from her bed.

"It's nothing." I whispered from outside the door, probably too low for her to hear.

Turning my attention away from the trailer, I crouched down so the Houston Patrol wouldn't see me, then speedily slid behind a tree. I looked around one side, then the other. I realized that the white nightgown was probably not the best camouflage, so I took it off and looked at it. What could I do with it? I certainly couldn't just leave it behind a tree. I balled it up and stuffed it down the back of my pants.

I snuck along the tree line on the other side of Santa Inez. Just as I was about to resume breathing normally, the headlights of a Houston Patrol Jeep came around the corner and raked the vegetation. I ducked down and froze. I could hear the crackling of the radio as one of the guards talked into it.

"Roger. 704 reporting in. All quiet in the Southwestern Quadrant."

He drove around far more than he needed to; I could have told him the only thing out there was me and he wasn't going to discover that but, instead, I waited stock-still until he moved out of earshot. I realized that by now it was no longer anywhere near 10:15, and Ann and Susan, if they had shown up at all, were long gone. I had only gotten about twenty feet from my bed and the wisest course would have been to hastily return.

Absolutely not. I was determined to have some fun. I crept farther into the underbrush and began to make my way down the steep and overgrown hill. I decided to put my nightgown back on for warmth and protection, then plunged through the blackberry bushes and young eucalyptus as quietly as I could, my internal dialogue half boasting, half desperately trying to convince myself that this was like being on a secret spy mission. I kept getting whipped by young branches and every so often there was a small rii-iip as the thorny vines caught at my flannel nightgown. Although I only fell down twice, it had rained recently so I got mud all over my hands and knees. Unimportant, I thought, compared to the magnitude of my mission. I scared myself. Visions of men with dogs and nuns with rifles flashed through my head, and I crouched down and listened. Nothing. I forced myself to calm my breathing but I couldn't control the wild beating of my heart. I plunged on.

Finally, at the end of this part of my journey, I was looking up through the trees at the six-foot, barbed-wire-topped fence. Again, I considered returning to the dorm, but somehow I couldn't: This was an odyssey, and the main event had yet to happen. It was hard climbing the fence, I had to scrunch the tips of my tennis shoes in between the chicken-wire holes. When I dropped down to the other side, the bottom of my nightgown got caught in the barbed wire. For a second I was held, suspended in mid-air, but then, ri-i-i-i-i-ip, luckily the nightgown tore and I fell to the ground. Scrambling up the ditch through a few feet of undergrowth to the road was easy, and once at the top I surveyed the road in both directions like an escaped prisoner, tucked the tattered bottom of my nightgown into the waist of my jeans and then trudged down the road.

I wondered if there was a way to find a party somewhere. Perhaps there were parties at Monterey Peninsula College, I thought, and determined to walk over there. Although I had never spotted anything but the science building and the library out the windows of cabs as we whizzed by, maybe you could hear parties from a long way off, and I figured there had to be some sort of student housing. It seemed worth a try.

I walked for a long time. When a car came by on the frontage roads, I crouched down by a tree or bush and remained motionless. I knew it was late because the highway would be completely empty for a long time, and then one car would speed past, rushing home. By the time I got to the college, there were almost no cars at all. I gazed up at the big hill, covered with grass, and then at some college buildings. When I climbed hopefully up the hill, it soon became clear that the buildings had not transformed themselves into dorms but steadfastly remained the dark glass and concrete science building and library. Sitting on top of the hill for awhile, I thought about how amazing it was for me to even be there, in that exact place, even though it was kind of a long way from being a party. I could look out over the lights of the city, and past them see the sand shining and the ocean sparkling, even in the meager light from the half moon.

Finally, the nature enjoyment paled and I tried to think of something else to do. I wondered if the blankness was something everyone felt or if it was only I who felt as if I were floating in an endless gray vacuum. It was possible that there was another 24-hour restaurant as fun as the Denny's near the college. I cheerfully set off down the hill and had just about gotten to Alvarez Street when, from far, far away, came the sound of many loud engines, motorcycles actually. I imagined they would just speed by on the highway, but bit by bit they got louder and louder. Hmmm. I wondered what they were doing out so late at night. Maybe the motorcycles would be ridden by cute boys who I could somehow befriend. It was far-fetched and, after all, what would the procedure be for me, a slightly plump girl in patched blue jeans and a tattered nightgown, to introduce myself to handsome boys on motorcycles? I mean, it'd look pretty stupid to flag them down.

Just as I reached Monterey Bay Drive, the motorcycles came around a wide curve. The lead motorcycle guy spotted me and yelled.

Uh oh! That wasn't a friendly yell, in fact I felt quite frightened and realized that perhaps it would have been a better idea to have stuck to my previous policy of hiding. I ran down Third Street and heard the sound of motorcycles slowing down very noisily to turn around and follow me. I was almost to the end of the short street when they came around the corner full throttle after me, whooping and shouting. It occurred to me that it was most likely going to turn out that they were not handsome either. I desperately turned the corner as the deafening roar of the engines filled the street and bounced off the buildings. I spotted an alley and saw, partway down the narrow, dank passageway, a group of full trash cans, garbage spilling out the tops and over the sides. Desperately, I threw myself behind them. I crouched down, peering around one trash bag, ripped open, spilling plastic, rotting vegetables and coffee grinds and I saw six or seven enormously, gigantically monstrous motorcycles speed by. The roar filled the street and bounced off the buildings. They didn't see me. That was lucky.

As the brain-crushing cacophony of the motorcycles faded in the distance, I got up, only shaking a little, brushed myself off and con-sidered what to do next. At this point, meandering in the direction of school seemed more appealing than venturing further into Monterey.

As I was walking home, I came across a small, 24-hour grocery store with a coffee counter. A gnarly old counter man, I guessed he was the owner, and a tall, gangly young man in glasses both looked at me strangely when I came in.

"Hello," I said cautiously.

"Aren't you a bit young to be out this late?" the grizzled counter man asked.

I sighed and stopped. I waited for him to act further on his suspicion, but he just stood there, holding the coffee pot, looking at me with a bored expression.

"Maybe so," I finally said, as if agreeably considering his idea, and turned my coffee cup over for him to pour me some. He did so and turned back away. Whew. I felt a tiny burst of triumph. Of course, I would have preferred tomato juice, but the risk that ordering juice might bring me under more rigorous scrutiny stopped me. Suddenly, I felt exhausted. Even though it seemed as though I'd said the secret password and gotten in the club, for some reason I drank my coffee hurriedly.

"More?" the counter man asked.

"No thank you," I politely replied. It was probably just about time for me to be getting back. The return journey seemed to take a lot longer, and this time I didn't climb through the woods but instead walked right up the front drive. By now the sky had lightened with the beginnings of dawn. It was a foggy day, nothing glorious and colorful, but I was filled with happiness as the gray lightened. I had done something no-one else had, I'd made myself different. Not that I was going to be rushing to repeat the experience next week or even, hopefully, ever—but still I knew I had changed.

As I was walking up the drive, I realized that all the dorm alarms were on, so there was no way for me to get in. I went around to the back of Senior Dorm to a little room where the cleaning service delivered the sheets and pushed five of the blue paper-wrapped bundles together for a bed, then opened another bundle, covered myself with six starched-cotton sheets, and slept.

91

At the awards ceremony it was business as usual.

"The National Student Merit Award recipients are: Teresa Barger, Diane Hull, Dana Hees, Kathy Thayler, June Smith and Ann Politzer. Will the winners please stand up." And we'd all stood beside our seats in Study Hall while the rest the student body clapped prolongedly.

"English awards, please stand up."

Teresa Barger, Diane Hull, Dana Hees and Kathy Thayler would stand up and more prolonged clapping would result.

"Achievement scores over 1900, please stand up."

And again it would be Teresa, Diane, Dana, Kathy, Ann and me. Any award that came from tests administered nationally, Ann and I got. Any awards determined by the teachers our school, Ann and I were sure to be excluded from winning.

92

Teresa and I were sitting, totally drunk, with our legs dangling over the edge of the Science building, looking down at the hockey fields four stories below. A few feet away, Joan was laughing and rolling around while Juana and Trish looked at her, grinning and passing a cigarette back and forth.

I painstakingly enunciated my words as I said, apropos of nothing, "Once someone said to me, 'Who do you think is the richest girl in our class?'" I paused.

"What did they mean?" a voice asked, though I didn't bother to distinguish who.

"They meant the fathers, of course. Who had the richest father or maybe family."

"So who did you say?"

"I had absolutely no idea."

Juana, Trish, Mary Pickering and Mary Meyers had invited Lucy, Teresa, Joan and me to a special party on the roof of the Science building after the awards ceremony on Thursday night. Their graduation was Saturday—the parents would arrive, shiny-eyed and proud in their luxury cars, the day would be brilliant, sun shining as usual, and after the ceremony, we'd all go home for the summer. I was lying on my back, looking up at the sky, idly throwing gravel off the edge of the building.

I continued. "I started guessing. 'Susan Weyerhauser?' 'No,' the person replied. 'Bobbie Bon? I was under the impression that her family owned every vegetable grown in Mexico.' 'No.' Suddenly I felt embarrassed for even guessing. 'I don't know,' I said to whoever it was."

I leaned over and took the bottle of white wine out of Teresa's hand. A full moon hung over the tennis courts.

"Well?" Teresa asked.

"Well what?"

"Who was it?"

"I don't know. They didn't tell me and I wasn't smart enough to figure it out."

I looked up at the perfect night sky, stars twinkling in all their appointed places, and thought about how nothing much had changed—but that I knew now that the future was inevitable. Teresa, Joan and I, and the rest of our class, had another year at Catalina to go, but really I knew we'd get through. It wasn't even going to be so painful, now that the die was cast. I wasn't going to be what I had been raised to be. I couldn't. And no matter how painful, how unsuccessful, how thwarted I might be as a result, I wasn't going to follow their path. I felt happy.

A little while later, I noticed that Teresa had gone over to the other side of the roof.

Mary Pickering was sitting next to me. I was lying down, looking up at the sky, too fucked up to support myself and not wanting to anyway. I could vaguely feel the tiny pebbles that lined the roof poking through my thin cotton shirt.

"You know June," Mary said, slightly embarrassed. "You know, it doesn't matter about the elections. You'll be student body president next semester."

It was nice of her to say so, but I didn't care. I didn't care about that, I'd already lost twenty pounds. I could do anything.